S0-AQM-605

ANGELS ON FIRE

ANGELS ON FIRE

a romantic dark fantasy
by
Nancy A. Collins

angels on fire	nancy a collins
cover art & interior illustrations	thom ang
jacket and book design	john snowden
art direction	richard thomas

Angels On Fire
Copyright 1998 © by Nancy A. Collins
All Rights Reserved.

All rights reserved. No part of this book may be reproduced or utilized in any form or by any means, electronic or mechanical, including photocopying, recording or by any information storage and retrieval system, without permission in writing from the Publisher.

The trademark White Wolf® is a registered trademark.
ISBN: 1-56504-909-8
Printed in the United States.

Published by
White Wolf Inc.
735 Park North Blvd. Suite 128
Clarkston, Georgia 30021
www.white-wolf.com

First printing September 1998
10 9 8 7 6 5 4 3 2 1

Dedication:

In Memory of Lou Stathis
1952-1997
Claimed By Greater Angels

part 1

up on the roof

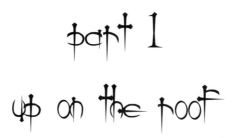

In Heaven an angel is no one in particular.
—George Bernard Shaw, *Man And Superman*

Angels may be very excellent sort of folk in their own way, but we, poor mortals in our present state, would probably find them precious slow company.
—Jerome K. Jerome

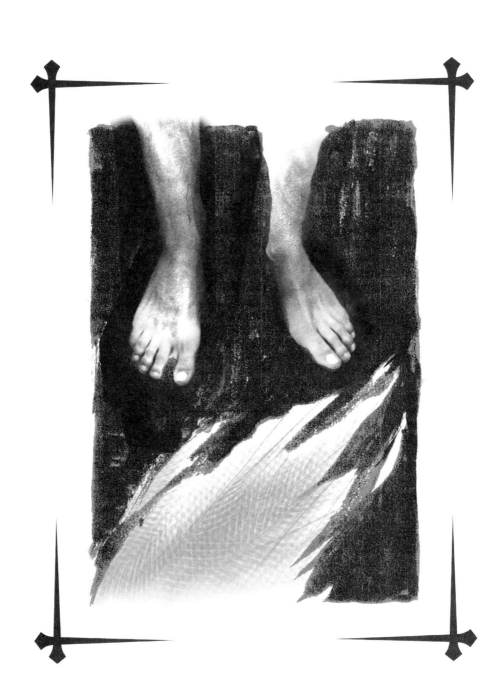

CHAPTER 1

Lucy wasn't sure whether she was going out for some fresh air or to commit suicide until she stepped out of the stairwell and onto the roof. But upon the sight of the heavy night sky, as impassive and uncaring as the eye of a baked fish, she cast her vote for extinction.

If only there'd been some stars. Maybe then she would have laughed at her folly and pain and gone back downstairs to her apartment and resumed her life pretty much as it had been the day before. Without him, of course.

But there were no stars to be seen on that night—or any night in the decade she'd lived in Manhattan. She had gone so long without catching sight of the heavens she often wondered if they were still there. New York City and its surrounding boroughs threw off so much reflective light, it muted the sky. Even on a clear night, such as this, only the moon could be glimpsed with the naked eye. The last time she'd *really* seen stars, now she thought about it, was three years ago. Had her mother been dead that long?

She remembered standing on Mam-Maw's back porch after the funeral—only it wasn't Mam-Maw's anymore. Cousin Beth owned it now. She'd modernized the kitchen, updated the plumbing and done all the things that the house had desperately needed done in the fifteen years since Pappy passed on.

But even with the alterations, there were still fragments of Lucy's childhood peeping out here and there: the cast-iron bottle-opener in the shape of a bulldog's head bolted to the kitchen door-frame; the Bavarian cuckoo clock Pappy brought back from the Second World War; the blue willow plates lined up edge-to-edge along the shelf in the dining room. These touchstones of her own private mythology were far more comforting, in their way, than the bevy of cousins clustered inside the house.

As she stood on the back porch of the house she had grown up in, Lucy could hear Beth in the kitchen (after all, it *was* her house, now), making sure there was enough coffee. Lord knows, you can't have Methodists over after a funeral and not have enough coffee to float a battleship. Although she liked her cousin well enough, she and Beth had never been particularly close, and the years spent away—first at college, then in New York—had done little to bridge the distance between them. She had left Seven Devils behind, while Beth had stayed. That alone spoke volumes, even if the cousins did not.

So Lucy stood on the porch of what had once been her grandparents' house, truly alone for the first time since arriving at the Little Rock airport the day before, watching the sky as twilight lengthened into night. She was surprised at how the stars filled the sky. She didn't remember the night being so full as a child. But then again, as a girl she had never imagined she would ever live in a place where the stars could not shine.

The scream of a passing police siren pulled Lucy back to her surroundings. She blinked rapidly as she stepped forward, allowing the stairwell door to swing shut behind her. After a day of absorbing the summer heat, the black tarpaper was slightly soft under her feet, as if she were walking on the back of a beached whale.

She had been on the roof only once or twice before, the last time being the previous Fourth of July. She'd thrown a barbecue with some friends and watched the fireworks over the river. That was shortly after she first met Nevin. Funny how all the events in her life were qualified as to whether they occurred before or after she met him.

She scanned the roof, surprised at its size. It was easily five thousand square feet wide, unbroken by skylights or chimney pots. After a decade spent living in the Lower East Side, it was strange to see so much empty open space. The building was relatively new for the neighborhood—dating back to the 1920s—and towered at least two stories over its neighbors.

As her eyes swept the area, she spied a couple of disposable syringes near the fire escape, the orange plastic caps clearly visible against the dark surface. It didn't surprise her that junkies came up there to shoot, but she couldn't help feel a surge of disgust. No place was safe from those fuckers. At least they didn't shit up here. That was what the lobby was for, after all.

"Motherfuckin' bitch! Don't fuck with me!"

Lucy glanced over the waist-high retaining wall to the street below. A crack whore was screaming at one of her sisters-in-trade as they were about to come to blows over the only working pay phone on the block.

One of the ever-present dealers trotted out from a nearby *bodega* and cursed out the women in Spanish, shooing them away like pigeons. The dealers didn't like it when the crackheads and junkies acted up on their turf. While the cops had long since given up cruising for drug crimes, disturbing the peace was another matter.

Lucy shook her head and returned her gaze to the skyline. There was a world of difference between New York and Seven Devils, and yet they had proven so pathetically similar. For all their touted sophistication, New Yorkers were just as fucked-up and shallow as the bow-heads and jocks she'd endured at Choctaw County High. Nevin had proven that to her in spades.

She closed her eyes and rubbed her brow, as if by doing so she could massage him out of her brain. She could still see the cruelty in his smile— as devoid of care and thought as the used syringes scattered at her feet. Had there ever been anything besides the void in his eyes as he closed the door on her—or had it been an elaborate hoax from the beginning?

That's what she got for getting involved with another artist. Creative people always ask for trouble when they mix love and art. She'd learned that more than once at school. She thought she'd smarted up since then. But Nevin was so handsome, so vital—so *inspiring*. She thought she'd finally realized the romantic fantasy all artists secretly nurse: the Soul Mate. Someone who understands the artist's needs, shares their passion for culture and experimentation, and with whom they can commune as an equal.

In Nevin she thought she'd finally found someone who would inspire her to great things. She introduced him to the artist's collective she belonged to, and together they labored on installations for the group shows. Granted, most of the ideas were hers, as well as the physical labor, but she didn't grudge Nevin his credit. After all, he was her muse. They were fighting together in the trenches—and that's all that mattered.

Until today.

When she got home from work, she'd found a letter waiting for her from the collective, notifying her that she'd been voted out of the group. The proposal had been put forward by Gwenda, a humorless trust-fund baby whose specialty was *faux* intensity. Her art consisted of making collages from glossy fashion and fetish mags, smearing a layer of black paint over the images, then gluing down "found" typography such as MURDER and JUMBO EGGS before putting a final layer of lacquer over it.

Gwenda often bankrolled the collective's installations and held a great deal of influence with the steering committee, and she had made it clear on more than one occasion that she considered Lucy's work too "commercial" and "accessible," and therefore not proper art.

As Lucy read the letter, her entire body trembled. She'd thought she would be free of Gwenda's type after high school, but they continued to dog her steps—ambulatory Barbie Dolls that couldn't be satisfied with their country clubs and sororities—they had to pollute the art world as well! Well, she wasn't in high school anymore, and she wasn't going to take being fucked with in such a heavy-handed manner!

Lucy succeeded in keeping her mad-on all the way to Gwenda's co-opt in Gramercy Park. As she hammered on the bitch's door, she was so pumped full of righteous fury she actually felt *good*. However, her exhilaration came to a crashing halt when, to her surprise, Nevin opened the door to Gwenda's apartment.

They stood there for a moment that could not have possibly been as long as it felt, staring at each other in dumb surprise.

The resulting scene was so loud and nasty that the tenants on the floor above left their apartments to peer over the railing of the stairwell, muttering amongst themselves.

It ended with Lucy being escorted from the building by a tired-looking doorman while Gwenda shrieked she was going to press charges if she ever darkened her doorway again.

When they got to the lobby, the doorman let go of her elbow and sighed as he took off his cap and smoothed back his hair. As he fished a Marlboro out of his shirt pocket, he'd given her a firm yet sympathetic look.

"I'm supposed to call the cops when shit like this happens," the doorman said as he lipped the battered cig. "You look like you've had a shitty enough day, though. There's no need'n makin' things worse."

She'd muttered a quick *thank you* and slipped out the door. As she headed back below Houston, the fires of her anger receded, leaving only ashes in their wake. The idea of going home to an empty apartment was enough to make her physically ill. She didn't want to face the thousand and one tiny reminders of the love she thought they'd shared. A love, she now realized, that had been a cruel, cynical lie. At least for one of them.

However, despite her unwillingness to face an empty apartment, Lucy had nowhere else to go, no one else to turn to. Since she started dating Nevin, what few friends she'd once had had gradually fallen away. It hadn't concerned her at the time. After all, she had Nevin, didn't she? What else could she possibly ever need?

Once she returned to her apartment building, she did not pause at her floor, but continued climbing the crumbling stairs until she reached the roof. Which brought her, full circle, to staring at the empty sky and remembering the night of her mother's funeral.

As she stood looking out at the city, she realized she had been deluding herself all along that the passion she had felt for Nevin had been mutual. He was no more than a highly polished mirror, reflecting what she had wanted to see. What she'd thought was love was merely a reflection of her own affection, not the real thing. Unfortunately, the pain she was feeling was real enough.

She stood on the roof's north-east corner, looking down at where the Super kept the garbage cans and recycling bins. Even six stories up she could still smell the sour reek of rotting food. As she wrinkled her nose in distaste, her brain calmly noted how the only thing keeping her from plummeting eighty feet into a pile of broken bottles, empty orange juice cans and coffee grounds was a three-foot-high barrier.

She closed her eyes, trying to blunt the terrible ache inside her, but it was no use. She was so tired. No. Not just tired. *Weary*. Yes, that was the word.

She was weary of dealing with shit. She'd spent her life slogging through torrents of it. It had started, as all things do, with her family. Then, one after another, came religion, school, work, the government and various lovers and supposed friends; all of whom had shit of varying colors and quantities to dump on her, so that it all ran together into a foul, hindering mess designed to drag her down and choke the life from her. Of course, moving to New York—the biggest shit pot of them all—hadn't made things any sweeter for her. Was this all she had to look forward to? A lifetime of struggle simply to keep her head above a torrent of raw sewage?

Could she do it? Could she bring herself to defy every instinct hard-wired into her being and turn her back on the madness once and for all? It would be so simple to surrender herself to gravity—to savor the split-second of freedom suspended between sky and pavement, free from all that had gone before and with nothing more to fear—for there was nothing left to concern her except her death.

Lucy glanced back down at the courtyard below, and was mildly surprised to discover she was already standing atop the narrow ledge of the retaining wall. The fact that she didn't remember climbing up worried her more than the chance of her losing her balance.

As she blinked in confusion, a sudden gust of wind caught her off-guard, causing her to pinwheel her arms as her right foot slipped into empty space. As she reeled atop her unsteady perch, she found herself thinking of the church bell.

Back when she was little, her family had attended church in a modest brick structure that would have been otherwise unremarkable except for the bronze dome that sat atop it like a verdigris-encrusted derby. It was there she came to know religion, if not God.

The faith of her fathers smelled of dust and tasted of warm grape juice and was composed of old people, tedium, and uncomfortable clothes worn only once a week. As far as she could tell, church was something to be endured in order to attain the pleasures of the Sunday table: deviled eggs, smothered chicken, snap peas in pot liquor and sweet tea.

The first thing anyone saw upon entering the church was a vestibule and the cloak room. A narrow set of winding stairs in the corner of the foyer led to the choir loft overhead. There were two doors flanking the pulpit. The one to the left led to the minister's office. The one on the right was the bell room, although there were other things in there as well—mostly spare hymnals, choir robes, and the three-quarter-size plastic Nativity scene placed on the church lawn during Christmas.

Lucy never actually saw the bell itself, just its rope, which dangled like the tail of an animal through the hole in the ceiling—thick and white and smooth to the touch. Now that she thought of it, the bell-rope had looked more like an umbilical cord than a tail.

It was Brother Peacock's job to toll the bell, just as it was Brother Hutchinson and Brother Landfair's job to serve as ushers, and Sister Helen's to play the organ. There was a good reason Brother Peacock was assigned the task of ringing the bell. He was not a young man, but neither was he small. A farmer like her father, he was rawboned and as weathered as a rockface, with hands big enough to hide a Bible. Even so, the momentum created by the bell as it swayed on its rocker arm was so strong it occasionally lifted him onto tip-toe.

She could see Brother Peacock as plain as day, even though he'd died long before she graduated high school, pulling on the rope, making the bell sway back and forth so that the clapper struck the interior rim. She could hear the tolling of the bell, still sounding as loud as it had to her three-year-old ears. *Dong-Dong! Dong-Dong!*

One Sunday, Brother Peacock smiled and motioned for Lucy to draw closer, showing her where to grab the rope. She peered upward, trying to see through the narrow hole cut in the ceiling and catch a glimpse of the bell. Brother Peacock gave the rope a mighty tug, then quickly stepped back and let go of the pull.

The moment Brother Peacock released his grip, Lucy sailed upward as if pulled by the hand of God. She felt no fear, only delight. And she knew, at that very moment, that this was how the angels flew. Then, as quickly as it had begun, Brother Peacock stepped back in and resumed control, forcing Lucy to drop reluctantly back to earth.

She had come closer to experiencing God during that brief moment than she ever had seated in the straight-back pews. But there was no way she could have explained that to her parents. She was too young and lacked the ability to express herself. Even if she could have, it still would not have changed things.

By the time she was old enough to enter elementary school the church's directorate voted to remove the old bell and replace it with a public address system that played taped carillons. It even chimed out 'Joy To The World' during Christmas time. The day the old bell was removed, the diminishment of her faith began. Odd that she would have forgotten it until that moment.

But with the resurgence of memory came a flash of insight so simple in its profundity she couldn't help but laugh. As far back as she could remember, whenever she dreamt of flying, the sensation she experienced in her sleep was not that of swimming, as everyone else described it, but of being plucked from gravity's relentless grip and drawn higher and higher—to the very vault of Heaven. To think that such a small thing, that happened so long ago, had kept itself alive in her dreams without her being aware of it. She was still shaking her head in amusement as she regained her footing and hopped back down to the safety of the roof.

This was no way to deal with all that had happened. For one thing, it would make that shmuck Nevin think he was important. She could see him sipping cheap chablis from a plastic cup while at an opening, shaking his head in disdain.

Poor thing. I guess she couldn't face life without me.

And she could well imagine what Beth and the others would make of it as they clustered in Mam-Maw's remodeled kitchen, guzzling coffee while their husbands stuffed their faces with deviled eggs and cold cuts.

If she closed her eyes she could almost hear Cissy Tilton, the town gossip, hissing like a goose: *"What did I tell you? Just like her mother!"*

And that, more than anything, was why she could not kill herself. She'd spent her life trying to prove she was nothing like her mother, and she was not going to give up now.

Her heart was still fluttering like a finch trying to escape its cage as she made her way back to the stairway. What she needed was a nice hot cup of tea liberally laced with whiskey. Then she'd put on some music that would help her put things in their proper perspective—say, some Janis Joplin or Bessie Smith—and take a good, long, hot soak in the tub; the kind that fogs your brain like a bathroom mirror. Yeah, that was definitely in order.

She was so preoccupied trying to recall whether or not there was still any DeWars left in the pantry, she didn't see the thing sprawled at her feet until she'd tripped over it.

"What the fuck?" she groaned as she struggled to get back to her feet. The heels of her palms stung from striking the roof's tarpaper surface, but she was otherwise unharmed.

She wondered what she could have fallen over. There weren't any TV aerials or vents anywhere around. Then she saw the outstretched arm near her foot—as white as marble against the roof-top. She gasped and dropped solidly down on her rump.

There was a man sprawled face down less than a yard away from her, a blanket of some sort draped over his back. Judging from his arms and legs, which were spread akimbo, he was otherwise naked. The head was turned so that the face pointed away from her, but she could tell that he had long, fair hair. She couldn't make out if he was breathing or not.

Her first thought was that some junkie had climbed onto the roof for a fix and o.d.'d instead. But that was impossible. She'd scanned the whole area the moment she got there. And there was no way someone could have come onto the roof without her noticing. And any junkie worth his salt who'd seen her half-assed balancing act wouldn't have stayed around to shoot up. They liked privacy, and they certainly didn't care for cops poking around asking questions.

So, if he wasn't a junkie, then where did he come from? He couldn't have dropped out of the sky—could he? Maybe that thing across his back was a parachute. Somehow she doubted nude night-time skydiving over Manhattan was a new fad she'd missed out reading about in the Lifestyles section of the *Times*.

Maybe he'd fallen out of a plane? But she hadn't heard an explosion overhead, and even if she *had*, that wouldn't explain the guy being bare-assed. Besides, she suspected that someone plummeting from a disabled aircraft—starkers or not—would have made a far splashier landing than this guy had. In any case, the poor bastard was probably dead.

Lucy eased forward, steeling herself for the sight of blood and brains. As she moved closer, the cloak across the man's back began to gleam, as if reflecting the dim light from the surrounding buildings. It possessed an iridescent quality that seemed oddly familiar, but she couldn't quite place it. As she bent to get a better look, her eyes widened and she gasped aloud.

It wasn't a blanket *or* a parachute.

They were wings.

They grew out of the shoulder blades and were roughly three feet wide and, although folded, easily twice that in length. The feathers were dark and shiny, like those of the hummingbirds that used to flit about Mam-Maw's back porch, sipping sugar-water from the feeders set out for them.

Even though she knew what she was seeing was indisputably real, her mind was still reeling even as, with trembling hands, she grasped the angel's bare shoulder and rolled it onto its back. She'd expected it to be heavy—or at least to possess the weight of a grown man—but it proved surprisingly light.

As shocked as she'd been by the wings, the rest of the angel left her speechless. One thing was for sure: it certainly wasn't the kind of angel she'd been taught about in Sunday School. Although it was at least six-and-a-half feet tall, with broad shoulders and a deep chest, it was as smooth as a Ken Doll between the legs. There wasn't even a hole to pee out of. The lack of sexual organs was so startling, it took Lucy a moment to register that the angel was also lacking a belly button and nipples.

The face was undamaged and an eerie mixture of feminine and masculine features, the chin as hairless as its chest and crotch. She gingerly pressed the flat of her hand against the angel's breastbone. It didn't seem to be breathing, nor did it have a pulse or heartbeat, yet the skin was warm to the touch. It must have crash-landed on the roof just before it died...That would explain that sudden gust of air that nearly toppled her off the ledge.

She didn't want to dwell on what might kill an angel. What was important was that she'd found it. But what good was a deceased angel—?

As she mulled that question over, she began to smile. It looked like things were finally beginning to look up for her, after all.

"You're coming with me, pal," she grunted as she hoisted the dead angel across her shoulder in a fireman's carry. "After all: finders keepers."

CHAPTER 2

For once she was glad she was living in New York City, where people minded their god-damned business, even when little old ladies screamed at the top of their lungs. She didn't want to have to explain herself to any of her neighbors if they happened to look out their door and see her hot-footing it down the stairs with a dead angel draped over her shoulders.

She was relieved to discover the body weighed no more than a large bag of groceries, and she was able to balance it easily enough with one hand as she dug into her jeans pocket for the keys to her door.

The apartment was dark—which was fine with her. She didn't want anyone across the way looking out their window in time to see her drag what looked to be a nude man into the living room and deposit him on the red velour couch she'd scrounged from the Broadway Flea Market.

What to do? What to do? Her mind was racing so fast it was almost impossible to think coherently enough to act.

The media. She needed to notify the media immediately. The newspapers, the networks, the tabloids...But which ones? And which one first? Should she call the *Times*? The *Post*? The *Daily News*? The *Journal*? *Newsweek*? The *Inquirer*? The *Star*? *Weekly World News*? Associated Press? Reuters? *Rolling Stone*? *Spin*? *Christian Science Monitor*? CBS? NBC? ABC? CNN? The BBC? Fox? UPN? MTV? CBN? Oprah? Sally Jesse Raphael? Geraldo? Or maybe she ought to call the big kahunas themselves direct—Rather, Jennings, Walters, Brokaw. Hell, maybe they could get ol' Walter and Dave out of retirement for this one.

She had a vivid image of herself splashed across the front page of the Choctaw County *Courier*, standing next to the dead angel, dangled by its ankles like a prize swordfish, with the banner headline: Local Girl Discovers Proof of Afterlife.

Yeah, that'd make 'em sit up and take notice at Dooley's Diner out on the highway, for damn certain. In your face, redneck muthers!

Telephone book. That's what she needed. The telephone book. She had to start calling around immediately. She frowned, scanning the darkened room for the phone. She liked being mobile when she talked on the phone, but she didn't trust cordless models. It was too much like talking on a kid's walkie-talkie for her tastes, so her phone had an extension cord long enough to use for a double-dutch jump-rope competition.

She spotted the length of white extension cord leading up the narrow hallway to her bedroom. She sprinted after it, dragging the phone out from under the bed like a recalcitrant pet.

She was going to be so famous her face would be on postage stamps! And she was going to be sooooo rich! Just thinking about it made her start to giggle. It was the same nervous, half-mad giggle she'd experienced at her grandfather's funeral years ago, only now she didn't bother trying to smother it with a clutch purse.

She was going to be so rich she could hire people to cook for her, clean for her, drive for her, even shit for her, if that's what she wanted! Hell, she'd be wealthier than a thousand Gwendas! She'd have more than enough money to bring Nevin running back to her, begging forgiveness.

And maybe—just maybe, mind you—she'd take him back.

No doubt the Smithsonian or the Vatican or some super-rich weirdo would want to buy the dead angel from her for several million. Maybe a billion or two. Or she could put it on tour, like they did King Tut, and charge people five bucks a pop to see a real-live dead angel. That was definitely worth thinking about.

Then there was the licensing, of course. T-shirts, coffee cups, satin baseball jackets, lunch-boxes, Under-Roos, the whole nine yards. She'd need an agent to handle that for her. She had a friend whose brother was a writer who was repped by William Morris…Naw. Not enough clout. It had to be CAA.

Then there was the movie version of her story—maybe they could get Winona Ryder to play her? Sissy Spacek to play her mom, maybe? If they got Johnny Depp for the angel, that would be really cool.

She tucked the phone under her arm and hurried back down the hall towards the kitchen, which was located just off the living room. She kept the NYNEX phone book on top of the refrigerator, alongside the cookie-jar shaped like a bear and an ever-growing pile of Chinese home-delivery menus. Surely the Yellow Pages had listings for all major news-gathering agencies in the city…

As she headed in the direction of the kitchen, a shadow moved towards her, blocking her path. Lucy screamed and dropped the phone, which struck the bare wood floor and shattered.

She took a rapid step backward, trying to distance herself from the shadowy figure blocking her path, but it moved forward as well. As it came towards her, light reflected from the street revealed that what was standing in front of her was not a man—but the dead angel.

Except it was no longer dead.

It towered over her, its golden crown brushing the eight-foot ceiling, looking down at her with strange, colorless eyes with distorted pupils. She hadn't realized the thing was so tall, then she realized the angel was levitating—although hardly the way David Copperfield floats Buicks and Claudia Schiffer around. The angel's multi-colored wings were beating so furiously they were blurs, allowing it to hover in place like a hummingbird, its arms outstretched.

"D-don't hurt me!" she whispered, her voice tight with fear.

The angel tilted its head to one side, a look of mild puzzlement crossing its androgynously perfect features.

"Get back!" she said, gesturing with her hands. "Get back or I'll *scream!*"

The angel tilted its head to the other side, its gaze fixed on her hands. It did not move away, but neither did it come closer.

"Just stay where you are—understand?" She had no idea if it understood English, but it seemed to find her hand gestures meaningful. "Don't come any closer, okay?"

The angel looked her in the eye and smiled the most beautiful, disarming smile she'd ever seen on anyone besides a baby.

"Okay," it said, in a voice like the dawn.

Relieved, she returned the smile and lowered her hands.

The angel promptly swooped towards her like an owl going for a mouse. Lucy turned and fled, shrieking, down the narrow hall back in the direction of her bedroom. She risked a glance over her shoulder and saw the angel looming behind her like a rogue Macy's balloon, its toes six inches above the bare floor. Choking on a scream, she dove into the bathroom and slammed the door behind her, locking it with trembling hands.

Gasping for breath, she dropped onto the toilet and, head in hands, stared at the door through her fingers. She could hear it moving about on the other side—or rather, she heard its wings. They made a sound like cicadas in summer. She closed her eyes and struggled to calm herself. She had to regain control. She needed to think her way out of this.

She could kick herself for freaking out and boxing herself in. Her bedroom might not have a lock on the door, but it *did* have a fire-escape that led directly to the street. While the bathroom door did have a lock, its solitary window was the size and shape of a gun-slit. Even if she were contortionist enough to wriggle through it, it still left her five stories up and nowhere to go but down—and quickly, at that. She was trapped. Plain and simple. Lucy slid down off the toilet and onto the cool of the tile floor, slumping against the bowl. "Shit," she groaned aloud, to no one in particular. Well, at least she was in the right room for it.

So, the angel wasn't dead after all. It must have been stunned or something. Although she could have sworn it hadn't been breathing and didn't have a heartbeat. Then again, maybe angels didn't have hearts or lungs. It's not like she was an authority on angel physiology.

Hell, now that she thought about it—maybe it wasn't even an angel. Maybe it was a member of some alien race that was the source of all the angel myths, kind of like those ancient astronauts.

She couldn't let this get her down. She had to look at the positive side of it. She would make just as much money with a live ancient astronaut as she would with a dead angel—it didn't really change much at all. If anything, this was actually an improvement! She just had to figure out how to work this thing to her advantage.

She just needed to think for a few minutes…

* * *

Lucy started awake, uncertain how long she'd been asleep. She knuckled her eyes and spat out fluff from the pink synthetic toilet cozy she'd been using as a makeshift pillow. At first she was confused by her surroundings, then remembered how she'd come to be locked in the bathroom in the first place.

She pressed her ear against the door, listening for the tell-tale drone of the creature's wings, but what she heard sounded more like human voices.

She opened the door a crack, peering around the jamb into the hallway. The voices became slightly clearer and seemed to be issuing from her bedroom. She recognized one of the voices as belonging to a particularly obnoxious early-morning talk show hostess.

Had she left the television on when she left the house for work the other day and simply forgotten to turn it off? No—she distinctly remembered the apartment being dark when she returned the night before. And when she'd retrieved the phone from under the bed, the portable set perched on her dresser had been as blank as a blind eye.

Lucy quickly closed the bathroom door and rested her shoulder against the jamb, chewing her thumbnail. She had to regain control of the situation, and there was no way she could do that by cowering in the john. Still, she was unwilling to sally forth unarmed against what was, quite literally, The Unknown.

She cast about the room, searching for a possible weapon. The only thing that came close was the plumber's helper under the sink. It wasn't much, but it had a wooden handle and the heavy rubber cup provided a certain heft she found comforting on a cave-woman level. And, if the thing tried to jump her, she could always spray it in the face with some Red Door, which might give her the time she needed to make her getaway.

Thus armed with a toilet plunger in one hand and an atomizer of perfume in the other, Lucy eased out of the safety of the bathroom and cautiously edged her way towards the bedroom.

The door was ajar and there were flickering shadows cast by the light from the television screen. Holding the plunger in front of her like a lion tamer's chair, she eased the door open a little further and looked inside.

Nothing had been moved, as far as she could tell. The dresser and wardrobe were in their usual state of disarray, the drawers half-open with their contents hanging out like tongues. The collection of purloined milk-crates that passed for her bookcase were still overflowing with used paperbacks scrounged from the Strand. Even her bed was still unmade from the day before. The only thing different, as far as she could see, was the angel perched on the back of the ratty easy-chair beside the bed, staring with rapt attention at the television's glowing screen.

As she moved farther into the room, she marveled that something as large as the angel could stay balanced atop the chair. It hunkered with its knees pulled up to its chin and arms wrapped around its calves, the wings occasionally twitching and shivering of their own accord without the angel seeming to be aware of their activities. As Lucy drew closer she could hear the angel muttering to itself under its breath, although it never once removed its gaze from the screen.

The early-morning talk-show hostess, her hair sculpted into something between a helmet and an ornate sea-shell, was blathering on about a certain celebrity's aerobic exercise video. When the camera cut to a clip of said celebrity hyperventilating to the Oldies, the angel suddenly swiveled its head toward Lucy, looking like a cross between a barn-owl and Linda Blair in *The Exorcist*.

Lucy gasped in alarm and jumped back, raising the plumber's helper over her head. If the angel perceived this as an aggressive gesture, it did not register in its face. Instead, it smiled the same disarmingly open smile as it had before and pointed at the television, announcing in a voice as clear and pure as an alpine spring:

"Free wee-wee pads at Puppy City!"

Lucy laughed so hard she dropped both the plunger and the atomizer. And all the angel did was watch, a slightly perplexed look on its perfect face.

CHAPTER 3

It was funny how the light of day—well, the crack of dawn—made things a lot less scary than they'd appeared in the dead of night. For one thing, Lucy now had an unobstructed view of all available exits, and, on its part, the angel did not leap from its perch and come flapping after her as it had earlier. Lucy felt a twinge of embarrassment as she replayed the events of the night before. No doubt the poor thing had been as disoriented as she was—probably even more so. After all, he—well, *it*, to be technical—was the one waking up in a strange place in a strange world, not her. If anyone had a license to freak out, it'd be—? Shit, she didn't even know what to call it, assuming it had a name.

She eased forward cautiously, just in case it decided to go after her like Tippi Hedren with a wigful of pumpernickel again. The angel remained motionless, except for its head, which tracked her with the steadiness of a bank-camera.

Lucy met its unwavering gaze, realizing her initial impression from the night before had been correct. The angel's irises were completely without color. This was made even stranger by the pupils, which were starburst in shape and appeared overlarge in the otherwise empty eyes. Even though it was obvious the angel could see perfectly well—especially in the dark—Lucy found herself thinking of her grandmother's cataracts.

"Uh—hi," Lucy said, clearing her throat.

The angel tilted its head, regarding her like a baffled hound.

"Sorry about last night. It's just that after living alone in New York for so long—you know how it is."

The angel's pale brow knitted slightly, as if trying to decipher a particularly difficult math problem, then tilted its head to the other side.

"Uh—well, I guess maybe you *don't* know, what with, uh, you being new here and all. But I think we ought to try and start off again on the right foot—don't you agree?"

The angel merely stared at her with its crystal-clear eyes which, she now realized, had yet to blink.

Lucy had no idea whether the creature seated in front of her was capable of comprehending human speech at all. Although it had spoken earlier, she was uncertain if it was any more than parroting sounds, the way a birdwatcher might imitate the warbling of a thrush to lure it into view.

"My name is Lucy. Lucy Bender." She spoke slowly and pointed to herself, tapping her breastbone with a forefinger. Then she smiled and pointed at the angel. "And your name is—?"

The angel's frown deepened for a second, then the knot of its brow loosened and it said in a voice as bright and soothing to the ear as a wind-chime stirred by a lazy breeze: "Joth."

Lucy let out a deep breath. Okay, at least communicating with the thing was easier than talking to a cab driver.

"You are a deathling, Lucy Bender."

Lucy's smile disappeared. Maybe speaking English wasn't going to make communication that much easier, after all.

"Uh—I'm a *human*, if that's what you mean."

"You die. You are a deathling."

Joth spoke as casually as if it was telling her the sky was blue. Lucy did not feel threatened or menaced by the statement, although had it come from anyone or anything else that most surely would not have been the case.

"Die? Me? Personally? Well, not yet—I mean—" She was quickly getting flustered. She wasn't sure what she'd expected to be the first statement out of the angel's mouth, but she certainly hadn't expected it to be, well, so *personal.*

Joth pointed at the television, which was still chattering away to itself on the dresser. "The creatures in the light-box are deathlings as well?"

"I guess you could say that."

"I want to see other deathlings."

Joth got to its feet so quickly she didn't see it move. One moment it was perched on the chair, knees drawn up to its chin, the next it was facing her, peering at her with its unwavering, translucent gaze.

Lucy was so startled she couldn't find the breath to cry out—all that came from her was a sharp, short gasp. The angel was so close it threatened to send her into a claustrophobic panic. Whatever it might or might not know about "deathlings," it was clearly ignorant of personal zones.

Lucy reflexively planted a hand on the creature's hairless chest, which felt as smooth as a firm peach, and gave it a gentle shove, pushing it back an arm's length. To her surprise, the angel flew backward, striking the easy chair with enough force to knock it over.

"Oh God! I'm so *sorry!* Are you okay!?!" she gasped. "I didn't *mean* to do that!"

"I do not understand—I have done wrong?" There was no surprise, no anger, no fear in Joth's face or in its voice.

"I really didn't mean to push you that hard! It's just—well, you can't *do* that!"

"What must I not do?"

"Get that close! And it's not just me—you can't do that to anyone! People—uh, deathlings—don't *like* it when someone else gets *that* close— it's considered hostile."

"*Hos-tile.*" Joth weighed the word as it spoke, swirling it in its mouth like a Beaujolais. "I do not understand *hos-tile.*"

"You know—angry, uptight, mad."

Again the blank stare. Lucy rolled her eyes and took a deep breath, trying to figure out a simple means of explaining basic human social etiquette to an angel.

"Joth, you can't get in people's faces like that—it's *rude.*"

"Rude."

"Look, just don't do it again, understand?"

Joth nodded. "It is not permitted. Therefore it is not to be done." The words had the ring of a rote recitation to them, like a liturgical response.

"What *are* you, Joth? Are you from another planet? Or did you escape from a genetics lab—is that it? Are you a mutant?"

"I am elohim."

"Is that the name of the planet you're from?"

"From?"

"Yeah, you know—your home. The place you were born."

"Born?" Joth's look of slight bafflement seemed permanent now. "Elohim are not born. We are Created."

"You're clones?"

"I do not understand this word. Elohim are servants of the Clockwork. We exist only to tend the Clockwork. We see to the Clockwork's every need. We regulate the Clockwork, we repair the Clockwork and maintain the Clockwork. That is what elohim do."

"Okay. Now we're getting somewhere. What does this Clockwork thingie do?"

"It Creates."

"It creates what?"

"Everything."

"Could you be more specific?"

"Worlds. Universes. Galaxies. Sea horses."

"You mean it's God?"

"That is one of the Clockwork's names; yes."

Lucy groaned and plopped down on the corner of her bed. Suddenly her legs seemed wobbly. Even though she'd called the thing an angel, part of her had always assumed it was really an alien lifeform from another planet where people had evolved from birds. Something weird but rational. Something scientific.

But if what Joth was saying was what it really meant—then she was sharing the room with an actual "Hark! The Herald Angels Sing" angel. Except this goober certainly didn't look like anything she'd ever seen gracing the top of a Christmas tree.

All the angels she'd ever seen—well, not personally, but in picture books and in the movies—had either looked like blonde women, Cary Grant or a beardless hippie in a long white dress with giant white wings like those of a swan—not the world's biggest hummingbird.

We're not born. We're Created.

Just like a gingerbread man.

"So, uh, Joth, is it? What are you doing here?"

"I am here."

"Yeah, I know. But *why?*"

"I am here."

"I can *see* that, but I want to know the reason for why you're here and not in Heaven, or wherever it is you're from."

"I do not know."

Joth was back on its feet again, although now careful to give Lucy plenty of space. It darted about the confines of the bedroom like a hummingbird on speed, picking up things and putting them down, opening and shutting dresser-drawers, repeatedly opening and closing the doors to her wardrobe and obsessively touching each and every one of her garments in a matter of a heartbeat.

"*Stop that!* Leave my stuff alone!"

Joth instantly stopped and came to rest in the middle of the room. Despite its having picked up and touched every thing that wasn't nailed down, Lucy couldn't tell if anything had been actually moved. Even the dresser drawers were back to their habitual half-open state.

"What the hell did you think you were doing?" she demanded.

Joth blinked. "I am here."

"Aw, Jesus, are we back to this again?" Lucy threw her hands up in surrender. "I give up trying to figure you out! I'll let the professional interviewers deal with your ass! Let them ask you answers until they're blue in the face! I don't care! Where's that damn phone?"

She stalked out of the bedroom and headed up the hall towards the living room, Joth following a few steps behind her. She found what was left of her phone lying in several pieces in the foyer.

"Cheap-ass piece of shit!" she groaned as she picked at the ruins. "That's what I get for not choosing AT&T! One thing's for sure—they don't make these things out of the same stuff as bowling balls anymore." She glanced at Joth, who was—literally—hovering just behind her. "Looks like I'll have to alert the media to the existence of God the old-fashioned way—by going to the city desk in person. Oh, and do me a favor—? Cut out the hovercraft routine, okay? Your wings are giving me a headache."

Joth's wings immediately halted their whirring and the angel's bare feet slapped against the floor.

"Thank you," Lucy sighed.

If Joth heard her, it gave no outward sign. Instead, its pellucid eyes were focused on something else entirely. Lucy followed its line of sight and realized that what had captured the angel's attention was one of her photographs— a hand-tinted print of the irises laid atop her mother's casket.

"What—? Do you like that?"

Joth walked over to where the picture was hanging and tilted its head first to one side, then the other, as it stared at the photograph. Then shoved its hand through the glare-proof glass.

Lucy cried out as the angel tried, in vain, to pluck the flower free of the photo, oblivious to the glass slicing its fingers. She quickly pulled Joth away from the shattered picture frame and into the kitchen, simultaneously turning on the faucet and snatching a fistful of paper towels from the dispenser over the sink.

"Are you all right? Does it hurt? How bad are you cut?"

"Hurt?"

"Just let me see your hand, okay?"

Joth obediently extended its left hand.

Lucy shook her head. "No, the *other* one! The one that's *bleeding*!" She looked more closely at the angel's proffered hand. "What the hell?!?"

There were several deep cuts along the angel's fingers and visible shards of glass jutting from its palm, but in the place of blood a milky substance leaked from the wounds. Even as Lucy watched, the lacerations began to seal themselves. Within seconds the angel's hand was whole again. Stunned, Lucy turned Joth's hand over, inspecting it for traces of scarring—there were none. Nor did Joth have any fingerprints.

She'd read of professional hit-men burning their prints off with acid or laser-surgery, but this went way beyond such self-mutilation. There weren't even lines on its palms. Joth's hands were as smooth and featureless as those of a rubber doll. And, now that she noticed, the angel also lacked fingernails. And there was something about the way its golden, shoulder-length tresses lay flat against its skull that suggested the angel didn't have any ears, either.

When she'd first found Joth, she'd perceived the angel as a winged human—but now she realized that Joth was actually an *approximation* of a human. Yet, for all its alien-ness, Lucy could not find it in herself to be repulsed or frightened by the thing standing in her kitchen.

After all, it certainly didn't possess the brainpower or malice to do her harm. If anything, it reminded her of a cross between a Labrador retriever puppy and the duck that had accidentally flown into the patio door when she was a kid. Plus, Joth's beatific good looks and lack of gender rendered even the unspoken tension between the sexes moot.

At certain angles Joth resembled an effeminate man, at others a mannish woman. The over-all effect was that of an attractive youth balanced on the cusp of adolescence, genderless in its perfection. The undercurrent of dominance/submission and the potential for sexual menace that existed between human males and females simply was not an issue with Joth. The fact that she was completely at ease with an utterly nude individual standing less than two feet away from her was a testament to that.

Still, she doubted she'd be able to hail a cab in the company of a bare-assed angel, even if it was Caucasian. From a distance.

"C'mon," she sighed. "Let's see about getting you something to wear."

Some digging in the foyer closet turned up a black ankle-length duster, a pair of baggy-fit jeans last used to repaint the dinette set, and a pair of battered leather moccasins used for schlepping garbage down to the basement.

"Here, these should do for now," she said, shoving the cast-offs into the angel's pale arms. Joth proceeded to rub the bottom of the moccasin against its cheek.

Fifteen minutes and a hasty explanation as to what clothes were and which item was to be used to cover what part of the body later, Lucy had succeeded in getting the pants and moccasins on Joth. She eyed the angel's gleaming wings, which were spread so that they framed its golden head.

"Can you, uh, hide those things?" she asked.

"Hide?"

The angel's habit of repeating every question posed to it was really starting to get on her nerves, but she supposed she ought to cut it some slack. After all, it clearly wasn't used to verbal speech. They probably used some form of telepathy in heaven or wherever it was from—and she still wasn't a hundred percent sure if Joth weren't some wacky space-brother from another planet.

"You know—fold your wings?"

"Fold my wings."

Lucy watched in amazement as the hummingbird-colored pinions folded themselves, one over another, and came to rest against Joth's broad, muscular back. Despite their size, they doubled over very compactly, seeming to hug the angel from behind like a second set of arms.

The simple grace and unspoken strength of the act reminded her of Mose, the black man who once worked for her grandparents. However, what she saw in her mind's eye was more like a film was unwinding in her head than a memory being sparked.

She could see Mose standing in the doorway of the old barn, harnessing the mule Pappy stubbornly insisted on keeping. Mose's denim work shirt was rolled up past the elbows, revealing arms the color of licorice that rippled with clean muscle. She could smell saddle leather, horse liniment and Mose's sweat, as well as hear his voice, surprisingly soft and sweet for a man his size, as he sang under his breath. She could even make out the beads of perspiration shining on his forehead and arms in the thick heat of an Arkansas summer.

She hadn't thought about Mose in years—not since Mam-Maw wrote during her junior year at college to inform her of his passing. He'd been a gentle, solid man—not very well educated, but far from unclever. He'd had a knack for working with wood, creating simple, but lovely, tables and cupboards. She'd been quite fond of him as a small child, before adherence to social taboos of race and station had been expected of her.

It was with a small shock that she realized she had never spoken of Mose to anyone outside her family—not even Nevin. She'd learned long ago that New Yorkers simply didn't understand how someone could grow up in rural Arkansas and not be a knuckle-dragging redneck with a Klan robe tucked away in the hall closet. They certainly wouldn't understand her waxing sentimental over the hired hand who used to help her grandmother turn over the mattresses and had made her a tiny matching table and chair for her seventh birthday.

"You are thinking of someone."

Lucy stiffened, automatically defensive. "Oh, yeah?"

"Mose."

Her heart skipped a beat, then began pounding furiously to catch up. So she'd been right about the angel being telepathic. Still, it was rather disconcerting to realize someone had actually read her mind.

"How do you know his name?"

"I look into your eyes and see him there."

"But—how?"

"I don't know."

She believed the angel when it told her this. After all, she wasn't exactly sure how she breathed, but she still did it. She wondered if the flashback was directly related to Joth. Maybe it was in the nature of angels to trigger fond memories in those near them. It probably wasn't even something it was aware of or able to control—like pheromones. Still, as pleasant a surprise as the memory of Mose had been, it had proven bittersweet—as only thoughts of times long past and people long dead can be. She didn't know if she could withstand a constant barrage of emotionally draining "snapshots" from her past.

"Here, put this on," she said, handing Joth the duster.

Joth slipped into the loose-fitting coat, consternation registering on its otherwise placid features as the canvas came to rest against its folded wings. The expression on the angel's face was similar to that of a dog forced to wear a sweater: one of mild discomfort mixed with the uneasiness that comes with doing something vaguely unnatural.

Lucy stepped back to eye her handiwork. While Joth would never make it past the doorman at the Limelight, it could pass on the street for a nondescript human being. At least in New York. In the East Village.

"Okay, that'll do—at least for now," she announced as she grabbed her leather jacket, groping the pocket to make sure she still had her keys. She headed for the door, dragging Joth behind her like a pull-toy.

"Come on, buddy—time's a-wastin'!"

"Where are we going?" the angel asked.

"Midtown, of course! We don't want to keep the media circus waiting do we?"

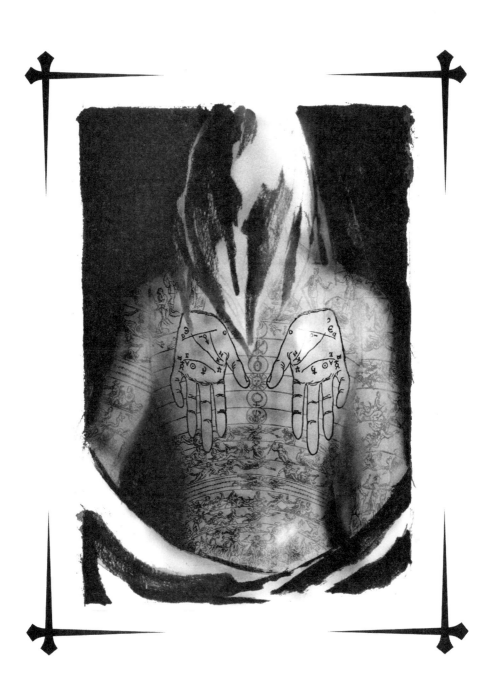

CHAPTER 4

Lucy stepped off the curb and onto Houston Avenue, lifting her arm to hail one of the canary-yellow taxis zipping up and down the divided street. To her relief, one of the drivers spotted her at the light and cut across from the far lane, coming to a sharp stop inches from where she stood. Lucy yanked open the back passenger-side door and hurriedly bundled Joth inside ahead of her. Judd Hirsch's tape-looped voice was already welcoming tourists to the Big Apple and reminding them to ask for a receipt as she closed the door behind her.

"Where to, lady?" asked the cabbie, reaching for his clipboard. While the driver was dark-skinned, she didn't have to check the license attached to the passenger-side visor to figure out he wasn't African-American. If his accent didn't give him away, the ritual scarification on his cheeks certainly did.

"Midtown. Rockefeller Plaza."

"Yes, ma'am."

She had learned the location of *The Terry Spanner Show*'s headquarters while doing temp work a year or so back for a law firm representing a family that had filed a suit against the production company. A guest had been outed on one of Spanner's shows–"Family Skeletons In The Closet"—which resulted in the father having a heart attack on stage and the son's suicide days later. Spanner got off scot-free, if she recalled correctly.

The Terry Spanner Show was famed for being a lower-middle-class freak show, with its parade of transsexual trailer trash, five-hundred-pound dominatrices, UFO abductees, cheating spouses, nympho grannies, and face-offs between pin-headed Born Agains and equally pin-headed heavy metal fans. It wasn't *60 Minutes*—but she had to start somewhere, and where better than with a show that wouldn't automatically call Bellevue when she told them she had a real live angel sitting in the lobby?

She glanced up as the cab came to a light and glimpsed the driver looking into the rear-view, a puzzled look on his face. The cabbie—whose license identified him as John Madonga—reached out and readjusted the mirror, his eyes widening as he got a better look at Joth.

Lucy tensed. *Oh, God—he's seen something—but what?*

Suddenly the driver's dark face split into a brilliant smile and he gave out a half shout, half laugh. The cabbie turned around and shot the grimy Plexiglas divider all the way back so that he could hook his arm over the front seat. Then, looking Joth square in the face, he began excitedly chattering in a language Lucy had never heard before. As she had never seen a New York cabbie do anything except honk and swear at traffic, she was too dumbfounded to do more besides stare.

As the cab proceeded fitfully up the avenue, Joth answered in the exact same tongue as the one spoken by the cabbie. The driver paid rapt attention to whatever it was Joth had to say, then proceeded to pepper the angel with what appeared to be numerous questions, to which Joth responded. After nearly a half-hour of this, the cab came to a halt at Forty-Ninth and the Avenue of the Americas.

"How much do I owe you?" Lucy asked, reaching for her purse.

"You owe me nothing, ma'am."

She shook her head, certain she hadn't heard right. "Beg pardon?"

"I would not dream of charging one of my own tribe!" the cabbie said, with a broad grin. "It has been many years since I left my village, and it is good to see a face from home!"

Lucy glanced at Joth, with its gleaming golden locks and alabaster skin, then back to the driver. "You mean him—?"

"Yes! Of course!"

"Uh—if you don't mind me asking, Mr., uh, Madonga? How can you tell my friend is from your village?"

John Madonga gave her a curious look that made the ridges of scar tissue under his eyes even more prominent. "Why—it is as plain as the nose on his face, ma'am." And with that the bright yellow cab surged back into traffic, to be lost amongst its brethren in Midtown gridlock.

Lucy stared after the cab for a long moment, then looked at Joth, who was standing patiently at her elbow, crystalline eyes fixed on her as if none of the towering skyscrapers and bustling pedestrians existed.

"Where did you learn to speak Swahili, or whatever the hell that was?"

"I am asked questions and I answer."

"You mean—you understood everything he said and were able to hold a conversation, even though you'd never heard the language before?"

"Yes."

Lucy had to admit she was impressed. "Wow! So you've got one of those Universal Translators like they have on *Star Trek* built into you? That's cool! But that doesn't explain why he thought you were from his home—I mean, what did he ask you?"

"Who has died, who has gotten married, who has been born in his village since he left it."

"And what did you tell him?"

"His second cousin is married to a woman from the next village, that his uncle has broken his leg while herding cattle but is doing well, and that his best friend from school has become the father of twins."

"You told him all that?"

"Yes."

"You actually lied to that guy?"

"Lied?"

"You know—said something that wasn't true."

"Everything I say is true. All those things have happened."

"But—how could you possibly know—?"

"I am of the elohim—a servant to the Divine Clockwork. All of Creation is known to me."

"Uh-huh. Okay. If you say so." Lucy grabbed Joth's wrist and took a deep breath. "Let's get going—the place we need to go to is on this block."

* * *

The lobby of Spanner Works, the production company responsible for *The Terry Spanner Show*, was surprisingly decorous, given the show's reputation. Lucy had expected something more in keeping with the audience—say, shag carpeting on the walls and vinyl bean-bag furniture—not muted colors, plenty of glass and chrome and light classical pouring from the sound system.

A neatly coifed secretary sat behind an ultra-modern black-matte reception desk. The only thing that hinted at the nature of the goings-on at the company was a poster-sized head-shot of the host leering down at visitors. Terry Spanner looked like a slightly demented TV weatherman—perhaps a debauched sports announcer—with a carefully groomed but patently bogus toupee worn at a jaunty angle. He certainly had a lot of teeth—all of them capped and trimmed to a uniform length—and he exposed them to good purpose in his trademark shit-eating grin.

Lucy glanced at Joth from the corner of her eye. In a way, Terry Spanner seemed more like an alien lifeform than the one standing beside her.

The receptionist looked up from her desk, smiling with blank inquisitiveness. "Yes, may I help you?"

"I'm here to see Mr. Spanner."

The receptionist's politely glassy gaze shifted from Lucy to Joth. Her eyebrow raised slightly. "Do you have an appointment, Ms.—?"

"Bender. Lucy Bender. And, no, I don't. But it's important."

"Of course. But I'm afraid no one sees Mr. Spanner without an appointment."

"I understand that, really I do. But this is different. Honest! I've got something big to show him! Really big! Bigger than UFOs! Bigger than Elvis, even!"

"I see—could you and your friend please sit over there, ma'am? I'll check to see if one of the assistant producers is in his office."

"Sure. No problem." Lucy guided Joth to one of the tastefully upholstered couches. It had been so long since she'd dealt with a sofa that didn't leak horsehair she almost didn't know how to sit on it.

The receptionist spoke into the receiver and a couple of minutes later a tall, slightly frantic-looking man in his mid-thirties emerged from the door behind the desk. He was missing his suit jacket, his tie was askew and his cheeks were flushed, and he spoke with the breathlessness of a man working on his first stress-related cardiac event. He shook Lucy's hand as she rose to greet him.

"Hello—Miss Fender, is it?"

"Bender. Lucy Bender."

"Well, Miss Bender—what is it you have to show us that's so groundbreaking?"

By way of explanation she pointed to Joth.

Talbot frowned down at the angel's upturned face. "I'm afraid I don't understand. Could you be a little more explicit?"

"I'll be more than happy to go into detail, but not here—is there somewhere else where we can talk? Somewhere more private?"

"Of course. Follow me."

Talbot lead Lucy and Joth past the receptionist and down a corridor that took them past rooms filled with partitions and computer terminals, with equally harried-looking men and women rushing from cubicle to cubicle.

"I should be able to find an empty interview room," Talbot explained, as he rattled the knobs on a couple of closed doors. The third one swung open. "Ah! Here we go!" he said, gesturing for Lucy and Joth to enter ahead of him. The interview room was only slightly larger than the boardroom-style table squeezed inside it. Framed pictures of Terry Spanner posed with various guests decorated the walls.

"Please, take a seat," Talbot said, motioning towards a couple of executive chairs. "As you can see, we're busy around here. But never too busy to check on a potential guest! Now—what is it that you and your friend have to show us that is so exceptional, Ms. Bender?"

Lucy smiled, leaning forward so that her elbows rested on the conference table, her fingers steepled. "What I am about to show you, Mr. Talbot, will make your boss one of the most famous men in broadcasting. If not *the* most! How does that sound?"

"Some would say Terry's *already* one of the most famous in the business…"

"How about respected? Do they say *that?*"

"Well—"

"What I have to show you will not only make Terry Spanner the most famous man on television—it will *also* make him the most respected tele-journalist ever!"

"*Ever?*"

"He'll come out looking like Edward R. Murrow! Hell, when he's through, Morley Safer won't be fit to fetch his slippers! How does that grab you, Mr. Talbot?"

"I'm intrigued, to say the least. You certainly talk a good game, Ms. Bender—but can you follow through?"

"This is hardly a question of empty boasts! What I'm about to show you will change the world forever!"

Talbot leaned back in his chair, fixing Lucy with a calculating look. "Okay. You've got me hooked. What's this earth-shattering secret you want us to have on our show?"

Lucy turned in her seat and motioned for Joth to stand. "Joth—could you be so kind as to remove your coat for Mr. Talbot?"

A look of genuine relief crossed Joth's face. It eagerly shrugged free of the duster, exposing its deep, hairless chest and wide, muscled shoulders. Talbot shifted in his seat, glancing from Lucy to Joth and back again.

"Joth—spread your wings, please."

With what sounded like the rustle of stiff silk, the angel's wings unfurled like the petals of an exotic night-blooming flower, pulling themselves up and away from Joth's torso. The light from the overhead fluorescent bars shone on the multicolored underpinning, and for a brief moment it was as if they were panes of stained glass. Lucy was so moved by the strange beauty of it all she had to cough into her fist before she could turn back to face Talbot.

"So—what do you think? Is this big or is this big?"

Talbot stared at Joth for a long moment then turned his gaze on Lucy. However, instead of the dumfounded delight she had expected, what she saw was rapidly rising indignation.

"Is this some kind of *joke?*"

"Huh—? What do you mean?"

"You come in here wasting my precious time—and for *what?* Tattooed men are a dime a dozen, lady!"

Lucy looked from Talbot to Joth, whose gleaming fourteen-foot wingspan all but filled the room, then back again. "*Tattooed*—? What the hell are you *talking* about—can't you see his fucking *wings?!*"

Talbot stood up rapidly, his face rigid. "Ms. Bender, I think I've seen all I need to. I'm afraid I'm going to have to ask you to leave."

"I can't *believe* this! I bring you the Eighth Wonder of the World and all you see is a *tattooed man?* Well, if you can't see the wings, maybe you'll notice a few other differences. Joth, would you take off your pants—?"

Talbot hurriedly raised his hands. "That's *quite* enough, Ms. Bender! I've already seen more altered genitals than a moil—I don't need to look at your boyfriend's!"

"He's *not* my boyfriend! He's not even a *he!*"

"And *that's* certainly not new around here, *either!*"

There was a sharp knock on the door and a burly man in a security-guard uniform thrust a bullet-shaped head into the room. Behind his broad shoulder Lucy glimpsed the receptionist and a couple of anxious-looking interns gathered in the hall.

"Mr. Talbot—is there any trouble—?"

Talbot straightened his tie slightly, a look of relief in his eyes. "No, Jamal. No trouble at all. However, if you would be so kind, please see to it that Ms. Bender and her—*friend*—leave the building?"

The security guard nodded his understanding. "Sure thing, Mr. Talbot. Come along, miss."

Lucy looked at the waiting security guard then back at Talbot, who was nervously tugging his necktie into a Gordian knot. For the second time in twenty-four hours she had done the unthinkable and Caused A Scene.

Doubtless Mam-Maw would have died of embarrassment, if she weren't already six feet under.

She glanced back at Joth, who was standing perfectly still, watching her with those strange, colorless eyes, head cocked to one side like an inquisitive robin. The angel was still stripped to the waist, its unmarked flesh glowing in the light from the overheads. She had to shake her head and laugh. To think Talbot had looked at such perfect, flawless flesh and seen swirls of pigment and ink!

"C'mon, Joth, put on your coat. This is no place for you. We're among Philistines here."

"Please, miss—if you'll just come along quietly—" The security guard motioned toward the hallway. He glowered at Joth, one hand resting on the butt of the revolver secured at his hip, apparently expecting some sort of trouble, but Joth merely smiled back. The security guard looked momentarily confused but quickly regained his composure.

It was a long march down the hall to the lobby. Heads popped in and out of open doorways to give Lucy and Joth a curious stare, then rapidly retreated, only to be replaced by another, different face. No doubt this would make for a couple of jokes at the water-cooler, then be quickly forgotten. Just another crazy white-trash viewer trying for her fifteen minutes, nothing more.

When they reached the lobby the security guard leaned between Joth and Lucy and pressed the call button for the elevator. Lucy could tell the guard was still watching Joth from the corner of his eye.

"Is something wrong?" she asked.

The security guard started slightly. "Oh! No—it's just that your friend reminds me of someone I used to know."

"Yeah. That happens a lot."

The guard cut his eyes to where the receptionist was sitting. "Uh, look, ma'am—don't worry about the cops, okay? Long as you and your friend leave the building everything's cool—understand?"

Lucy smiled ruefully and nodded. "I understand. You're just doing your job."

The elevator chimed and the doors opened. Lucy stepped in, Joth following on her heels. As the doors closed behind them she glimpsed the security guard still standing there, staring after Joth, rubbing the back of his neck. The look on his face was that of a man trying to talk himself out of thinking he'd just seen a ghost.

* * *

Angels On Fire

Lucy hadn't really been expecting to have to get back home on her own. She'd imagined that once the TV people caught sight of Joth's magnificent wings she would be squired back to her apartment in a limo. But that was clearly not going to be the case. While she still had the money she had planned to pay the cabbie for the drive uptown, something told her she better hang onto it if she expected to eat and buy toilet paper later that day. Which meant taking the subway home. Luckily, she happened to have a couple of tokens on her.

She paused outside the entrance of the Rockefeller Plaza subway station and turned to Joth. "Look, we're going to take the subway back home—"

"Subway? This is like cab?"

"Sort of. Except that there are a lot more people, you don't talk to the driver, and it's underground."

"Underground?"

"Yeah. Beneath the surface of the earth. Below the street."

Joth glanced down at the gray pavement, then back up at Lucy.

"Below belongs to the Machine," the angel announced, with the dire seriousness of a five-year-old convinced that there is a tiger living under the bed.

"Whatever," she sighed, taking Joth's hand in her own. "Just don't let go of me while we're down there, okay?"

Having said that, they descended into the maze of interconnecting tunnels that led, eventually, to the F Train.

* * *

The production meeting was already under way when Talbot arrived, a bulging file-folder tucked under one arm. He smiled anxiously as he took a place at the end of the table, mopping his brow.

"Sorry I'm late, everyone." Although his excuse was supposedly to the entire group, his eyes were focused on the head of the table.

The executive producer glanced up at the interruption, fixing Talbot with a pair of eyes that were as dark and unreadable as those of a cobra. The eyes seemed even darker when taken in contrast to their owner's hair, which was as red as freshly spilled blood.

Terry Spanner turned toward Talbot, flashing a smile that possessed more teeth than one would have thought possible to fit in a human mouth. "No problem, Carl. We really hadn't started yet. What was the hold-up?"

"I had to give another crazy the bum's rush."

"I thought I heard yelling a little while ago. Anything interesting?"

"Not really. I thought I'd gotten better at spotting these types. Well, the man was dressed like a street person—but the woman looked okay enough. Turns out she was just another East Village burn-out trying to palm her performance-artist boyfriend off as the Eighth Wonder of the World. Granted, the guy had some nice tattoos—"

The Assistant Director looked up from her notes and frowned at Talbot. "Tattoos? Are you talking about that woman Jamal showed out?"

"Uh—yeah. Did you see them?"

"They walked right past me! And whatever that guy was, he sure wasn't tattooed! I mean, it was kind of hard to get a good look, what with the dreadlocks and all, but those were ritual scars he had all over him—you know, like African shamans or Australian aborigines…"

"Dreadlocks—?" Talbot laughed, shaking his head. "I don't know who you were looking at, but the guy I'm talking about didn't have any hair at all! He had this big yin-yang symbol tattooed on his skull…"

"I saw Jamal escorting two women out of the building earlier, but I didn't see any guy at all—black, tattooed or otherwise. There was a woman dressed in black jeans and a motorcycle jacket, and then there was the Chinese woman in the black duster," the head writer said as he picked at his cardboard container of fried rice.

"Chinese woman? Are you sure about that?"

"I think I'd recognize someone from my own ethnic group, don't you? Surely you couldn't have missed her, Carl! After all, she was topless under that coat!"

Spanner's shit-eating grin had disappeared, replaced by a far less amiable scowl. "Wait a minute, Carl—how many nuts did you have escorted out of the building today?"

"Just those two, I swear, Terry! I have no idea what they're talking about—!"

Although the Executive Producer had remained silent throughout the exchange, his gaze was now directly on Talbot. Talbot felt his stomach tighten and a bead of sweat race down his back and head for the crack of his ass. He'd never felt very comfortable around the Executive Producer. There was something—strange—about the man. Not that he ever did or said anything untoward. But Talbot couldn't escape the feeling that there was something very unpleasant going on behind those unnaturally dark, glittering eyes. When the Executive Producer finally spoke, Talbot flinched as if he'd been struck.

"Did you get the young lady's name, Talbot?"

"Y-yes, Mr. Meresin! She filled out the standard forms! They should still be with the receptionist."

"Good. Very good."

Meresin smiled and Talbot quickly looked away, for fear of what he might see looking out from behind the other man's eyes.

* * *

Luckily for Lucy and Joth it was still early in the day and the subway car was relatively uncrowded. Lucy sat on the hard plastic bench and stared forlornly at the bilingual placards advertising wart removal, warning about AIDS, and posing the eternal question: *Hammertoes?*

All her fantasies of multimillion-dollar marketing deals, licensed T-shirts and being interviewed by Larry King had disappeared as quickly as they had arrived—but taking more than mere high expectations with them. What good was it to have an angel no one else could see for what it was? She might as well have stumbled across a singing and dancing bullfrog. She glanced over at Joth, who was openly staring at the faces of the other riders in the car as only small children and the utterly mad are wont to do. She quickly leaned over and nudged Joth in the ribs with her elbow.

"Stop that!" she stage-whispered.

"What?"

"Looking at people! It's rude to stare like that!"

"Rude?"

"Rude is—well, *rude*. It makes people feel threatened, understand? Like when I told you to back away. You can look at people, but you can't *stare* at them like that! See how I do it? You start off by looking at the floor, then you let your gaze drift up a little bit at a time—it doesn't stay in one place too long. Just watch me, okay?"

By way of example, Lucy let her gaze drift across the length of the subway car, touching on, but never settling upon, an old woman with a stringbag full of groceries; a teenaged boy tricked out in baggy hip-hop fashions; an older African-American man dozing with a copy of the *Post* steepled across his lap; a pair of Orthodox rabbinical students bent over their prayer-books. Finally her gaze came to rest on a tall, lean man dressed in unbleached linen pants and leather sandals, with shoulder-length snow-white hair pulled back into a loose ponytail. What caught her attention was his shirt—an eye-hemorrhaging Hawaiian print depicting sunset on Oahu.

With a sudden start, Lucy noticed the man in the Hawaiian shirt was looking back at her. She blushed and quickly looked away. When she risked a quick glance back she realized the white-haired man in the Hawaiian shirt hadn't been staring at *her*, but at *Joth*.

Before she could figure out what that might mean, the conductor announced the Second Avenue stop. Lucy got to her feet as the train slid to a halt, Joth's hand still in hers. As they moved toward the doors, Lucy glanced over her shoulder in the direction of the man in the Hawaiian shirt, but he was no longer anywhere to be seen.

CHAPTER 5

It was with greatly reduced spirits that Lucy returned to her humble Alphabet City apartment, Joth still in tow. They had trudged the six blocks from the subway station without incident. While the angel's ragged appearance might have raised the occasional eyebrow in Midtown, on Houston and Avenue B it didn't even warrant a glance.

Lucy's depression, however, was quickly replaced by alarm as she reached, keys in hand, for the door to her apartment, only to have it slowly swing inward.

"*Shit,*" she hissed under her breath, her heart lurching into turbo-powered overdrive.

There was someone in her apartment, all right. She could hear them moving around. She contemplated running downstairs and fetching the Super, but then she would have to explain what Joth—who wasn't on the lease—was doing there, and she wasn't really up to that right now. She was still agonizing over what to do when the door was yanked open from the inside, and she found herself staring face-to-face with the intruder.

"Oh, uh, hi," Nevin said, as unprepared to see Lucy as she was to see him. He was dressed in what she had come to think of as his Downtown Art Uniform: a pair of tight-fitting black Calvin Kleins, a black Armani T-shirt, black hi-top Doc Martens, and a black half-jacket of calf's leather. His dark, short-cropped hair looked fashionably bedraggled, and his strong, jutting chin was, as ever, cloaked in five o'clock shadow.

While inwardly relieved that it hadn't turned out to be a crackhead or a junkie going through her apartment, Lucy was far from pleased to discover he had entered the apartment while she was out. Still, a part of her thrilled at the sight of him. Perhaps he'd come to his senses and was going to beg that she take him back. Then she saw the empty space on the walls behind him. Looking down, Lucy spotted the artwork that had been hanging in the foyer propped against the hall closet's door, bundled in old blankets and bound with twine.

"What the hell do you think you're doing!?!" she shouted, pushing her way past Nevin.

"I just came by to pick up what belongs to me, that's all."

"*Yours?* Those are *my* pictures, damn it! *I* was the one who paid the models, bought the film, photographed them, developed the negatives and paid to have them framed! *I* was the one who paid for the nine sets of slides for the NEA Grant!"

"But *I* was the one who gave you the idea!" Nevin sneered in reply. "You even let *me* sign my name on the bottom! So they're just as much *mine* as *yours*. Besides, I was the one who filled out the grant forms—which were approved by the way. In my name."

"*What?!?* Of all the *nerve*—! You lousy stinking *poseur!* You're nothing but a thief and a whore! You couldn't just dump me for that rich-bitch mall vampire, you had to steal my work, *too!* I hope that cunt chews you up and spits you right back on the street where you *belong!*"

"You're one to talk," Nevin snorted, nodding at Joth, who was still standing in the hall, watching them placidly like a cow chewing its cud. "Honestly, Lucy—couldn't you do better than a squatter?"

"Leave him out of this! He's got *nothing* to do with you—or me, for that matter! But if you think you're going to waltz out of here with those pictures, you've got another think coming, asshole!"

Lucy moved to block the door, hands on her hips, eyes seething with indignant rage. Nevin shifted his tactics, smiling and softening his voice.

"C'mon, Lucy—lighten up! After all we've meant to one another, it shouldn't end like this! Neither of us wants this to get ugly—"

"It's a little *late* for you to be worried about that, isn't it?" she replied tartly.

"Lucy—please! Be reasonable!"

"You're *not* leaving here with those pieces, Nevin!"

Seeing he was not going to get any farther, Nevin's eyes narrowed and his voice quickly lost its honeyed edge. "I'm not going to argue with you any longer, Lucy! So get out of my way!"

Nevin picked up one of the bundles and headed for the door, but Lucy blocked him, pushing him hard enough that he staggered backward a couple of steps. Nevin's face darkened as he righted himself.

"Get *out* of my fuckin' *way*, bitch!" he snarled.

Lucy's growing rage forced her voice to climb into a shriller register. With a slight shock of surprise, she realized she sounded exactly like her mother. "That's it! I'm calling the cops!"

Nevin struck her so fast she didn't even realize she'd been hit until she rebounded off the wall and fell to the floor. He stood over her prone form for a long second, breathing hard, the way he used to do after they had sex.

Joth stepped forward, tilting its head to first one side, then another, looking at Lucy as she lay sprawled on the floor, then at Nevin. Nevin tensed, preparing for some kind of retaliation, but relaxed when the angel merely continued to stare.

Mistaking the angel's passivity for cowardice, Nevin leaned forward until his nose was a millimeter from the other's and sneered disdainfully, "Whatchoo looking at, *pussy?* You keep that crazy bitch out of my hair, or I'll kick *your* ass, too!" Nevin gave a nasty laugh and snatched up the remaining bundled artwork, then sprinted out the door and down the stairs.

Lucy groaned and rolled over. Joth was crouched over her, watching her every move intently, but making no effort to help. The back of her head throbbed fiercely from where it had struck the wall and there was blood coming from one of her nostrils and a cut on her lip.

As she struggled to sit up she kept telling herself she wasn't going to cry. Crying didn't solve anything. Then she realized the pictures were gone.

"You didn't stop him," she said, her voice so tight the words came out squeaky. "You let him take my stuff! Why didn't you stop him?"

"Stop?"

"Not let him leave with the pictures!" she sobbed. "Do I have to tell you how to do *everything?*"

The tears were hot and scalded her cheeks. She took a deep, shuddering breath, trying her best to suppress the sobs that threatened to shake her apart. She was *not* going to cry! Crying was losing control. Crying was feeling sorry for yourself. Crying was letting someone get to you. She'd sworn she would never cry like this again back in junior high, where she had suffered the taunts and jeers about her mother.

Lucy flinched as Joth's fingers caressed her tear-stained face, although its touch was light as a spiderweb's. The angel was hunkered down beside her, leaning so that its features were inches from her own. It held up one hand to stare in fascination at the dangling teardrop it had scooped from her right eye.

"Why do you excrete essence? Does something require Repairing?"

"I'm *crying*, you stupid bastard!" she snapped in mid-sob.

"Why are you crying?"

"Because, for your information, I've had a *really* crappy day!" she retorted as she wiped the tears from her eyes. "First I get strong-armed out of the artists' collective, my boyfriend dumps me, I nearly jump off a roof, the art for my next opening gets stolen, I find out I've been swindled out of a grant, and my asshole ex-boyfriend slaps me around for a few laughs! And, if *that's* not bad enough, I'm stuck with a stupid fucking angel who I can't even get *cab fare* for! So, as far as I'm concerned, this has been one of the *shittiest* days of my life—!" She looked up at Joth, hoping for some sign of understanding in the angel's colorless eyes, but saw only emptiness. "Oh, *forget* it! I should know better than to expect sympathy from you! Well, at least there's no way things could possibly get any *shittier.*"

Lucy sniffed as she got to her feet, wiping her eyes on the back of her hand. She leaned her shoulder against the now-barren wall before limping across the foyer to close the door. An explosion of black dots momentarily filled her vision, swarming like clouds of mosquitoes off a stagnant pool. She winced and rubbed the back of her head. There was a lump the size of a duck egg on the back of her head, just below the crown; she could tell combing her hair was going to be a *lot* of fun over the next few days.

As she locked the door and slid the security chain into place, she was suddenly aware of a prickling on the back of her neck. She'd only felt its like once before: on a picnic when a tree ten feet away from the pavilion was struck by lightning.

Although she dreaded doing so, Lucy knew she had no real choice but to face whatever it was that was making every hair on her arms stand at attention. She turned around and saw what looked to be a rip in the fabric of time and space in the middle of her living room. At least she assumed that's what it was, not being overly familiar with such things.

There was a long, slightly ragged horizontal tear from which a bluish-white light poured forth. It was as if her living room was merely a piece of painted scenery that someone had cut a slit in from backstage. As the edges widened on the vulva-shaped portal, arcs of blue-white electricity shot forth. Accompanying the electric light show was a sourceless wind that rattled the windows and kicked up small whirling dervishes of dustbunnies and grit. Lucy shielded her eyes with a raised arm and gripped the doorjamb to keep her balance as the wind grew in intensity. Although her eyes were all but squeezed shut, she could see a figure of some sort framed against the light. She looked to where Joth was standing and saw that the angel was pressed against the far wall, cowering in fear, its hands raised in ritual supplication.

There was a final, explosive burst of bright light and the wind from nowhere fell still. When Lucy dared to look again, the rift in the living room had disappeared and in its place were two figures, the sight of which made her realize that the shittiest day of her life was, indeed, far from over.

The first figure was humanoid in appearance, in the sense that it stood upright and had two arms, two legs, and a single head. However, it was also a lion. But not a big, fuzzy, cuddly *Wizard of Oz* Cowardly Lion with a ribbon in its mane. This was an eight-foot-tall lion which, much unlike Bert Lahr, had a muzzle full of razor-sharp teeth and long, curved claws of brass. Its mane, which fell to its muscular chest, was composed not of fur but tongues of fire. The lion also had huge wings of flame, which it flexed and twitched in time with its tail. However, despite the crackling flames, the temperature in the room did not rise appreciably, the paint on the walls and ceiling did not bubble and blacken, and the smoke alarm remained silent.

As fearsome and disturbing as the winged lion was, it was nothing compared to its traveling companion, which hovered by its side at shoulder-level. It was roughly the size and shape of a beach-ball, surrounded by a corona of the same heatless fire the lion's mane and wings were composed of. A mass of twitching, writhing tentacles, like those of a jellyfish, were tightly clustered beneath it.

At the sound of her gasp of horror, the floating orb swiveled in Lucy's direction, revealing a cornea as big as a dinner plate and a pupil the size of a saucer. Lucy shrieked once and quickly clamped her hands over her mouth. The giant floating eyeball looked her up and down, then seemed to lose interest quickly, swiveling back in the direction of Joth, who was still cowering in the corner, looking like a deer trapped in the headlights of an oncoming tractor trailer rig.

Although it did not open its mouth, a deep, gravelly voice came from the direction of the winged lion.

"Joth of the Lesser Elohim, you have left the Clockwork without permission of the Hierarchs. It is my duty, as a servant of the Clockwork, to escort you back to the Host."

Lucy frowned. These creatures—whatever they were—were Joth's superiors? Which meant they must be angels, too—although nothing she'd ever heard tell about. At least Joth more or less fit the part of an angel—but these two were more along the lines of what she imagined batted for the away team.

The winged lion beckoned with its brass talons. "Come forward, Joth, and present yourself so that you might be Cleansed before your return to the Host."

Although Joth was clearly frightened out of what little wits it possessed, the angel did as it was told and took a hesitant step forward, looking like a child who knows he's about to be beaten within an inch of his life, but can't understand why.

The sight of the normally placid creature's trembling limbs and fearful expression struck Lucy like a fist. Whatever intergalactic moving violations Joth might have committed, surely they didn't warrant such trepidation on the poor shmuck's part. It seemed so unnecessary. These weirdoes were simply power-tripping on the poor guy. And nothing pissed her off more than bullies.

"*Hey!* Who said you jerks could come in here and start ordering people around?"

The winged lion glanced over its shoulder in her direction, wrinkling its snout in displeasure.

"What is a *deathling* doing here?" it growled.

"I *beg* your pardon? I happen to *live* here, thank you very much! And I *don't* remember inviting you—whoever *you* are!"

The winged lion blinked with a second pair of eyelids, which momentarily turned its blazing eyes into clouded marbles. "I am Nisroc of the Seraphim. This is my appointed Watcher, Preil of the Ophanim. All of Creation is ours to traverse."

"Oh, *yeah?* Well *this* piece of Creation happens to be *mine*, pal! And I *don't* take kindly to strangers showing up and harassing my house-guests!"

Joth stood riveted, watching the conflict between Nisroc and Lucy with uncertainty. The floating eyeball pivoted on its invisible axis and fixed Lucy with its unblinking gaze.

"This is most irregular," said the ophanim in a high-pitched whine, like a dentist drill given voice. "This deathling is apparently capable of perceiving us, Lord Nisroc!"

The seraphim shot the ophanim a sour look. "So I observed, Preil. She wears the halo, can you not see?"

The mass of tentacles clustered under the eyeball shivered and flushed pinkish red as its pupil swiveled towards the floorboards in what passed for chagrin.

Lucy wasn't exactly sure what Nisroc meant by her wearing a halo, but there was no time to worry about such things. She motioned to Joth, catching the angel's attention.

"Joth!"

The angel looked at her, but taking its colorless eyes away from Nisroc was difficult.

"Listen to *me*, Joth: you *don't* have to go with these bozos if you don't *want* to! You can stay here, okay?"

"Deathling! You have no idea what you are meddling with!" Nisroc growled. "It is my appointed task to retrieve the prodigal and return it to its rightful station amongst the Host! Your interference places much in jeopardy! If you would heed divine counsel, stay out of this, if you are wise! In a brief span of time—the turning of your world—all that has passed will be of no more substance than a tissue of dreams."

The seraphim motioned once more to Joth, mesmerizing the angel with the light reflecting off its gleaming brass talons.

"Come forward, Joth. Come forward and be bathed in the Fire, so that you may once more serve the Clockwork."

"Joth, snap out of it!" Lucy yelled. "*Stay!*"

Joth blinked and swayed like reed in a high wind. Then its eyes rested on Lucy and it stood still and steady. Nisroc glanced uneasily in Lucy's direction, plucking at its mane with its claws.

"What say you, Joth of the Elohim? Will you come with us, or stay with the deathling?"

"Stay."

Nisroc took a deep breath, its chest swelling like a balloon, and issued an ear-splitting roar that shook the windows in their panes and made Lucy jump in fright.

"So it was marked that this was the first Question," Nisroc growled.

The seraphim gestured with its right hand, tracing elaborate patterns in the air. With each movement of its brass-tipped fingers, sparks flew and there was a smell of hot metal. A glowing doorway appeared, this time without the fireworks and wind-machine.

Nisroc pointed a finger at Joth, glowering at the angel. "We go now—but we will return, as it was decreed before the race of Man crawled from the seas. Three times the Question shall be asked. You have answered the first of these. Should you answer the same two more times, forever shall you be cast out from the Host."

"Yeah, well, thanks, buddy," Lucy interjected. "Don't let the door hit you on the ass while you're leaving! And make sure to take Mr. Peepers with you!"

Nisroc cast a final glance over its shoulder at Lucy as it stepped through the portal. "The folly you have wrought is far more than you could ever imagine, little deathling. If I did track the elohim here, the Machinists will not be far behind. A grounded angel is like blood in the ocean, or a wounded zebra on the plains. You would do well to mark these words—and live in fear."

And with that, they were gone as if they had never been there to begin with.

Lucy glanced down at her wristwatch and was stunned to see that no time had passed. Either her watch was broken—which was not impossible—or time itself had halted while Nisroc and Preil had manifested in her living room.

Now that the heavenly skip-tracers were gone, Joth slid onto the floor of the living room, knees drawn up to its nose, arms wrapped about its thighs. It was hard to tell if it was thinking, deeply depressed, or asleep.

Lucy could feel how hard her heart was beating. Good thing she hadn't realized she was so terrified at the time. Then again, it's not every day a girl gets to tell a high-ranking member of the Heavenly Host to hit the road, jack.

Plus, now that she had the time to think, there were a lot of things the seraphim said that bothered her. Especially that part about blood and wounded zebras. And what the hell was that bit with "the Machinists" all about?

Her train of thought was interrupted by a knock on the door. She stood there for a long moment, debating whether to answer it or not. It was probably one of the neighbors coming to complain about the noise. She wouldn't be surprised if Nisroc's roar had shattered stemware for blocks around.

But then again, after appointing herself a Good-Will sponsor for an overgrown Christmas ornament, being bullied by a shit-heel ex-lover, and receiving obscure threats from heavenly civil servants, arguing with Mrs. Dinkelmeier from 4C seemed positively quaint.

To her surprise, the man standing on the doorstep was tall, lean and handsome in a hard-to-pinpoint way. He was dressed in an exquisitely tailored dark gray suit with a red silk tie that matched the bold color of his hair. But most unusual of all was that his eyes were as black as a beetle's back.

"Ms. Bender? Ms. Lucille Bender?"

"Yesss—?" she said slowly, suspicious as to exactly why this decidedly prosperous gentleman was standing outside her door.

"Allow me to introduce myself," he said, a business card appearing in his hand with the speed of a magician's bouquet. "My name is Meresin. I am the Executive Producer of *The Terry Spanner Show*. I believe you came by our offices earlier today—?"

"Look, man—I'm sorry about all that. You're not here to arrest me, are you?"

Meresin laughed, revealing very white, very uniform teeth. "Oh, no! Far from it, Ms. Bender! If you'll invite me in, I'll be *more* than happy to elaborate—"

Lucy backed up, motioning for Meresin to enter. "Oh, uh, sure—come on in—please excuse the mess—I'm afraid I haven't been able to do much cleaning up around the house lately," she explained while snatching up dirty laundry and loose trash that the wind from nowhere had redistributed throughout the apartment.

"Don't worry about such things on my account, Ms. Bender," Meresin said. "After all, I imagine you have *far* more to handle than simple housechores, what with having an angel fall into your lap!"

Lucy froze, clutching an armload of dirty brassieres, and stared at Meresin. "Angel—? You—you know about Joth?"

Meresin sniffed the air, his nostrils quivering like a hound's. "My, the atmosphere is positively rank with ozone! Have you been recently visited by Celestials?"

"If you mean Nisroc and Preil—you just missed them."

"Good. I simply can't abide the things! While the elohim have their obtuse charms, I find seraphim to be pompous boors! And the less said of their secretaries, the better!" He clapped his long-fingered hands together and rubbed them expectantly "Now! Let's see this Joth of yours!" A worried look crossed his face. "The angel *is* still here, is it not? It didn't return with the others, did it?"

"N-no. It's still here. But, look—how do you *know* all this? Who *are* you?"

"As I said, I'm the Executive Producer of *The Terry Spanner Show*—"

"Yeah, but that *still* doesn't explain why you know about all this weird crap!"

A deep, mellifluous voice emerged from the direction of Lucy's bedroom. "Haven't you figured it out yet, Ms. Bender? He's from the other side," said the white-haired man from the subway.

Lucy hurled the armload of dirty laundry onto the floor and angrily stamped her foot. "Now that *really* tears it! When the hell did my apartment turn into fucking Grand Central Station?!?"

Meresin gave no sign of noticing Lucy's outburst, but instead nodded a greeting to the white-haired stranger, displaying a smile that was both knowing yet menacing.

"Ezrael. Still playing the guardian, I see. As ever."

"And you the deceiver, Meresin. As ever."

There was a sudden burst of light, as if a flashbulb had gone off in a darkened room, illuminating what had been present all along but unseen. Where Meresin stood was a humanoid creature with the lower quarters of a goat and a long, lizard-like tail that lashed back and forth like an angry cat's. The upper torso was human in appearance, as was the head, although the ears were sharply pointed and the tongue forked. Boar-like tusks jutted from the lower mandible and leathery bat-wings were folded against its back. The only things that remained of Meresin that Lucy recognized was the shock of supernaturally red hair, which grew along its spine, and the black eyes.

Meresin seemed genuinely miffed. "Come now, Ezrael! That was *totally* uncalled for so early in the game!"

"Be gone, Infernal beast!"

"Oh, very well! Have it your way, if you must. For now."

Meresin snapped his fingers and was, once again, clothed in the guise of a handsome television producer. "If you don't mind, I'll leave as I came, instead of in the traditional belch of sulfur. I have a car waiting at the curb." With that, the demon turned on its heel and strode from the apartment.

"That's odd. Meresin usually puts up more of a fight than that," Ezrael muttered as he watched the demon go.

Lucy turned to the stranger in the Hawaiian shirt, wagging a finger at him. "Look, mister, I remember seeing you on the subway, and it's not like I don't appreciate the way you showed up that sleazeball from the Spanner show for what he truly is—but *who* the *hell* are you and what the fuck are you *doing* in my house?"

"I understand your anger and confusion, Ms. Bender. But you have nothing to fear from me..."

"It still doesn't explain *how* you tracked us down and got into my apartment! You didn't abracadabra yourself in here, did you?"

"Tracking a grounded angel is not difficult to do, if you know what to look for. Besides, I spotted Meresin's limo parked downstairs, so I knew I was at the right address. And as for how I entered your abode—I needn't resort to anything as grandiose as teleportation when the fire-escape works just fine. You really should talk to your Super about getting a better lock on that window in your bedroom, by the way."

"So—*why* are you here?"

"To help the angel."

"How do you know he's an angel?"

"Because I know one when I see one."

"That's impossible—!"

"My dear Ms. Bender!" Ezrael laughed. "After all you have experienced in the last few hours, you *still* cling to such concepts as the impossible? Believe me when I tell you that I recognized the angel the moment our eyes met—just as birds know one of their feather from that of any other. We are kin, of sorts—" Ezrael lifted his garish Hawaiian shirt and pulled on the waist of his khakis, exposing a midriff that was unremarkable—except that it lacked a navel—"you see, once I was as it is."

CHAPTER 6

"Come, I know this is too much to handle in so short a time," Ezrael said with a kind smile. "Why don't I fix you some tea while you try and relax? And since our friend is in a fugue state, we might as well make use of the down-time."

"Fugue?" Lucy frowned. "You mean he's depressed?"

"Not mentally or emotionally, no. Elohim do not sleep, as you understand the term. However, they do have periods of inactivity, usually after physically or spiritually draining events, that permit them to regenerate their energies." Ezrael motioned for Lucy to take a seat.

Too weary to argue, she sat and watched the white-haired stranger locate clean cups and saucers and put the kettle on the boil. He moved with surprising speed and grace for a man of his apparent years, with a minimum of wasted movement. Lucy was surprised at how Ezrael's puttering about in her tiny kitchen did not make her feel in the least anxious, despite the fact she had known him less than five minutes. Then again, she was nowhere near as territorial as Mam-Maw, who had been notorious for snapping a wet tea-towel at intruders into what she considered her private domain.

Within minutes the kettle was whistling and Ezrael poured the hot water into waiting cups and dropped tea bags in.

"Mind if I join you?" he smiled, sliding a mug of herbal tea across the dinette in her direction.

"No, go ahead."

As Lucy lifted the chamomile to her lips, she looked the old man square in the face and noticed for the first time that his eyes were golden, like those of a cat. But after all she'd seen today, such things were interesting, but hardly startling.

Ezrael sighed and put down his tea cup, glancing out the window into the air shaft before returning his gaze to her.

"What I am about to tell you, Ms. Bender, is something that pilgrims have frozen on the rocky soil of Tibet attempting to learn, that crusaders sacked the Holy Land to protect, and countless heretics died under hideous torture for daring to question. I am going to divulge to you the exact nature of the creature you know as God."

"What?!?" Lucy choked, sending chamomile tea out her nose.

Ezrael laughed, shaking his snowy head. "Come now, my dear! Having been witness to angels, seraphim and daemons, surely God is not so hard a stretch?"

"It's just that, well, I—I don't really believe in God."

"That's okay. The God you're referring to doesn't exist, anyway. Nor does Buddha. Or Krishna. Or Zeus. Or Ishtar. Or any of the other millions upon millions of names for the Clockwork. But that is not to say they are completely invalid, either. They are all aspects of the Clockwork— imperfectly perceived and imperfectly translated, but there is truth in each, just as there is falsehood.

"But for me to explain, at least as it relates to you, I'm afraid it's necessary to start at the Beginning. And I *do* mean *the* Beginning. Do you mind?"

Lucy shrugged. "Naw. I kind of expected it might be a, um, *complicated* story."

Ezrael smiled and nodded. "You're a wise woman, for this day and age. Let me start by stating that that which is responsible for Creation is not a giant old man with a long beard and flowing white robes, seated high up the clouds. That which makes all things is the Divine Clockwork.

"None know where the Clockwork first came into being, or how it did so. Not even the Clockwork itself, for it is incapable of what you and I understand as thought or speech."

Lucy frowned. "Wait a second—are you telling me God is *dumb?*"

Ezrael shook his head. "You must not confuse the Clockwork with anything you have ever known, Ms. Bender. The Clockwork is a vast organism without beginning and without end. It excretes galaxies and exhales asteroid belts. What thoughts it may have—if any—are as far removed from mortal comprehension as opera is from the singing of quasars. The Clockwork is genuinely unknowable on that level.

"It exists in a dimension beyond this one—a realm where symbolism and metaphor are as real as atomic energy and steel are in this. That dimension is the protoverse; it is removed from Time and Space, existing separately from the rest of Creation. I guess it could be called Heaven, although the average mortal would be hard-pressed to recognize it as such.

"The Clockwork dwells in the protoverse, and the Host dwells within and upon the Clockwork. The Host are immortal and composed of rigidly observed castes, of which you have met three so far. They are, in descending order: archons, seraphim, ophanim, cherubim, and elohim. The elohim themselves are divided between the Greater and Lesser varieties."

"What's the difference between the two? Elohim, that is," Lucy asked as she sipped her tea.

"Greater Elohim have fiery wings, like those you saw on Nisroc. They are in charge of the Lessers during work details. The archons are the most powerful of those who tend the Clockwork. It is they who are most often mistaken for the gods mortals worship. They are the Lords of Creation, the Keepers of the Scales, the Protectors of the Clockwork. They are nearly as obscure as the Clockwork itself, but they have made themselves known from time to time.

"Below the archons are the seraphim, such as the one called Nisroc. They hold great power amongst the Host, serving as judges, inquisitors and administrators. They see to it that timetables are met and rituals observed. They are also Keepers of the Fires of Righteousness and Creation."

"What about the eyeball-guy?" Lucy said, visibly suppressing a shudder. "I don't remember anything about giant floating disembodied eyeballs in Sunday School."

Ezrael snorted a laugh. "Ah! Yes! The ophanim! I was just getting to them! They are what the Christian Bible refers to as 'Thrones,' I believe, and which the Talmud called 'Watchers'. The creature called Preil is one such ophanim. They are the eyes of the Clockwork, recording all things that occur in Creation so that the truth may be known when needed. They're a cross between stenographers and a video crew, if you will.

"Below the ophanim are the cherubim, who act as immediate supervisors over the elohim, constantly relaying orders and information up and down the chain of command. The elohim, however, are by far the most numerous of the Clockwork's spawn. There are countless flocks of them, for they are the drones who tend the Clockwork. They minister to the Clockwork's every need from the moment they first draw their heads from under their wings.

"Elohim are task-oriented, but their minds do not register the concept of individual accomplishment or action. They tend the Clockwork because, well, that's what they were created to do. If something is broken, they fix it. It's that simple. They give their actions as much conscious thought as a weaver bird does the construction of its nest. It is all instinct. There is no learning process. None of them are taught what to do or how to do it. They simply do whatever it is that needs to be done, whatever it may be, whenever it may be required. Those that are quick at maintaining the Clockwork when it malfunctions survive and continue.

"Those that are too slow are destroyed by the Clockwork when it malfunctions. I have seen hundreds of elohim boiled at once in a geyser of live steam, or melted in a explosion of bile. Once, I saw an entire aerie crushed by a prolapse—only to be re-created anew by the Clockwork, moments later. There is no telling how many times an elohim is destroyed and re-created, as they have no true memory."

Lucy blinked. "No memory? But—how do they learn or remember?"

"Elohim are like dogs, if you will. They live constantly in the Present, the immediacy of the Now. The Past does not exist, except as something that is not Now. And the Future is an even more abstruse concept. It is impossible for a human to imagine an existence such as the elohim's. After all, what is a man or a woman but the sum of their experiences? Experience is what one learns from and, eventually, develops into wisdom. If these memories are stripped from a man, he becomes a stranger in his own skin.

"Without a Past there can be no Future—only the Present. An eternal and unending Now. That is all our friend—what is its name, by the way? I assumed it named itself for you?"

"Joth. He said his name was Joth."

"Very good. As I said, this is all Joth has ever known—however long that might be. Joth might be no more than twelve minutes old—or more ancient than the seas. The protoverse operates outside of Time, as human understand the term. Certainly the Celestials would have gone insane long ago if they possessed memory of any sort.

"But now that it has pierced the veil into Creation itself, Time can no longer be denied—although the Host has been known to cheat it now and again. And now Joth is beginning to remember those things that have gone before. Memory is a dangerous thing for those unaccustomed to it. One is constantly discovering what is good, what is bad, what works, and what does not. It is a never-ending cycle of discovery and surprise—but also anxiety and uncertainty, where every defeat is always crushing, because it is always the first.

"Try, if you can, to imagine what Joth is undergoing: the last time you were in such a position you were a tiny baby—and it was so frustrating, so traumatic, your memory has mercifully erased nearly all of it from your mind. If a baby had the recall capabilities of an adult, they'd never learn to walk or talk! Why bother to get up, if all you're going to do is fall back down again? Why attempt to communicate if all that comes out of your mouth is gibberish? You must be patient with Joth, although it will be exceptionally trying at times. As a true stranger in a strange land, the elohim will need your help, as there is nothing to guide its course except whatever instructions you might provide."

"I still don't understand—how did Joth end up on my roof?"

"While the Clockwork exists in a dimension removed from this one, it can be easily accessed, provided one knows the proper rituals. Indeed, there are spots where the barrier between worlds is exceptionally fragile—and occasionally elohim that have lost their way from the body of the Host plummet through these portals and into the mortal plane, streaking across the sky like falling stars. I was one such prodigal—as is Joth."

"So, the Cowardly Lion that showed up in my living room was a truant officer?"

"Roughly speaking, yes. Although perhaps a better analogy would be that of a park ranger sent to retrieve an animal that's wandered off its preserve. Since the Beginning, whenever an angel has fallen into the mortal world, Nisroc has been assigned to retrieve it before it is corrupted. Most of the prodigals return as soon as they are located."

"Corrupted—? Are they afraid I'll teach Joth to smoke, play cards and swear?"

Ezrael shook his head. "It's not *that* sort of corruption that concerns them. You've already had a brush with one such agent."

"That devil Meresin, or whatever he called himself?"

"He's a daemon, actually. He's get of the Infernal Machine, just as Nisroc is a spawn of the Clockwork."

"So—these Machinists that Nisroc mentioned, they're daemons?"

"Yes. However, the Horde, much like the Host, are not what you might think they are."

"Nisroc also said something about me having a halo—what was that about?"

Ezrael grunted and rubbed his brow with the ball of his thumb. "The Clockwork is geared to one thing and one thing only: Creation. It is a generative force. It does nothing but eat positive energy and excrete galaxies. All living things are part of Creation—be they daffodils, jellyfish or orangutans. By reproducing and continuing their genetic structure, they feed the Clockwork.

"Yet all living things serve the Infernal Machine as well, for in order to survive, all things must consume other things, and, in the end, all things must die. War, disease, misery—these things feed the Machine.

"The creation of *anything*, whether it is a bird's nest, a pointed stick or a thatched hut, serves to feed the Clockwork. Science and the discovery of new things feeds the Clockwork, as does the service of justice and the healing of the sick. But it is not as simple as it might first sound. When a disease is conquered, the Clockwork is enriched. Yet when plague is rampant on the land, the Clockwork still thrives, for diseases are living things as well—things that breed and live and die, in their tiny, destructive way. So to destroy a disease is also to strike a blow against the Clockwork.

"The Clockwork cannot operate without the Machine, nor can the Machine exist without the Clockwork. This is the First and Oldest Truth, as reflected in Ouroboros, the Great World Serpent, the Everlasting Circle and the I-Ching. The Clockwork and the Machine are the Consumer and the Consumed, the Dual Natures That Never Meet—except in one place, and one place only."

"Where is that?" Lucy asked.

"In the heart of Man," Ezrael said with a wise, sad smile. "Humankind is the fruit of the union of the Undivided Twin. In your way, you are demigods. You hold within you the seeds of Heaven and Hell. Every child born into Creation is a potential Merlin, Buddha, Jesus, or Athena—although most end up as accountants, mothers and farmers.

"You've no doubt noticed the physical differences between Joth and the average human. The lack of genitals and fingerprints is nothing compared to what they lack within."

"You mean angels don't have souls?"

Ezrael shrugged. "Souls are no big thing. Many mortals live their lives without them. No, what the Celestials and Infernals lack is free will. Celestials are the spawn of the Clockwork, Infernals the get of the Machine. Yet your breed was born of the Machine and the Clockwork's convergence. The results are as different as those of masturbation and copulation.

"You see, the richest source of positive energy resides in those things created by mortal hands, for they are imbued with a tiny spark identical to that which fires the Clockwork at its heart. A thing of True Beauty awakens something of the divine in all who behold it, be it a painting, sculpture, pottery or a poem. These icons have the power to inspire those who look upon them throughout the ages and are loci of immense energy, providing the Clockwork with its most potent food source. The best I can compare it to is the royal jelly that turns a drone into a queen bee.

"Art, music, literature—none of these things would exist without the driving force that motivates humans to do more than hunt and gather and reproduce. This is the heritage bequeathed you by the Clockwork. And it is a precious one, indeed. Yet, mankind also has a genius for destruction, inherited from the Machine.

"Animals do not destroy. They kill only out of hunger or self-defense. Man destroys because it pleases Man to do so. Animals do not create. They breed and build, spurred only by the need for food and survival. Man creates because its pleases Man to do so. And that, in the end, is what counts.

"You hold the universe inside you. You're not all one thing or another, but a combination: good and evil, wise and foolish, innocent and corrupt, hero and coward. In the heart of every sinner is a glimmer of saint—just as in the holy man lies hidden the sinner's taint. To be absolutely Good or Evil is to be barren—bereft of the drive to create a world beyond one's self. Humanity is not an inferior copy of the angels—they are but poor shadows of you!

"Your power lies in your diversity. For only through verisimilitude can creativity emerge. Mortals are the only players on the board who have the capacity for surprise. A pawn may turn into a knight, while a king might prove to be worth no more than a rook. Animals are predictable in their actions and reactions to stimuli. Even their panic and aggression can be foreseen, given proper knowledge of the individual species. But humans— while you still possess a strong herd instinct, you are capable of foiling any number of well-laid plans by your simple unpredictability! Humans are creatures of chaos and order, law and misrule. You possess a capacity for duality which Nisroc and Meresin lack.

"Meresin is a corrupter of souls, a sower of discord, a tempter of the weak and base—not because he chooses to be, but because it simply is his Nature to do those things, just as it is in the nature of a bird to fly or a fish to swim. Conversely, Nisroc is compelled to oppose Meresin's machinations, not because it is motivated by any desire for the Greater Good, but because it is impossible for it *not* to do so. It would be like a duck sinking to the bottom of a lake—anti-nature.

"While you would do well to fear Meresin, you are far from helpless in the face of the supernatural. You see, Meresin is at the greater disadvantage, so he must use all the powers at his disposal. It is Meresin who should cower and quake at the mere thought of crossing swords with you!"

"That's really nice of you to say, speaking as a human and all," Lucy replied. "But what does *any* of that have to do with the halo Nisroc was talking about?"

"Hm? Oh, forgive me—I did get sidetracked, didn't I? Well, as I warned you, there are no simple answers in this situation."

"So it would seem."

"The halo Nisroc mentioned is a reference to your aura, Ms. Bender."

Lucy rolled her eyes. "Angels! Auras! The I-Ching! You're not going to start talking about chakras next, are you?"

"Only if you insist. Now, allow me to explain: all things possess an aura, invisible to the human eye. The nature of the aura varies from individual to individual, but its strength is determined by the individual's alignment…"

"I knew it," Lucy muttered under her breath. "Here come the chakras."

"Please! Allow me to finish! This alignment shows how greatly influenced the individual is by the Clockwork or the Machine. There are other factors involved—such as emotions and physical illness—that affect the halo, but alignment is the most important."

Ezrael fell silent for a moment as he studied Lucy, his lips pursed while he looked her up and down. "In you case, your halo shows extremely heavy influence from the Clockwork—you look shocked. Why is that?"

"I guess I'm surprised—I've never considered myself particularly religious."

"Ms. Bender—religion has *nothing* to do with whether one is influenced by the Clockwork or not! The simple fact of being a female ties you to the Clockwork at its most primal level. You are also an artist, which binds you even tighter yet. Thirdly, you bear the genetic mark of those sensitive to the invisible world. Is there insanity in your family?"

Lucy blushed furiously and dropped her gaze to the floor. Ezrael smiled and gave her hand a pat.

"Come now—you need not be ashamed. Was it your mother?"

Lucy lifted her eyes to Ezrael's and nodded, too shocked to speak.

"Your mother had the sight, Lucy, but not what was necessary to endure it. Often it lies dormant until a grave emotional or physical shock awakens it, usually far too late in life to do more than damage. But *you* are an artist, which means that your inner sight is constantly active—like an old dog that dozes with an eye half-open."

"Is that why I can see Joth's wings and no one else can?"

"In part. But, more importantly, you were at ground-zero when Joth fell to earth. That is why you can see its true nature while others do not. They see only what they *expect* to see. As I said, your kind is gifted, but that doesn't mean they aren't fools."

"You keep saying 'your kind,' and 'you humans,'" Lucy frowned. "You're not still an angel—are you?"

Ezrael laughed and shook his head. "No, I haven't been one in quite some time! I am, however, what is known as a Muse."

"Muse—? But aren't they supposed to be women tricked out in sheets?"

"—wearing a laurel wreath and carrying a lyre? Hardly. While some of us are female, not all of us fit such a strictly classical definition. And before you ask, while I am not a human, I assure you I am mortal. While killing me is exceptionally difficult, as my enemies have discovered over the centuries, and I age very, very slowly, I *am* capable of dying. I surrendered my immortality a long, long time ago, under circumstances very similar to Joth's."

"What? I don't understand—?"

"As I said earlier, it is not unheard of for angels to fall from their world to this. And, as I said, Nisroc is usually quick to retrieve them, for the longer a prodigal elohim is away from the Host, the more unstable it becomes. But should something interfere with the initial retrieval—then the prodigal has only two more chances to return to the Host."

"What if next time Joth tells them he wants to return?"

"It will have to undergo purification in the Fire of Righteousness, in order to burn away all the impurities it has acquired from Creation. The Fire is fierce and terrible, and Joth would have to dwell in its heart for a year or more before being allowed near the Clockwork."

"Well…what if Joth *didn't* return?"

"Then it will probably turn into a daemon."

Lucy gasped audibly, glancing first in Joth's general direction, then back to Ezrael.

"Wait a minute—I thought you said you *weren't* on Meresin's side!"

"Don't worry, I'm not!" he chuckled. "The transformation from angel into daemon is not Joth's only fate. It will only become a daemon if its refusal to return is *not* of its own choosing. If Joth makes a *deliberate* decision to remain on earth of its own free will—then the fires of Creation shall burn away its divinity and it will be as other mortals.

"It will be as if Joth was born into the world a full-grown human, knowing hunger and want and cold for the first time—but also discovering joy and warmth and love. What happens after that is up to Joth. Not all former angels are muses, though most of us are—although we can be as unpredictable as any human. However, most of us find ourselves drawn to the Blessed; those humans who possess within them the divine spark—creative types, such as artists, builders, inventors and the like.

"I, personally, have a predilection for the visual arts, although I know a fellow muse who leans more towards playwrights. By using my magics in subtle ways, I encourage to greatness talent that might otherwise find itself thwarted or consumed. In this way I still serve the Clockwork. But now the service is of my own choosing."

"So—Joth will become mortal if he—"

"*It!* Joth is an *it*, not a *he*. Besides, there's no guarantee, should Joth choose to remain on earth, that it would become male."

"Okay, whatever. As I was saying—Joth will become normal if *it* chooses to remain on Earth of *its* own free will. Right?"

"Right."

"But you said angels don't *have* free will."

"Yes," Ezrael sighed, sipping his tea. "Bit of a Catch-22, that."

CHAPTER 7

Lucy glanced out the window and saw the sun going down. "Oh, Jesus!" she moaned as she slapped her forehead. "I can't *believe* I forgot to call in sick!"

Ezrael grunted as he ferried their empty cups to the sink. "Where do you work?"

"A brokerage firm on Wall Street. I'm a clerk-typist. It sucks, but it pays the bills."

"I'd say you had other things besides work on your mind today."

"Yeah," Lucy sighed. "I really thought the sky was the limit this morning. Now I feel like I'm looking up at it from the bottom of a dry well." Lucy shook her head in disgust. "That's what I get for having great expectations!"

"You shouldn't be so hard on yourself," Ezrael smiled. "After all, you're only human."

"Which puts me in the minority around here," she said, resting her chin on her fist. "So what do I do now?"

"We prepare ourselves."

Lucy turned to fix Ezrael with a quizzical stare, cocking one eyebrow. "What do you mean *'we,'* white man?" she asked.

Ezrael laughed as he squeezed her shoulder. "I am here to *help*, Lucy, whether you choose to believe it or not."

The older man fished an antique pocket watch out of the breast pocket of his Hawaiian shirt and frowned at it. "You are right about one thing, however—time *is* slipping away. If I am to be ready for what lies ahead, I must make a few errands before it gets too late." He snapped the watch shut and returned it to his pocket. "I will try be as quick about my business as I can. You stay here and keep watch over Joth. Do you have a spare key?"

"Look in the cookie jar," Lucy said, pointing at a large ceramic bear set atop the refrigerator. "Uh—don't get me wrong. It's not that I don't appreciate what you're doing, Mr. Ezrael—"

"Ez," he said, plucking the spare key from where it was taped inside the bear's head, pocketing it as easily as a magician would a coin. "Call me Ez. And I'm doing this because I owe it to Joth—and to the memory of someone I cared for a long time ago."

The former angel motioned for her to follow him. "I need you to make sure the door is locked behind me when I leave. And while I'm gone, allow absolutely *no one* entry! Meresin is far from the *only* Machinist in New York City—any one of which would most gladly surrender a horn or a hoof to make Joth one of their number."

Lucy followed Ezrael to the front door, trying her best not to let the fear rising within her show in her eyes. Muggers and serial killers were nothing compared to the Unknown—the fear of which, countless eons ago, had given form and reason to such half-glimpsed things as Joth and Meresin in the first place.

As she moved to close the door, Ez grabbed the door jam and thrust his face back in one last time. "Remember—allow *no one* entrance until I return!"

"I understand. Just hurry back, okay?"

Lucy quickly locked the door and shot the deadbolt into place. She hurried through the apartment, turning on all the lights, banishing the shadows back to their corners. She hadn't realized how late it was until she turned on the lights in the living room, causing the walls to leap out like guests at a surprise party.

Once all the lights were on and the doors and windows shut tight, Lucy sank down onto the red velour sofa, chin propped atop her fist, and stared at her peculiar house guest. Joth remained motionless, hunkered on the living-room floor like a living gargoyle, eyes fixed on some unknown point. In a way, Lucy was glad Ezrael was gone. She needed time to marshal her thoughts and try to digest all she had been told. Up until now, things had moved too fast for her to do anything but react.

Assuming everything Ezrael told her was *true* and she *wasn't* tied to a bed in Bellevue talking to the ceiling-tiles, she had no other choice *but* to trust him. It had been a long time since she had to do that. After all, Manhattan was hardly a city that encouraged its citizens to put their faith in absolute strangers. Everyone here was out for themselves, as Nevin had amply proven.

Thinking of Nevin made her wince and rub the back of her head. Now that all the lights were on, it was impossible to ignore how bare the walls looked. She sighed and bit her lower lip. There was a down-side to catching her breath—up until now she hadn't had time for feeling used.

What she felt was anger aimed at herself, not at Nevin. She was mad at herself for being so damned stupid—again. The signs had been there for her to see, but she had—as usual—chosen to ignore them. She used to think she was unlucky in love, but now she was beginning to wonder if she wasn't just out-and-out masochistic.

The lump in her throat had grown so large and heavy it was strangling her. She grabbed a short, tight gasp of air around it, blinking rapidly in a desperate attempt to keep the tears from spilling, unbidden, down her cheeks.

So much of her time, self and money had been tied up in those photographs. Losing them was like having a pet taken from her. Now all she had left was the one picture—the hand-tinted print of the irises lying atop her mother's casket. And the only reason Nevin hadn't taken that one as well was because the frame was damaged.

She had been upset when Joth broke the frame earlier—now she was glad it happened. She didn't know how she would have handled Nevin taking that piece as well. She glanced over at where the print rested in its ruined frame, propped against the wall.

"Oh, Mama," she sighed, shaking her head. "What *would* you make of all this, huh?"

The tears came then. She had not cried at her mother's funeral. Nor had she cried in the three years since. Now, she finally let her grief come forth.

"*Mama,*" she whispered, her throat so tight she could barely squeeze the words out. "I'm so *sorry.* I'm so very, *very* sorry."

Lucy had spent most of her life trying not to think about Mama. First out of shame, then out of guilt, but mostly out of fear. The fear that if she thought too much about Mama, she would end up like her.

Mama had her first breakdown at Daddy's funeral. Lucy had only been six and a half when the tractor rolled on her father, but she remembered how Mama went into hysterics at the cemetery—insisting she could see Daddy watching the mourners from a distance. She worked herself into such a state Doc Moody had to give her a shot just to get her into the car. When the doctor stopped giving her shots, Mama moved on to more freely available medication prescribed by men with last names like Beam, Dickel, and Walker.

Mama was in and out of the state hospital in Benton on a regular basis after that. By the time she was eight, Lucy was living more or less full-time with her grandparents. After a few years of electro-shock therapy and heavy medication, the doctors let Mama come home. While Mama's delusions were under control, the alcoholism certainly wasn't, so Lucy continued to live under her grandparents' roof.

During junior high Lucy had been forced to suffer the shame and embarrassment of being the daughter of the town's crazy drunk. Doc Moody had tried to explain to her that what was wrong with Mama was beyond his—or anyone's—ability to fix, but Lucy was convinced her mother's behavior was deliberate.

When Pappy died during Lucy's junior year in high school, Mama's craziness came back in spades, landing her in Benton for another protracted stay. She was still in a padded room when Lucy graduated. By the time Mama was finally released, Lucy was off at college. Mam-Maw pretty much looked after her after that, and for a while it seemed like Mama might have finally put her demons behind her.

Then Mam-Maw passed away, and suddenly Mama was on her own for the first time in her life. She sold her parents' house to Beth and bought herself a trailer on the edge of town, where she pretty much lived the life of an alcoholic recluse for two years. Then one night Lucy got a call from Mama in the middle of the night, rambling on about how she could hear them walking around outside the trailer—meaning Mam-Maw, Pappy and Daddy. She pleaded with Lucy to come back to Seven Devils, to look after her. Lucy told her no and to go to sleep. Sometime after Lucy hung up on her, Mama took a double handful of pills and washed them down with a quart of George Dickel.

And now, if what Ezrael told her wasn't utter bullshit, it seems Mama wasn't crazy after all. At least, not at first, anyway.

Poor Mama—one moment she was just another rural Arkansan housewife who enjoyed making peach cobbler, crocheting socks and listening to Loretta Lynn, the next she was seeing beyond the veil into the Great Beyond. She simply wasn't prepared for it.

Lucy liked to think she'd stretched her consciousness far beyond the narrow limits of what was considered possible in Choctaw County, but even she was having trouble absorbing what was happening to her. She could just imagine how having the doors of perception thrown wide must have shattered Iris Bender's grip on reality—and Mama never claimed to see anything as *outré* as angels or giant floating eyeballs, just dead relatives.

Still, what Ezrael told her explained a lot—such as Mam-Maw's side of the family's reputation for witchy ways. Lucy always had the feeling that Mam-Maw knew a lot more about what was plaguing her daughter than she let on. Lucy could remember several occasions where her grandmother stopped whatever she was doing to stare off into space, or appeared startled by something Lucy could neither see nor hear.

Her grandmother had been a no-nonsense woman whose creative energy manifested itself in hand-made quilts and elaborately embroidered hankies and pillow-cases. What memories Lucy possessed of her mother before the illness were dim—she remembered Mama had a fondness for puzzles and crosswords, but nothing genuinely creative. In fact, one of the few things she'd brought back with her when she went to Seven Devils for Mama's funeral was her mother's collection of jigsaws puzzles, which she kept stashed in the hall closet. They were one of the few things that reminded her of her mother from happier days.

Perhaps whatever it was that enabled members of her family to see into the Protoverse, or whatever Ez called it, was augmented by the creative impulse. That made sense, in a way—maybe the creative side of the brain was what kept Mankind from permanently freaking whenever it glimpsed the Unknown peeking in through the kitchen window.

Still, buffer zone or not, Lucy was starting to wonder if her neurons might be deep-fried to a crackly crunch. She now knew, beyond a shadow of a doubt, what numberless mystics, philosophers, and saints had died trying to discover—that, yes, Virginia, there *is* an Afterlife, a God, and a Devil, and all because she was unlucky enough to trip over an angel and drag it back to her apartment like it was an old lamp someone had set out on the curb with the garbage.

However, none of this inside info was providing her with much in the way of warm-and-fuzzy religious awakening. The only thing worse than discovering that There Is No God is discovering There *Is* A God—but that it doesn't know or care that you exist.

Frankly, she preferred it when the Universe was a cold, cruel place devoid of reason and where all life was motivated only by the need to create more of itself.

She wept until she fell asleep, wearied from the emotional stress that had accompanied the events of the last twenty-four hours. The last thing she saw before her heavy eyelids closed was Joth squatting on the living room floor, as silent as a stone.

The next thing Lucy knew she was being roughly shaken. She struck out blindly, catching Ezrael in the gut. The former angel groaned and dropped the gym bag he was carrying.

"Watch where you're punching!" he snapped. "It's just me!"

Lucy knuckled her eyes and looked around, feeling slightly dazed. "Sorry—I thought you were my ex-boyfriend."

"Never mind that!" Ezrael replied. "Where's Joth?"

"What do you mean—?" she said stifling a yawn. "He's right over there."

Lucy pointed where the angel had been squatting. Except that he wasn't there. "Where—? Where did he go?"

She jumped to her feet, looking around frantically. "Joth? *Joth*—!?!" She hurried down the hall and looked in the bedroom and the bath, but Joth wasn't to be found in either one.

"You didn't open the door, did you?" Ezrael asked. "I *told* you not to open the door!"

Lucy opened the hall closet and peered inside. "I didn't! I swear!"

"Then where is Joth?"

"I don't know! Maybe he went back to heaven or whatever the hell it is he's from?"

"I *seriously* doubt you would have been able to sleep through a portal being opened," Ez commented dryly.

"So where *is* he?"

The former angel peered into the kitchen then quickly motioned for Lucy to join him.

"I think I may have an answer." Ez pointed to the open window facing the air shaft. "Wasn't that closed earlier?" He plucked a pin feather from the window sill and held it up between thumb and forefinger. "That's what I was afraid of—it looks like Joth has decided to go sight-seeing."

part 2
the devil you know

Those who consider the Devil to be a partisan of Evil and angels to be warriors for Good accept the demagogy of the angels. Things are clearly more complicated.
—Milan Kundera, *The Book of Laughter & Forgetting*

CHAPTER 8

Deathlings were a curious breed. As far as Joth could tell, they were noisy, smelly, and always in a big hurry, rushing here and there at a furious pace, whether alone or in groups. Some deathlings had traveling companions, while others were solitary. There was even an entire sub-group that appeared to be alone, but spoke into small devices clutched in their hands.

And it wasn't just the deathlings—the creatures they traveled in were also in a hurry, even though they spent much of their time sitting still and honking at one another. Indeed, the deathlings' world was in such a hurry its skin rumbled beneath Joth's feet on a regular basis. Hurry-hurry-hurry. That's all this world seemed to be about.

This need for constant and frantic motion of the part of the deathlings appeared to be the result of Time. Time seemed to matter to deathlings as much as the Clockwork did to the Host.

Joth could not understand why the deathlings pushing past it seemed so determined to get from where they were to somewhere they were not. After all, there were no ducts that needed clearing, no valves requiring turning, no mouths to feed, no colons to flush. What possible function could these deathlings be serving, scampering to and fro at such a pace?

This city, as Lucy called it, was tiny, but there was much about it that reminded the angel of the Clockwork. But where were its servants? Occasionally Joth spotted deathlings with shiny yellow skulls emerging from holes in the world's surface that burped steam or smelled of sewage, but it did not spot any Repair Squadrons wheeling about the spires towering overhead.

As Joth continued to wander through the city, it followed no set path or predetermined course, instead allowing itself to be pushed along by the human tide that surrounded it, much like a cork riding a wave.

The neighborhoods the angel passed through went from yuppie to trendy to sleazy to scary, the middle-executives and secretaries gradually replaced by far rougher types of more dubious employment. The Starbucks and bagel shops were replaced by XXX marquees and check-cashing businesses. Joth, the ultimate tourist, observed it all, from the street vendor selling Coco-Lada from a wheeled cart, to the shop windows overcrowded with cheap electronics, to the *botanicas* with their storefronts full of saints and multi-colored candles.

* * *

Julio leaned against the front stoop of his apartment building and scowled openly at the wino ambling past, then turned to the youth beside him, spitting in disgust.

"You see that, Juan? Fuckin' juicer couldn't steal a fuckin' shirt. Like we want to look at his skanky chest."

The other members of the gang—four in all, ranging from fourteen to nineteen years old—laughed over-loudly. They wanted the butt of their joke to know he was the focus of their derision, but the wino appeared oblivious. The other boys muttered amongst themselves and looked to Julio, who was taller, sported a light mustache and had gold-capped front teeth, which made him the nominal leader.

Julio's derisive sneer quickly turned into a frown. "Yo! Asshole! What you doin' on our side of the street?"

The wino smiled vacantly at the sky, the pavement, the fire hydrant, showing no sign that he'd heard Julio in the first place.

"Mother*fucker*!" He reached out and roughly grabbed the wino's shoulder, spinning him around like a rag doll. "Yo! I'm *talkin'* to you—you a retard or what?" he snarled, throwing gang sign in the bum's face.

There was no anger or fear in the old man's eyes—not even surprise at being manhandled. Instead, the wino regarded Julio with an open, slightly unfocused gaze.

"I am Joth," the wino replied, smiling.

"What he say, Julio?" asked Juan, trying not to giggle.

"Say he Josh," Julio replied over his shoulder. "Fucker's trippin'." He returned his attention to the wino. "What you doin' this side of the street, asshole?" he snapped, pushing the wino's shoulder in provocation. "This *our side* of the street, motherfucker! What you lookin' at?"

"I am just—looking," Joth replied.

Julio twisted his mouth into a wicked parody of Joth's smile. "Oh, you *looking*? You lookin' at *what*, asshole? Our women, no? Mebbe you lookin' at my dick, huh? I tell you what you lookin' at—you lookin' at *trouble*, asshole!"

"I am looking at everything."

Julio's scowl deepened as the other members of his gang exchanged slightly baffled glances. The wino wasn't responding to their taunts and insults with anger or to their threats with fear, and it was making them uncomfortable.

"What you tryin' to pull, asshole—you gettin' *Kung Fu* on me?"

"C'mon, Julio—leave him be," Juan snorted, clapping a hand on his friend's shoulder. "Fucker's weak in the head."

"Fucker's *dissin'* me is what he is!" Julio snarled, angrily shrugging Juan off his arm, fixing his angry gaze on the wino. "Yo! *Fuckhead!* You know who I am?"

The wino nodded.

Julio smiled and his chest swelled noticeably. "Oh? Who am I, then?"

The wino's voice was as placid as that of someone reeling off information they have learned phonetically and committed to memory without ever understanding its true meaning. "You are Julian Alvarez, known as Julio. You were born in 1981 to Ernesto Alvarez and Concha Rodriguez. In 1985 your father broke your arm. In 1987 he sexually molested you—"

Julio's chest rapidly deflated as his eyes bugged out of their sockets. "*Shut up!*" he screamed. "Shut your lyin' mouth—!"

"In 1992 you began molesting your younger sister, Maria. In 1996 you stabbed to death Elvira Mae Johnson, aged sixty-seven, when she caught you stealing her Social Security check from her mailbox…"

"I said *shut up!*" Julio's voice climbed the register, becoming a shriek of mixed pain and anger.

Julio did not know how the wino knew these things about him and he didn't want to know. These were things not even his mother or Social Services knew. All Julio wanted was to shut the wino up—shut him up good—and there was only one way he knew how to make things go away.

The wino stared at the knife in Julio's hand as if it were a flower or a shoehorn. He didn't try to run away or dodge the attack as Julio plunged the knife into his bare chest.

Julio looked into the wino's eyes, expecting to see pain and fear in their depths, but all he saw was himself, as if reflected in the windows of an empty house. Julio was nose-to-nose with the wino, his fist still gripping the knife hilt, yet the old man did not cry out or even seem aware that he'd been stabbed through the heart. Julio glanced down at the blade jutting from the wino's chest, just to make sure, but there didn't seem to be any blood.

"What the fuck kinda shit *is* this?" Julio wailed, panic making his voice crack. As he yanked the knife free, something that looked like milk spurted from the wound, drenching his hand. It glowed like the goop in the glow-sticks he bribed Maria with to keep her from telling Mama about the stuff he made her do.

Julio staggered backward, trying to shake off the white liquid dripping from his fingers. It was cold but it somehow seemed to burn. He continued to back away, clutching his afflicted hand.

"What did you do to me?" Julio screamed at the wino.

But the wino wasn't standing there anymore. In his place was Mrs. Johnson, a crimson stain spreading across her withered chest. Julio had known Mrs. Johnson all his life. She had lived on the block for as long as he could remember. She handed out lollipops and bubblegum on Halloween. But that hadn't kept him from putting the knife he used to jimmy her mail box open into her heart when she fought him for her check. Mrs. Johnson looked at Julio from her place beyond the grave and pointed an accusing finger at her killer. Julio screamed like a man who has looked into the eye of hell and seen himself burning in its depths.

Julio dropped the knife and fled back up the stairs to his apartment. His friends exchanged frightened glances and immediately broke ranks, scattering in every direction.

* * *

Joth watched the deathlings run away, somewhat baffled by the exchange that had taken place. The elohim had never seen such negative energy focused through a deathling before. Lucy's halo surrounded her head like a rainbow, the colors oscillating with her mood. The cab driver's halo had been as warm and red as a sunset. The TV man's was weak and gray, like a wispy fog. Julio's halo, however, was all sharp and pointy, like black lightning bolts. The Machine was in ascendance in all the young deathlings that had been gathered around Joth, but it had been strongest in the one called Julio.

* * *

The moment the gang members fled, Estrella Martinez darted out of the doorway of a nearby *bodega*. She had seen the hoodlums terrorizing the poor woman, but was too frightened to come to her aid. Estrella grabbed the young girl's sleeve.

"Honey, you okay?" she asked. "You need a doctor?"

The woman shook her head.

"I am Joth," she replied, her smile identical to those of the plaster saints for sale in the *botanica*.

Estrella clucked her tongue in pity. The poor girl was crazy in the head. The woman's smile suddenly disappeared and she said out loud to no one in particular. "Julio's coming back."

Estrella glanced over her shoulder in the direction of the tenement the Alvarez kid had disappeared into, then turned back to assure the young woman that there was nothing to be afraid of, only to find her daughter Nina, who had died of leukemia thirteen years ago at the age of nine, smiling at her. Estrella gave a tiny cry and grabbed the woman's hand, covering it with kisses, her eyes filling with tears.

* * *

Joth tried to pull its hand away from the deathling female, but she refused to let go. The elohim saw a deathling child—her body wasted by disease—lying in a hospital room, tied to machines by tubes and wires. The image filled Joth's mind, threatening to push everything else out.

"Motherfucker!"

Estrella gave a cry of fear and let go of Joth's hand to look in the direction of where Julio now stood at the top of the tenement's stoop.

The youth shivered and twitched like a man in the grips of malaria, skin blanched and drenched in sweat, his eyes hot and wet. His halo, however, belied his physical appearance. It was blacker than before and throwing off sparks in all directions, like a reverse-negative Fourth-of-July pinwheel.

"Get *out* of my *head!*" Julio howled as he pulled the Glock semi-auto out of his warm-up jacket and aimed it at Joth.

Estrella Martinez screamed her daughter's name and put herself between Julio and Joth. The bullets tore through the older woman and into the angel's upper torso. Estrella spun about like a marionette caught in its strings and collapsed onto Joth, knocking the angel to the pavement.

Julio stared at where the wino and the old woman lay sprawled on the sidewalk like lovers and wiped the sweat from his brow with his gun-hand. He didn't want to look at the hand with the wino's blood on it. It was like someone else's hand, not his.

At the sound of the approaching sirens, Julio's eyes suddenly cleared. It was like he'd been awakened from a deep sleep only to find himself walking down the middle of a busy street. The woman he'd shot was screaming in pain—calling out for someone named Nina.

Julio gave a convulsive cry of horror and dropped the gun as the wino slowly dragged himself back onto his feet, looking more confused than hurt. As the wino took an unsteady step in his direction, Julio screamed and fled down the street, knocking garbage cans and pedestrians over in his desperation to escape what he now was certain was a fiend from Hell.

* * *

Joth watched Julio until he disappeared from sight. It had no desire to pursue the deathling, but it was puzzled by its actions. Why had he done such things?

"Nina—?"

Joth looked down at where Estrella Martinez lay dying on the street. She had a hold on the elohim's pants leg and was trying to pull herself into sitting position. Joth stared in fascination at the fluid pouring from the woman's mouth, nose and chest. It was so red, so bright, so—vital. The elohim knelt beside the dying woman and touched the blood bubbling from her wounds. Joth held its hand up before its eyes and tilted its head to one side to stare at the ruby droplets dripping from its fingertips. So this was what fueled the deathlings' flesh. Joth could feel its innate power, even in these tiny drops.

But, more importantly, Joth knew what must be done. The deathling called Estrella Martinez was Broken. It is in the nature of the elohim to Repair that which is Broken, to set right that which is askew. Joth glanced down at its own chest, where the bullets had lodged after traveling through the deathling called Estrella. The wounds were large—each the size of a silver dollar—although they were already beginning to pucker and shrink. Instinctively, Joth cupped a hand underneath the largest of the bullet holes, catching the milky essence, then poured it directly into Estrella Martinez's open wounds.

Joth then stood up and stepped over the woman's body and continued in the direction it had been traveling before Julio stopped it. Joth did not need to stay and watch the deathling's wounds seal themselves to know that it happened. Besides, the sound of the approaching sirens was too much like that of the cherubim for its liking.

There was much about this world of time and mortality Joth did not understand. Why was the deathling Julio so angry? Why did the deathling

Estrella allow herself to be Broken? Why did the deathling Nevin act in much the same manner toward Lucy? Perhaps Lucy could explain these things to Joth. After all, she was a deathling. But Lucy was not here for Joth to ask.

A shiny black car with mirrored windows pulled up to the curb, inches from where the angel stood. The rear passenger window powered down and a man with bright red hair and eyes as shiny and dark as the car in which he rode smiled out at Joth.

"Going my way?" asked Meresin.

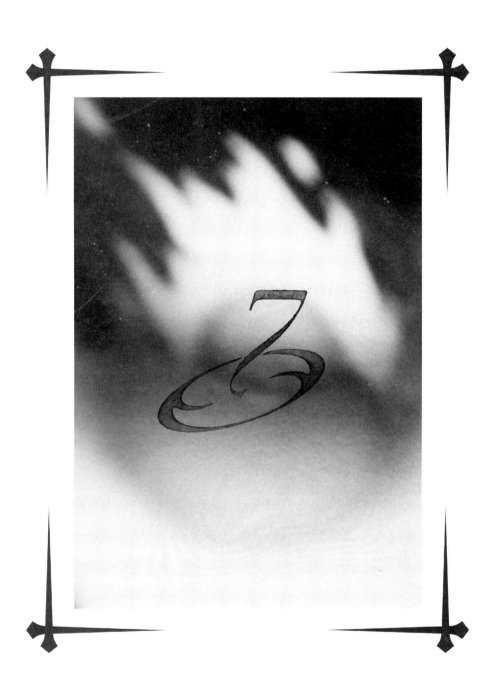

CHAPTER 9

"My-my—what a mess you've made of yourself." Meresin said, clucking his tongue. "This world was not made for the likes of you, I fear."

Joth frowned and stared at the red-haired deathling seated beside it. As the angel focused its attention, the halo surrounding the stranger leapt into bold relief. It was blacker than the Void and arranged in elaborately jagged strokes that resembled a ritual head-dress.

"You are a Machinist!" Joth gasped.

"Well, we can't all be perfect, *can* we?" the daemon sniffed. "Allow me to introduce myself—I am Meresin. We have a friend in common, I believe—Lucille Bender."

Joth blinked. "Lucy?"

"Indeed! She's very worried about your whereabouts."

"Worried?"

"Yes, indeed. Dear Lucy is concerned for your well-being. She knows that deathlings are *very* treacherous creatures, Joth! Their mortality makes them prone to madness. Because of that, they can never be fully trusted."

The angel's brow creased in unaccustomed thought. "But—*Lucy* is a deathling."

"Yes, well—like I said—we cannot *all* be perfect."

"I want to talk to Lucy."

"Then you are in luck!" Meresin smiled. "I'm meeting her for drinks!"

Joth frowned. "You are going to drink Lucy?"

"Merely an expression, my fine feathered friend. As it so happens, I was on my way to keep my rendezvous with the delightful Ms. Bender when I happened to spy you on the street. She will be *most* pleased to see you!"

"But you are a daemon—"

"One of the Sephiroth, to be exact—the counterpart of your Seraphim," Meresin interjected.

"Why should you help me?"

Meresin smiled, showing more teeth than was physically possible for a human. "That's a *very* good question! One I will be *more* than happy to answer once we arrive at the club! All shall be answered in time."

* * *

Lucy paced the floor of her apartment, anxiously wringing the hem of her T-shirt. "What do we do now?" she groaned aloud. "He could be *anywhere!*"

"Calm down, Lucy," Ez said. "We'll find him."

"Stupid-stupid-*stupid!!!* This is all my fault!" Lucy said, striking herself repeatedly on the forehead with the heel of her palm. "If I hadn't fallen asleep, *none* of this would have happened! How could I have been so damn *stupid!?*"

"It's *not* your fault." Ez unzipped the gym bag he'd brought with him and began rooting around in it. "You have to sleep. Joth doesn't. There's no point in beating yourself up for being human."

"Why should I stop now?" she sighed. "I can't *help* but worry about the poor bugger, even though he's been *nothing* but a major pain in the tuchis since I found him! Still, I can't hold it against Joth. He may not be the brightest button on the shirt, but he honestly doesn't seem to have a mean bone in his body—assuming he *has* bones! And now he's wandering around loose in New York City without a chaperone! I feel responsible for what happens to the guy, you know what I mean?" Lucy halted her pacing to frown down at Ezrael. "What *are* you looking for in there?"

Ez gave a shout of triumph and held up a polished crystal the size and shape of a goose egg. "A-*ha!* Found it!"

"Great! Wonderful! Splendid! What the hell is it?"

"It's a scrying device." Ezrael replied, polishing it on the front of his shirt like he would an apple. "It will show us where our angelic friend has gotten off to."

As Ezrael held it up to the light, Lucy glimpsed a faint blue-white glow at the center of the scrying device.

"You mean it's a crystal ball?"

"Crudely speaking, yes. Hand me Joth's feather, please."

Ezrael took the angel's feather from Lucy and brushed it lightly over the surface of the scrying device while chanting under his breath in a language she didn't recognize, then exhaled three times in rapid succession until its surface clouded, then held the crystal egg back up to the light. The bluish glimmer at the heart of the crystal trembled, then rapidly intensified, filling it like a miniature sun.

"This should do it," he explained. "I'll be able to get a fix on Joth's location now."

"Can you see him?" Lucy asked nervously, craning her head so as to try and glimpse what might be transpiring within the depths of the crystal. "Is he okay?"

"Yes—I see Joth—I—*uh*-oh!"

The scrying device flared nova-white and with an audible *pop!* went dark. Ezrael lowered the crystal egg and held it out for Lucy to see. It lay smoking in his hand, blacker than a burnt-out lightbulb.

* * *

The club was located in the Meat Packing District, on the far west side of Greenwich Village, within a few blocks of the Hudson.

During the day the neighborhood was busy and blue collar, with trucks rumbling in and out, dropping off and picking up carcasses. After sundown, the selling and inspection of meat continued—although along guidelines far removed from those approved by the Food & Drug Administration.

Meresin's limo pulled up before a converted storefront with black mirrored windows that boasted the numeral '7' within a elliptical circle. Blocking access to the door was a hulking giant outfitted in a pair of black leather chaps, a leather jockstrap and a leather vest. The bouncer stood with arms folded, features set in an intimidating scowl. Outside of its utter hairlessness and the slightly scaly appearance to its skin, there was little to hint that the bouncer was not human—except for the lack of eyelashes and the tip of a fang poking out from under its upper lip.

As Meresin climbed from the back of the limo, the bouncer quickly snapped to and opened the door to the club. But when Joth emerged from the car, the bouncer quickly moved to block the entrance, its throat sac filling with venom.

Meresin held up a hand to stay the bouncer's attack. "It's okay, Spitter! The angel's with me!"

Although the hulking daemon's throat sac rapidly deflated as it moved out of the elohim's way, it continued to glower at the angel with open hostility.

"Don't mind Spitter," Meresin stage-whispered. "He takes his responsibility as gatekeeper *very* seriously. After all, the Seventh Circle is one of Manhattan's most *exclusive* clubs."

The building's interior was cavernous, and the walls and floor being painted black made it seem even larger still. The ceiling was hung with heavy wine-colored velvet drapes and an elaborate crystal chandelier dangled over the whipping posts, stocks, pillories, racks and catherine wheels arranged across what would have been, in other clubs, the dance floor. To one side of the huge central room was an antique walnut bar with ornately carved nymphs and satyrs that boasted a solid gold foot-rail. Behind the bar was a huge, gold-veined mirror that reflected the faces, human and otherwise, of those there to drink and dance.

Although the evening was still early, house music thumped in the background like the heart of some great beast, and several patrons— human and daemon alike—clustered at the rail. Many of the daemons had shed their mortal guises upon entering the club, while those that were still in masquerade were easy enough to spot, their auras crackling above their heads like summer thunderclouds. Yet even the most casual survey made it clear that no one in the Seventh Circle boasted a halo as imposing as Meresin's.

Upon sighting Joth, the assembled daemons became visibly alarmed and began muttering amongst themselves. Meresin quickly turned to glower in the direction of the hissing gossips. As the sephiroth fixed his gaze on them, the lesser daemons lowered their eyes in ritual surrender, acknowledging his superiority.

Satisfied that he had asserted his dominance properly, Meresin turned to share his amusement with his guest. "My, aren't *you* causing a stir!" he chuckled. "Come along, Joth. I have a table here—Joth?"

Joth was standing in the middle of the dance floor, oblivious to its surroundings, staring up at the chandelier directly over its head. Colored baby spots shone through the hundreds of dangling pendants, fracturing the light so that tiny rainbows chased one another over the walls and floor. Joth lifted its hands to catch the swirling lights, like a child trying to snatch fireflies out of the air. Meresin sighed and stepped forward, taking the elohim gently yet firmly by the hand and leading it to a booth at the farthest corner of the club.

"Here you go, my friend," the daemon said. "The best seat in the house."

Joth looked around. "You said Lucy would be here."

"And she'll be here *soon*," Meresin assured the angel. "There is one thing immortals must learn in this world, Joth—and that is patience when it comes to waiting for a lady!"

Joth tilted its head to one side, uncertain as to the meaning behind Meresin's laughter, but did as it was told. As Meresin moved to join his guest, the daemon heard his name being called from across the dance floor.

The sephiroth smiled at the two lesser daemons hurrying towards him. One was an oni with grayish-blue skin, horns, long black hair that hung down its back like a horse's mane, and three eyes; the other was an imp with fluorescent black skin, bat wings and long, monkey-like arms.

"Gaki! Nybbas! How *good* to see you both! Please—have a seat! After all, this *is* your club, is it not?"

The daemons exchanged anxious glances before dragging a couple of chairs over from a nearby table. The infernal partners sat side-by-side, doing their best to avoid getting too close to Joth. Meresin seemed to take a perverse pleasure in the daemons' ill ease, his smile growing wider as he watched them squirm.

"I would like to introduce you to a friend of mine—Joth. Whom I trust we will seeing *much* more of in the future."

While the oni's double-row of razor-sharp teeth were displayed in an obsequious smile, its forehead eye rolled in consternation. "Meresin—you do us *great* honor in gracing our premises, as always—*however*—"

"However *what*, Gaki?"

"Sephiroth or not—have you lost your *mind*, daemon?" snapped the imp, bat-wings flexing like a nervous fist. "Having an angel on the premises is bad enough—but you *know* what you risk bringing it here!"

"You doubt the wisdom of my tactics, Nybbas?"

The imp glanced at its partner for support, but all three of the oni's eyes were looking elsewhere. Nybbas drummed its taloned fingers on the table-top nervously, its wing membranes trembling like sails in a rough wind.

"It's not *that*, Meresin—it's just, should the seraphim come, this place will be contaminated for a decade or more—probably longer! We'll lose our business—!"

"And we just got the liquor license straightened out!"

"What is more important—your liquor license or serving the Machine?"

Gaki and Nybbas exchanged a nervous glance.

"*Well?*" Meresin asked, black energy crackling from the tips of his fingers.

"*The Machine!* The Machine, of course!" Gaki said hurriedly.

"I am glad to hear it," Meresin said icily as he fished a platinum cigarette case from the breast pocket of his Savile Row suit. "I appreciate your concerns, but you both know the rules. 'Whenever a daemon locates a downed angel, it is that daemon's responsibility to bring said angel to the nearest gathering of its fellows for Harrowing.' The rules must be observed, below as above. There can be no variation, there *is* no variation. The angel *must* be Harrowed, and it shall be done *here*. Have I made myself understood?"

"Yes," Nybbas and Gaki muttered in glum unison.

"Good," the Arch-daemon said, selecting a thin black cigarette from the case and tamping it against the table top. "I *do* hate having otherwise useful subordinates destroyed." Meresin turned to smile at Joth. "How about you? Are you having a good time, my friend?"

"Where is Lucy? You said—"

Meresin held up a hand, his smile stretching his lips so far it looked as if the corners would meet behind his ears. "*All* in good time, my angel! All in good time!" The daemon slid out of the booth, motioning for Joth to follow. "Come. First, I would introduce you to my kin."

* * *

"*Ez! Hold your horses!*" Lucy shouted as the muse charged down the stairwell. She was a landing behind him, struggling with one of her Air Walks. "At least wait until I've got my shoes on—!"

"*There's no time for shoes!*" Ezrael's voice echoed up from somewhere between the third and second floor. "*The Mechanists have Joth!*"

Lucy tucked her shoe under her arm and headed after Ezrael, taking the stairs two at a time until she caught up with the Muse in the lobby.

"Where are we going?" she gasped. "Do you even *know* where he is?"

"The scrying device held out long enough for me to get a fix on him," Ezrael explained. "They're at a Machinist speakeasy called the Seventh Circle."

Lucy's jaw dropped. "The Seventh Circle? Are you *serious*? I've heard of that place—! It's a membership-only s&m club over in the West Village! It's supposed to be pretty exclusive…"

"More than you realize," Ezrael replied. "Come on, let's go!"

"But, my shoe—!"

"Your shoe can wait!" Ezrael grabbed Lucy's elbow and dragged her out of the lobby and onto the street. Ezrael jumped off the curb into the avenue, waving his arms frantically. "*Taxi! Taxi!*"

It was a bad time of the evening to hail a taxi on Houston. There were dozens of yellow cabs speeding up and down the avenue, but it seemed they were all either going in the wrong direction or already carrying fares. More than one empty cab sped past the wildly gesticulating muse and the disheveled woman hopping on one foot while waving a shoe, only to stop a few hundred feet down the block to pick up passengers.

"Damn it!" Lucy groaned. "We'll *never* get a cab in time!"

Suddenly one of the yellow taxis swerved from across two lanes of traffic to come to a screeching halt beside Ezrael. The cab driver rolled down the passenger-side window and smiled up at Lucy.

"You are the lady-friend of my tribesman, are you not?" said John Madonga. "I was just about to go off duty—but then I saw you…Do you need a ride, Miss?"

* * *

Joth followed Meresin to the center of the dance floor. At a gesture from the sephiroth, the prerecorded music halted in mid-beat and the gathered daemons and their human *confreres* turned to face him.

"Greetings, my brethren—and fellow travelers. I, Meresin of the Sephiroth, bring before you Joth of the lesser elohim, for you to welcome as your nature commands. Let the Harrowing begin."

A mixture of growls and coarse laughter arose from the assembly. Meresin glanced at Joth, who was standing beside him, its attention once more fixed on the crystal chandelier dangling over its head. The daemon then glanced at the tip of the cigarette it held between index and middle fingers, causing it to ignite.

Joth was still smiling up at the chandelier, oblivious to the danger it was in, as the group moved forward, forming a tight circle around the captive angel. Meresin stood apart from the Harrowing and silently watched while smoking his black cigarettes.

"Milord, why aren't you taking part?" asked one of the witches, clearly baffled by the arch-daemon's behavior.

Meresin rolled his eyes. Warlocks and witches always felt it necessary to address him as 'milord' or 'your satanic majesty.'

"It is enough that I brought the angel here," he replied. "My work is done."

The Harrowing began tenuously; at first all they did was push and poke at the elohim. When it became obvious the angel was incapable of physically defending itself, the group became more aggressive, tearing at its clothes until the elohim's hated form was fully revealed.

An imp with shaggy legs and corkscrew horns fluttered forward and spat on Joth, its fluorescent green saliva striking the angel full in the face. A pig-snouted daemon with curving boar tusks muscled its way forward and with a squeal of devilish glee, cut loose with a stream of scalding piss that struck the elohim square in the chest.

But it wasn't until an oni the color of boiled shrimp boldly jumped forward and snatched free a handful of feathers, that the angel finally flapped its wings in a belated attempt to escape, but there were too many hands holding it down.

A daemon with the head of a three-horned black goat roughly caressed its prodigious member to erection while laughing at the angel's attempts to free itself.

"What's the matter, elohim?" taunted the goat-headed daemon. "Is our company not to your taste?" The daemon's laughter dissolved into raucous bleating as semen shot from its arm-sized penis like water from a fire-hose. Joth coughed and spat as the vile green mess splashed its face.

The daemons' screams of delight grew louder and wilder as they continued to pummel and insult the helpless angel. They struck it with clenched fists, kicked it with hooves and feet, butted it with their heads, pinched it with their talons, yanked on its hair, pulled out its feathers. They spun it around and around and pushed it back and forth as if playing a vicious game of Blind Man's Bluff. They even knocked it to the ground and dragged it across the floor by its heels. Whichever way Joth attempted to dodge or run, the daemons and their attendants blocked its way. Their twisted features filled its vision, their shrieks and brays of laughter stuffed its ears.

Joth tried to shelter itself with its wings, but it was no use. There were too many of them. Joth had battled imps while on Repair patrol, but always in the company of a squadron of fellow elohim. And then the imperative was not to protect itself, but to protect the Clockwork. Confused, frightened and surrounded by its enemy and unable to escape, Joth cried out for deliverance with a piercing cry like that of an eaglet calling to its parents for help.

Nybbas, clamped its hands over its ears and grimaced. "It's calling the Host! Silence it! Shut it up before it's too late!" shrieked the imp.

One of the warlocks, driven wild by the frenzy, grabbed an empty beer bottle from the bar and smashed it against the foot-rail. Shrieking maniacally, he lunged at Joth, slashing the angel's throat from ear to ear.

There was a hideous wail—horrible beyond all comprehension—but it did not come from Joth.

"You *idiot!*" Gaki screamed at the bottle-wielding warlock. "You've *ruined* everything!" The oni's mouth opened wide enough to swallow a basketball and bit the warlock's head off at the neck, leaving the body to drop onto the floor.

The pig-snouted daemon shrieked in pain as it staggered past Meresin, its eyes and upper torso smoldering as if doused with vitriol. The sephiroth sighed and dropped its half-finished cigarette and ground it out with a swift twist of his heel.

Leave it to deathlings to screw things up.

* * *

By the time the cab reached the block where the Seventh Circle was located Lucy had finally managed to get her shoe back on. She peered out of the back of the cab at the club. So this was the Seventh Circle. She'd heard various stories about the nightclub, some of them intriguing, all of them sordid. Rumor had it as a genuine no-holds-barred sex club, where the rich mingled bodily fluids with the famous, and the Beautiful People did less-than-beautiful things to each other's persons. Only now it seemed that some of the Beautiful People were neither.

Lucy leaned forward and tapped on the plexiglass partition between driver and passenger. Madonga reached over and shot the divider back.

"Yes, Miss?"

"Look, Mr. Madonga," Lucy said. "My friend—your, um, tribesman—is in that club. He's in trouble, and he needs help."

Madonga's eyes grew serious. "Should I call the police, ma'am?"

"*No!*" Ezrael interjected. "No—that shouldn't be necessary. We just need you to wait for us to come back out. Can you do that?"

John Madonga nodded. "Of course. We are of one blood, your friend and I."

"Good man!" Ezrael said. "We'll try to get in and out as fast as possible. C'mon, Lucy!"

Lucy hesitated as she caught sight of the bouncer. "Sweet Jesus!" she whispered. "How are we supposed to get past *that?*"

"Leave it to me," replied the muse.

The bouncer scowled at Lucy and Ezrael as they approached the velvet ropes of the club, holding up a webbed hand the size of a catcher's mitt.

"Members only," Spitter growled.

"There must be a misunderstanding," Ezrael smiled up at the bouncer. "We're here at the invitation of one of your members—a Mr. Meresin."

Spitter blinked. "Meresin?"

"Yes, he assured us he would leave our names at the door. If you check your clipboard, I'm sure you'll find us there—Ezrael and Lucille Bender—?"

As the bouncer reached for the guest list, Ezrael motioned for Lucy to slide past while the daemon's head was turned.

Spitter turned back around, frowning down at the clipboard.

"I don't see your names here—" the hulking daemon looked around, a suspicious look on its face. "Hey—where'd the girl go?" Spitter dropped the clipboard, its throat sacs swelling as it bared its fangs in a fierce growl.

Ezrael narrowly dodged the stream of venom that arced from the daemon's mouth. It struck the wall behind the muse, causing the bricks to smolder. Moving incredibly fast for a creature its size, Spitter caught the front of the muse's Hawaiian shirt in its ham-sized hand.

"You ain't gettin' past *me*, bastard," it rumbled, drawing Ezrael towards its dripping fangs.

There was the sound of screams and smashing furniture from inside the club and a living wall of flesh, scales, and claws smashed its way through the door as the Seventh Circle's membership stampeded out of the club. The fleeing club-goers knocked the bouncer to the ground, trampling him underfoot.

Freed from Spitter's grasp, Ezrael pushed past the panicked daemons and witches, trying his best to avoid the bouncer's fate. He found Lucy just inside the door, pressed against the cigarette machine, her face pale and her body trembling.

"Are you okay?" Ezrael, asked, giving her a quick visual check. "None of them spat on you, did they?"

"N-no," she managed to gasp. "They—they didn't seem to notice me. Jesus, Ez! Did you see them? They looked like something out of Bosch! And there were so *many* of them!"

"Like I said—it's a popular place. This is one of the few clubs where they don't have to worry about keeping up appearances. You're not going to faint on me, are you?"

Lucy shook her head and pushed a stray lock of hair out of her hair. "M-maybe later. But I'm okay for now."

The interior of the Seventh Circle looked like a tornado had touched down on the dance floor. Tables were overturned, chairs toppled, stemware smashed. The club's trendy torture equipment had been reduced to expensive kindling during the stampede to escape.

Lucy wrinkled her nose in distaste. The place smelled like a cross between the monkey house at the zoo and a distillery. A human body, minus its head, lay sprawled in a pool of blood near the bar. Lucy grimaced and quickly looked away. She was relieved to see the corpse didn't have wings.

As she scanned the ruins she finally caught sight of the angel, cowering with its head tucked under its wing, beneath a huge crystal chandelier that was suspended from the ceiling.

"*Joth!*"

The angel lifted its head from under its wing and looked about uncertainly.

"Ez! There he is!"

Lucy started to go the angel's side, but Ezrael grabbed her arm and jerked her back. "Don't touch it!"

"What's the *matter* with you? Are you nuts? Let me *go!*" She tried to yank her arm free of the muse's grasp, but his grip tightened further.

"I *said* don't touch it!" Ezrael repeated, his voice hard as steel. "Look," he said, nodding his head at Joth in way of explanation.

Most of Joth's body was glowing greenish-yellow, as if the angel had been splashed with day-glo paint. Lucy glanced up at the ceiling, but did not see any black-lights suspended from the lighting tracks.

"Ez—what does this mean?"

"Nothing good," he replied. "Neither one of us can physically touch Joth until I can work a cleansing ritual. That will take a little time."

"Time you'll never get, Muse," said Meresin. The daemon was seated in a booth in the far corner of the bar, smoking a foul-smelling black cigarette and sipping a pink martini.

"You *bastard!*" Lucy shrieked. "What did you *do* to him?"

"*Him?*" Meresin raised an eyebrow as he finished his drink. "Oh—you mean the *elohim*? I assure you, Ms. Bender, *I* did nothing to your precious angel. I didn't have to. My lesser kin and their, um, companions, were all too eager to welcome Joth to our ranks. Think of it as a fraternity hazing, if you would."

Without taking his eyes off Meresin, Ezrael whispered in Lucy's ear. "I need you to go over to the bar and find a bottle of white rum."

"You want me to fix you a drink?" she asked, baffled.

"Just *do* it, okay?" Ezrael let go of Lucy's arm and moved slowly in the direction of the daemon, all the while keeping Joth between them. "Looks like things got a little out of hand," he said to Meresin, pointing to a wide stretch of the black floor that was now bleached white. "Somebody got a little too rough during the Harrowing, am I right?"

"You *could* say someone lost their head," Meresin smirked, flicking a half-smoked cigarette in the direction of the corpse sprawled near the bar. "You know what witches and warlocks are like, Ezrael. They think it's all black sabbats, orgies and icy semen. Morons!"

"The material we have to work with nowadays is so shockingly shoddy! I never thought I'd see the day I longed for alchemists and corrupt priests! You have *no* idea how trying it is to work with quasi-literate headbangers, bad poets and politicians."

"My heart bleeds, sephiroth," Ezrael replied frostily. "But if you think you're going to claim this prodigal as your own, you're sadly mistaken."

"Oh, am I, then?" Meresin slid out of the booth with the grace of a panther. "Those are bold words indeed, Muse, considering your batting average. You've lost the last two of your kinsmen to the Machine. You're getting old, Ezrael—best to stick to your white magicks and hanging out at East Village coffeehouses.

"Face it—the elohim is *ours!* Why don't you and the lovely Ms. Bender simply leave while you still can? I'll guarantee you safe passage. Come the dawn, it will be as if none of this ever happened—at least as far as the fair Lucille is concerned. Or Joth, for that matter."

Ezrael shook his head. "I'm afraid I can't do that, Meresin."

"No more talk, then," agreed the daemon. Meresin snapped his left wrist, as if shooing away a bothersome fly, sending a tongue of black flame arching towards Ezrael.

The muse lifted his hands, palms outward, and a disc of blue aether appeared in mid-air, shielding him from his opponent's fiery whip. Tendrils the color of sky wrapped themselves about the daemon's upper body like fingers of ivy. Meresin growled throatily and flexed his muscles, causing the aetheric restraints to shatter.

Lucy didn't know how long Ezrael could keep Meresin busy, but something told her it wouldn't be for long. Careful to avoid slipping in the pool of blood from the headless corpse, Lucy made her way behind the bar, hurriedly scanning the display of liquor bottles for white rum. But as she reached for a bottle of Bacardi, a blue-gray hand with long, black nails closed about her wrist.

"What do we have here, Nybbas?" Gaki growled, its forehead eye looking in the direction of its partner while its other eyes were fixed on Lucy.

Lucy gasped and tried to wrench herself free of the oni's grasp, but its grip was unbreakable.

"Looks like we got us a gatecrasher," the imp chittered from its perch on the bar, its pinions opening and closing like a butterfly drying its wings.

"You know what we *do* with gatecrashers?" Gaki grinned, exposing a double-row of razor-sharp teeth.

As the oni's mouth moved closer, Lucy found herself too frightened to scream or move or even close her eyes. She wondered if this was how the mice pet shops used to feed the boa constrictor felt.

Just as Gaki began to unhinge his fearsome jaws, a wind from nowhere began to blow. The imp Nybbas threw back its head, sniffing the air with alarm. Its nervous chittering turning into frantic ultrasonic pips. The oni's third eye blinked then rolled toward the ceiling.

"Damned sephiroth—I *told* him this would happen!" Gaki snarled as it roughly tossed Lucy aside.

Lucy watched in amazement from where she lay sprawled as Gaki rolled itself up like a window shade, becoming a blue-gray ball of foxfire that shot through the ceiling of the club. The oni was quickly followed by its business partner, who took to the air like one of the winged monkeys from *The Wizard of Oz*.

As Lucy got back onto her feet, she saw reflected in the mirror behind the bar the reason for the daemons' sudden departure: a portal identical to the one the seraphim Nisroc had opened in her living room was now in the middle of the Seventh Circle's dance floor.

Meresin shrieked like an angry cat, his face knotted in consternation. "No fair summoning the seraphim! *No fair!*"

"*I* didn't summon it, daemon," Ezrael shouted over the howl of the rising wind. "It comes of its own accord!"

"*No!*" Meresin yelled. "I'm not *ready!*"

As Nisroc stepped out of the portal and onto the dancefloor of the Seventh Circle the black paint coating the walls of the club began to bubble and swell, the chandelier shook like the bells on a sleigh, and the heavy tapestries draping the ceiling began to smolder.

The seraphim stood and regarded its surroundings with obvious distaste, the ophanim Preil bobbing in its master's wake, its solitary pupil expanding and contracting as it recorded the scene before them.

"What have we here?" the seraphim growled, wrinkling its muzzle in revulsion at the sight of Meresin.

The sephiroth gnashed its teeth, its mortal guise melting away like soft wax, revealing the daemon underneath the suit. He pointed a trembling talon at Ezrael.

"You may have won this round, Muse! But not by the strength of your own hand!" With an angry roar, the daemon wrapped its huge bat-like wings about its body like a cape and disappeared in a puff of brimstone.

"Ez—is this the frying pan or the fire?" Lucy asked as she handed him the bottle of white rum.

"Depends on how you look at it," he replied.

The seraphim sniffed the air. "Where is the elohim called Joth? Its cry for deliverance was what drew me to this stinking hell-pit."

Preil shot forward like a pinball, coming to a sudden halt over where Joth lay huddled on the dance floor. "I have located the prodigal, Lord Nisroc," the ophanim announced. "However, it is heavily contaminated."

"I'll take care of that, if you don't mind," Ezrael said, shooing the ophanim away like a bothersome horsefly.

The muse opened the bottle of white rum and handed it back to Lucy, then fished a small unmarked packet from his pants pocket and emptied a colorless powder into the liquor. Muttering in an unintelligible language, Ezrael took the bottle and shook it vigorously, placing a thumb over the open neck. He then took a mouthful of the clear liquor and shot it out in a fine spray over Joth, moving clockwise as he spat. Within seconds of the rum striking the angel's body, the fluorescent green splotches began to fade.

Ezrael turned to Lucy as he wiped the rum dripping from his lips and chin with the back of his hand. "It's okay—you can touch Joth now."

Lucy smiled with relief and knelt beside the dazed angel. "Joth? Joth, are you okay? It's me, Lucy—?"

Joth lifted its head from under its wing. "Lucy? Meresin said you would be here, but you weren't."

"He was lying to you," she said, smoothing Joth's hair out of its face. "But now I *am* here. I've come to take you back home."

"No, deathling," growled Nisroc, stepping forward. "That is what *I* have come to do. The elohim called out for Deliverance, and the Host has answered."

"And we got here *first*, Nisroc," Ezrael said sharply.

The seraphim turned to fix Ezrael with a withering glance, its brass claws fingering its mane of liquid fire. "Do I *know* you, wizard?"

"I am Ezrael, late of the elohim, once and future servant of the Clockwork."

"You are out of your league, Muse," Nisroc warned the former angel. "The elohim cried for Deliverance, and its cry was heard. If one of the Sephiroth flees at the sight of me, what chance have you and your magics?"

"You want to try me and find out?" Ezrael replied, squaring his shoulders. "I'm no longer a worker drone without will or thought of my own, Nisroc. I stood against the Horde to protect Joth, and I'll stand against the Host just as readily."

"*Apostate!*" shrieked Preil, wrapping its tentacles about Ezrael's neck and upper torso, stinging like a jellyfish. Ezrael cried out in pain, clawing at the ophanim, but was unable to wrench himself free of its grip.

"Let go of him, you—you—eyeball!" Lucy shouted angrily.

She looked around for a weapon and spotted one of the cricket bats used for 'disciplining' certain of the Seventh Circle's patrons. She swung at the ophanim and connected solidly, sending Preil flying end-over-end across the room until it smashed into the mirror behind the bar.

Before she could check to see if Ezrael was okay, Lucy was wrapped in a blanket of flame. The fire was all over her, licking at her arms, her legs, her hair. She swatted at the flames, as if she might somehow knock them off her body, but it was no use. The flames were so cold—colder than ice—yet she burned—burned without end or relief.

She could see Joth through the curtain of flame, its brow furrowed in confusion, as it watched her burn. The look on the angel's face was exactly the same as when it stood by and watched Nevin beat her.

* * *

Ezrael stared in horror as Lucy screamed in pain and fell onto her knees, clawing at the fire that enveloped her from head to foot. He had not expected Nisroc to loose the Fire upon a deathling. These were not the worldly flames that burned down houses and reduced mortal flesh to ash, but the fires that burned souls and scorched minds. This was the divine punishment that, in ancient days, had once been known as the Fire of Righteousness—and there was only one thing that could save her.

Ezrael grabbed Joth and shook the angel so hard its wings trembled. "*Tell it you don't want to go back!*"

Joth smiled at Ezrael. The angel recognized the stranger's blue halo from earlier in the day. "I saw you in the subway—are you Lucy's friend?"

"*Tell Nisroc to go away!*"

"But—"

"*Do as I say, Joth!*"

Joth looked at Nisroc, who was watching Lucy writhe on the ground, then back at the white-haired stranger with the blue halo.

"*Go away!*" the angel yelled.

Nisroc halted its scourging of the deathling and turned to stare at Joth. Ezrael hurried to help Lucy got to her feet.

"I was on fire," she mumbled, staring in stunned disbelief at her unburned clothes and skin.

"*What* did you say?" said Nisroc.

Joth trembled as the seraphim's fierce gaze was turned onto it and glanced at Ezrael, who nodded sternly. "I-I said 'go away.' I don't want to go back."

The seraphim fixed a disapproving eye on Ezrael as it smoothed its mane. "So be it." Nisroc opened its mighty jaws and issued a roar that shook the building to its foundations. Lucy clapped her hands over her ears at the sound of the seraphim's roar. The whole bar trembled as if it was in the grips of an earthquake. She looked up just in time to see the crystal chandelier above Joth detach itself.

"Joth! Look out!" Lucy screamed, pushing Ezrael aside as she dove forward and knocked Joth out of the way of the three-hundred-pound chandelier as it came crashing to the floor.

When Lucy dared open her eyes again, she was astonished to see that all of the walls, floors and furnishings of the Seventh Circle that had once been black were now whiter than a swan's wing. The only thing that proved that she was in the same building as before was the shattered crystal and twisted metal that had once been the chandelier. Nisroc and Preil were nowhere to be seen.

"You're a brave woman, I'll give you that," Ezrael said as he helped Lucy to her feet. "Foolhardy—but brave. Not many humans would dare use a Celestial for batting practice."

"I couldn't just stand there and let it sting you, or whatever the hell it was doing. Are you okay?"

"I'll live—what about you?"

"I guess I'm okay. It hurt like hell while it was going on—kind of like getting tattooed all over my body at the same time—but now the pain's completely gone. What the hell *was* that shit, anyway?"

"The Wrath of God."

"Remind me not to piss him off like that again." Lucy looked around. "What about Joth? Is he okay?"

"Well—it depends on how you define 'okay.'"

"What do you mean?"

Ezrael took a deep breath and turned to look at Joth, who was poking at what was left of the chandelier.

"Joth—show Lucy your wings."

The angel did as it was told, obediently stretching its wings to their full span. What Lucy saw was enough to cause her to cover her mouth with her hand as she gasped aloud.

The brilliantly colored feathers lining the inside of Joth's wings were turning color and, in some spots, actually starting to molt. And in these bare spaces Lucy could plainly see the leather of a bat's wing.

CHAPTER 10

John Madonga hopped out from behind the wheel and hurriedly opened the passenger-side door as Ezrael and Lucy emerged from the club with Joth. The angel was on the verge of another fugue, so its companions were forced to support its body between them like a drunken sailor.

"Is he okay?" Madonga asked. "Does he need a doctor?"

"Our friend will be fine once we get away from this place," Ezrael assured the worried cab driver. "And the sooner the better."

Madonga nodded his understanding as he shut the door behind Lucy. The taxi wasted no time leaving the scene and losing itself in one of the city's major traffic arteries. As they headed back downtown, John Madonga glanced into the rearview mirror to check on his passengers.

"If you do not mind my asking, sir, what was going on back there? The moment I lost sight of you, there was a great rush of people out of the club. One strange gentleman attempted to jump inside my cab, but I was able to lock the doors in time. He was most curious indeed—he looked as if he had no ears or nose. I was very frightened."

"They were having a costume party, that's all," Ezrael explained. The muse met and held the cabbie's eyes in the rearview mirror. His voice was very deliberate as he spoke. "Somebody set fire to a wastebasket as a joke, and it got out of hand. Our friend here got a little too much smoke, that's all—he'll be fine once we get him back home."

John Madonga nodded his head, as if in agreement, and returned his attention to driving. Once they reached their destination, Madonga left his cab running at the curb to hurry ahead to hold the door of the building open for Ezrael and Lucy.

Lucy paused and looked at Ezrael over the top of Joth's nodding head. "You think you can get him up the stairs okay?"

"Sure. No problem," replied the muse. "He's not heavy."

Lucy nodded and handed Joth over completely to her companion. She turned back to face the cabbie. She didn't have much money, but she couldn't stiff the guy after he'd been so helpful. But the moment Madonga saw her reach in her pocket, he shook his head.

"I cannot take your money, Miss," he said solemnly.

"Please—at least let me give you something—won't you be in trouble with your supervisor for not turning your cab in on time?"

Madonga shrugged. "What does that matter? Your friend is my brother and he needed help. If I could not do more, then I could certainly do no less."

Lucy blushed and shifted about awkwardly. "Thank you, Mr. Madonga. I really don't know what to say…"

"If you wish to repay me, Miss, then you can do it by looking after my kinsman," the cab driver smiled. "See that no more harm comes to him."

Lucy nodded and extended her hand. "I'll do my best."

"That is all anyone can promise," Madonga agreed, shaking her hand. "Good luck to you, Miss." With that he hurried back to his waiting vehicle, pausing only long enough to wave one last time from behind the wheel before disappearing back into Manhattan traffic.

* * *

There were feathers on the stairs.

There were three or four brilliantly colored plumes per landing. While it was nowhere near as bad as finding the contents of a down pillow leading to her door, the sight did not ease Lucy's mind.

Ezrael looked up from his gym bag as Lucy entered. She held up the fist full of angel feathers she'd collected.

"He's molting," she said. "That's bad, right?"

"I'm afraid so," sighed the muse.

Joth was perched on the far end of the living-room sofa, its forearms locked about its knees, staring off into space. There were feathers on the cushions.

Lucy pulled her espresso machine out of the cupboard and blew the dust off it. It had been a Christmas present to herself a few years back, when she still had time to waste grinding beans and brewing coffee before going to work. It was a pain in the ass to set up and work, but something told her that freeze-dried Folgers was simply not going to cut it tonight.

"Can I be of any help?" Ezrael asked from the kitchen doorway.

"Yeah—just stay out of my way," she grunted. "Thanks for the offer, though. There's not enough room for anyone to be helpful in here. But there is one thing you *can* do…" She glanced up at the old wizard as she worked. "Tell me where you know this Meresin asshole from. It's clear you and this guy—or whatever he is—have got history."

Ezrael sighed and shook his head. "Are you sure you want to know? It's a long story."

Lucy smiled crookedly as she took a half-pound bag of arabica out of the freezer. "Look, if I didn't want to know, I wouldn't have asked."

"Fair enough," Ezrael smiled, pulling up a chair at the kitchen table. "It all started a thousand years ago. No! Don't laugh! It's the truth! It was during what is now called the Dark Ages. Those were years when the Machine's influence was indeed strong upon the hearts and minds of humankind, even those who believed they served the Clockwork.

"Printing with type had begun in China only sixty-seven years earlier. The horse-collar wasn't a century old. Hell, the horseshoe was still relatively new-fangled! Leonardo would not be born for four hundred and fifty-three years, Michelangelo another twenty-four beyond that. Shakespeare and Marlowe would not take their first, squalling breaths for five hundred and sixty years. Milton would not enter the world for six hundred and ten.

"Even though the age was dark, there were still glimmers of light to be seen on the horizon, promising rebirth: the Bridge of the Ten Thousand Ages was on the verge of completion in Foo-Chow; Sridhara was on the cusp of recognizing the importance of zero; the Lady Sei Shonagon was beginning the journals that would become, in time, *The Pillow Book*. European peasantry was on the verge of replacing its wooden plows for ones of iron, and the Vikings were striking across the frigid Northern Sea towards Greenland and beyond, discovering new lands, new worlds. And then there was Constantinople, seat of the Byzantine Empire, gateway to the East, the first and last bastion of Graeco-Roman culture.

"Constantinople was as New York City is now—a thriving, bustling metropolis, home to nearly five hundred thousand souls. Its people were proud—and rightly so—of upholding the standards of Ancient Rome and Hellenic Greece. While Rome had fallen to the barbarians, the long walls of Constantinople had stood strong. Where the light of civilization was all but extinguished in the West, literacy and the arts burned bright in the heirs of Byzantium.

"That is not to say that cruelty, barbarity, and inhumanity were unknown to them. Indeed, the elaborate bureaucratic system created to strengthen and maintain the empire bred bloody thoughts and bloodier deeds in those who sought power. Nor was Constantinople free of the religious strife that pitted Christian against Pagan, Christian against Jew, and, finally, Christian against Christian.

"A year before I fell into your world, all Christendom—Catholic and Orthodox alike—was swept into a frenzy, fearing Judgment Day was at hand. Peasants left their fields, nobles abandoned their castles, and merchants closed their shops to travel to Rome and Antioch in hopes of begging final favors before the return of Christ. Some were so confident the end was at hand they burned all their worldly goods in huge bonfires. To the immense relief of many—and the chagrin of some—it so happened that Judgment Day did not come with the Second Millennium. But none were considered fools for having thought it would happen. This was the world into which I fell—a world that held angels to be as real as bread, and just as necessary to Mankind's survival. It was a world that saw God and Satan manifest in every aspect of Nature.

"I crash-landed in the courtyard of an artist named Miletus, who served as apprentice to a master iconographer, who worked for the imperial family and other nobles. In time, Miletus would take over the workshop and assume his master's clientele. I guess he was what you'd call an up-and-comer on the art scene of the day. Miletus had no trouble accepting an angel in his courtyard, given the beliefs of the time. But being of artistic temperament, he saw me as being more female than male. I know what you're thinking! How could anyone see me as anything but a man? I realize it's hard to picture me as being anything but what you see before you today, but a thousand years ago I was as Joth is now—perhaps even more androgynous in appearance. In those days my hair was golden red and hung between my wings, like a horse's mane. I was delicate of frame, fair of skin, soft of feature, and with a light, honeyed voice. When Miletus first looked upon me, his heart was lost for good—or so he always insisted. It was Miletus's love that gave me the strength to renounce the Host in favor of mortal existence."

The muse sighed and leaned back. "But it is useless to tell you my story. There is so much that is different—so much that has changed—between that world and this. How can you hope to comprehend?"

"No, go on," Lucy pleaded. "I really want to hear what you have to say."

"Then perhaps it is better I show you, rather than tell you," he smiled.

"How so?"

"Permit me, if you will," the muse said. "Close your eyes, please." He placed the index and middle fingers of his right hand on Lucy's shut eyelids.

* * *

She was no longer sitting in her kitchen but somewhere far away and long ago. It was as if she were watching a movie, yet at the same time was part of it as well. She was looking down from some occult vantage point as a burning body contorted on the stone floor of a cluttered workshop.

The body was without sex and had wings like Joth's. It had long auburn hair that hung to the small of its back. Standing nearby, watching the angel burn, was a human male with dark hair, dressed in a knee-length tunic, tight-fitting wool tights and leather sandals.

The angel cried out in pain and fear, throwing back its head to reveal a decidedly masculine jaw and Adam's apple as it reached out towards the dark-haired Miletus. The iconographer's face registered horror and disgust, as if Ezrael was some sort of vile insect.

"*Abomination!*" Miletus shouted, fleeing the workshop, cursing and wailing like a thing gone mad.

Exhausted and dazed, the newly transformed Ezrael sat up and looked down at the penis between his legs, blinking in confusion. For some reason, this piece of flesh had something to do with driving away Miletus. Struggling to his feet on legs as wobbly as those of a newborn fawn, Ezrael used an old robe to cover his nakedness and set out in search of his lover.

Ezrael wandered the winding streets of Constantinople, harried by dogs and rebuffed by strangers who thought him a beggar. The newborn muse wept and wailed openly, as would a frightened child separated from its parent, but no one came to his aid, thinking him drunk or mad.

As he continued to wander, Ezrael eventually found himself outside the relative safety of the city's tower-studded walls. Hungry, cold and alone, he stumbled through the surrounding countryside, completely unaware of the dangers that might befall a solitary traveler. Ezrael walked, shivering and wracked by hunger, in the ditches along the road, until eventually he came to the walls of a monastery, from which hung a rope attached to a bell. Ezrael rang the bell and after a time a monk stuck his head out of a hole high in the wall and looked down at him.

"What is it you want of us, my son?" he asked.

"I am looking for Miletus," Ezrael replied.

"There is no one named Miletus amongst our cloister," said the monk, hoping this would be good enough to send the stranger on his way.

"I am very tired and very cold, and my belly burns with fire. This world is strange to me and I have never known these things before. All I want is to find Miletus."

The monk stared down at Ezrael for a long moment, then said, "I shall fetch the abbot."

A few minutes later a different head stuck itself through the hole in the wall. The abbot was older than the monk, and his eyes seemed to shimmer like gold coins in the fading daylight. Something like recognition flickered across the older man's features.

"Unlock the gate. I would speak to this man, for he is known to me," the abbot announced.

There was a sound of a huge bolt being drawn aside, and the heavy metal door in the monastery's wall swung open, allowing a glimpse of orderly gardens tended by robed men. The abbot stepped forward, a large wicker basket covered with a rough cloth hanging from one arm. He smiled when he saw Ezrael, despite his tattered clothes and the filth caking his limbs.

"Come, my brother," the abbot said, gesturing for Ezrael to follow him inside the walls. "Come and sit with me."

Ezrael followed without hesitation, although there was consternation on the face of the monk accompanying the abbot.

"Your Grace," murmured one of the brothers. "Do you think this wise—?"

The abbot turned to his subordinate and waved him away. "I have nothing to fear from this man. Now leave us, Brother Jokannan; I would speak to my kinsman alone.'

The abbot led Ezrael to a bench set beside a pool, in which was reflected the likeness of the Virgin Mother, her arms lifting high her precious burden. The abbot set the wicker basket down between himself and Ezrael and threw back the cloth, revealing a loaf of bread, a jug of water, and a small wheel of cheese.

"Tis a horrible thing to die of starvation and yet not know how to eat," the abbot observed quietly. "Even worse to die of thirst, yet hold water in your hand, unaware that it will save you." He took the loaf of bed and broke it into two sections, handing Ezrael the larger piece. "What is your name, my brother?"

"Ezrael."

The abbot smiled and nodded knowingly. "Do as I do, Ezrael, late of the elohim."

The former angel watched as the abbot placed the bread in his own mouth and proceeded to chew it, then followed suit. The moment Ezrael's teeth closed on the crust, saliva filled his mouth and he proceeded to chew voraciously.

"Slow down, friend Ezrael," the abbot warned, placing a gentle hand on his arm. "Or you will soon discover the pain that comes from filling a shrunken belly too fast."

The abbot uncorked the bottle and took a drink from it, then handed to Ezrael, instructing the muse in the basic elements of survival that most mortals learn at their mother's breast—how to eat to fill his belly and drink to slake his thirst.

"You are most fortunate, little brother, that your wandering brought you here," said the abbot. "There are not many of our kind in this world. The Machine is in ascendance, and its spawn are everywhere. Should they come across a newborn muse—well, you are lucky you are not already lying in a pile of your own intestines along the road. Now, may I ask you what brings you here?"

"I seek Miletus."

The abbot nodded as if he understood everything. "This Miletus—he is the human for whom you denied the Host?"

"Yes."

There was a shimmer of sadness in the abbot's eyes, as if Ezrael's plight had awakened memories. "And he fled after the Fire?"

"Yes."

The abbot took a deep breath and raised his golden eyes skyward. "The mortal world is a rose armed with angry thorns, my friend. In the days since I came to be as mortals are, I have seen Rome fall, muses put to the sword, and the West stained red with blood and black with ash. It is a dangerous time for creatures such as ourselves.

"The brothers cloistered within these walls are scholars, working on illuminated manuscripts. They believe they serve the glory of God, although none know how great their service truly is. I do what I can, with my meager magicks, to protect the fruits of their labor until the day the Clockwork regains ascendancy in the heart of Mankind. You are welcome to stay here with us, Ezrael, if you so desire."

"I thank you, brother, but I must decline your offer. I am determined to find Miletus, and I will not rest until I do."

"I wish you well, then, little brother," the abbot replied, patting his hand. "I shall send you back into the material world with a loaf of bread and my blessings. Soon you will once again be hungry and thirsty, but at least you now know how to eat and drink!"

As Ezrael continued his journey, he came across bodies in the fields along the road, their limbs twisted by death and torn by scavengers, lying cold and nameless under a bleak and heedless sky. Weakened by fatigue and hunger, he eventually collapsed in the doorway of a house in an abandoned village that had been recently attacked, only to come awake to find a stranger bent over him, attempting to strip him of the meager rags he was wearing. Ezrael cried out and struck out blindly in hopes of escaping. The looter, surprised to find Ezrael wasn't dead, quickly scuttled away.

As Ezrael stared after the half-starved, wild-eyed fellow, he saw a halo form about the looter's head—a halo tainted by the Machine. The muse had been lucky that he had been assailed only by a very wretched specimen, best suited to stripping the dead of their belongings and unaccustomed to live victims.

Ezrael's flesh burned with fever and his limbs trembled with ague. The muse was ill unto death—yet he would not rest until he had found his lover. When he grew too weak to walk, he crawled. When he could no longer crawl, he collapsed in the mire at the side of the road, near a stone marker. As he lay there trembling in the filth, Ezrael heard the hooves of an approaching horse. He struggled to raise his head to see who the rider might be, but his illness had made him all but blind.

The horse came to a halt and the rider cried out Ezrael's name. Miletus was near tears as his strong arms embraced Ezrael's wasted body.

"Forgive me, Ezrael!" Miletus wept. "When I returned home and found you gone I nearly lost my mind! I've been looking for you ever since! Praise be to God that I found you!"

Suddenly things began to speed up, the time melting before Lucy's eyes as weeks dissolved into months, then into years, as Ezrael returned with Miletus to Constantinople and was nursed back to health. She saw how their love evolved, as Ezrael's gender ceased to be of any importance—or hindrance—to Miletus. The artist loved Ezrael as he would love a wife, at least within the privacy of their household. Upon the streets of the city was a different matter, as homosexuality was forbidden by the emperor.

Ezrael's general physical appearance was that of a comely youth in his early twenties, the only telltale signs of his having once been of the Host his golden eyes and lack of a belly-button. Ezrael discovered that humans did not seem to notice the color of his eyes—but he was careful never to undress in the public baths, in case his lack of a navel proved more obvious.

Ezrael lived with Miletus for twelve years, posing as his apprentice. And since Constantinople was a fairly cosmopolitan city, as such things went in those days, nothing was said of their 'closeness' as long as they remained 'discreet.' Miletus thrived as an artisan, turning out some of the most accomplished work of the period. He was in great demand amongst the nobles of the city, who wished to commission quality icons for their private chapels and shrines. He had his pick of clients and could name his price— an enviable position for a man to be in.

Yet, although Miletus was successful, part of him was dissatisfied. While Byzantine art—especially that of the iconographers—valued technical proficiency, it considered the individual vision of the artist to be of no importance. While the work was exquisite, it consisted of the repetition of the same themes, the same poses, the same characters, again and again, with little variation.

Miletus set to work on an icon of his own design—a radical and dangerous thing, since the Church, both East and West, denounced all art except that which glorified its god and saints. The subject of Miletus's masterpiece was no apostle or suffering martyr but a god born of ancient myth, depicted as a handsome youth, naked save for a carelessly draped leopard's skin, and holding a lyre in one hand and a laurel wreath in the other. At the young god's feet lay a docile lion, while stars arced over his head, tracing auguries in the skies.

The left side panel of the icon depicted the seraphim Nisroc standing rampant, claws outstretched, like the seal of the Frankish kings. On the right-hand panel stood a more orthodox angel, save that its wings gleamed with all the colors of the rainbow. The icon stood three feet in height and was hinged so that the side panels closed tightly shut over the central image, rendering it indistinguishable from any other icon in Christendom.

It took Miletus six years to compose his masterpiece. He worked in his spare time, bringing home tiny cast-off chips of precious gems and fragments of gold leaf from his commissioned projects in order to give gradual shape to his vision. Amethyst, garnets, emeralds, rubies, mother-of-pearl and diamond chips—most no larger than the nail of a baby's little finger—were laboriously glued into place. And then, as it was nearing completion—disaster struck.

Ezrael was away from the house when the emperor's guard arrived. They were lead by a bureaucrat Miletus had been unwise to speak of publicly in the most disparaging of tones. They were there to arrest the iconographer for theft. When Ezrael returned later that afternoon, it was to find his lover gone and their home sacked. None of the neighbors would open their doors to answer his frantic questions as to what had happened. Ezrael finally went to Miletus's former master, the man who had trained him in his craft.

The old man told Ezrael that Miletus had been charged not only with theft from the imperial person, but idolatry as well. Granted, every Orthodox Christian in the empire bent their knee before stylized representations of their god—but the god on display in Miletus's triptych was certainly not Christ.

The old master advised Ezrael to flee the city, for he would be considered Miletus's partner in crime and share his fate, which was not to be a pretty one. Although the old man's words were wise and well-meant, Ezrael could not turn his back on Miletus.

After disguising himself and utilizing bribes, Ezrael succeeded in gaining entrance to the prison where Miletus was being held. For an extra bag of silver, he was allowed to enter his lover's cell, which was cramped and filled with rotten straw that stank of rat piss and human shit. Miletus had been stripped of his clothes and placed in the ragged robe of a heretic. And, most horrible of all, they had taken his eyes and hands.

Ezrael hunkered down in the reeking straw and whispered his lover's name. Miletus's blinded head turned in his direction and the artist reached out as if to touch him, then quickly yanked his arm back, pressing the mangled stump to his chest.

"You shouldn't have come here! They'll catch you!" he whispered fearfully.

"You know I couldn't leave you, Miletus!" It was all Ezrael could do to keep from weeping as he spoke. "I'll get you out, somehow!"

Miletus laughed bitterly and shook his head. The pain and weariness in his voice was plain to hear. "I am to be burned with the other heretics a fortnight from now—Better I die that way, than to live like this!"

"Don't talk like that, Miletus! I will bribe the guard to let you out! We can still be together! I'll take you to this place I know—a monastery! You'll be safe there—"

Miletus shook his head. "What kind of life would I have to look forward to? They took my eyes! They took my hands! They were tools by which I made my living. In truth, without them I am as good as dead. Better I should let it end in fire than continue this way! Go now—please, Ezrael, I beg of you! If you were to be captured, it would destroy me more completely than anything they have done to me. Go now, if you truly love me, go—! And do not look back!"

Ezrael stroked his lover's head, now turned gray, and Miletus's body shook, but there were no tears, for they had been burned away with his eyes.

The muse fled the city and made his way to the monastery he had visited a dozen years before. The abbot was still in residence and welcomed Ezrael warmly, providing him with the robes of the order. In a fortnight's time, Ezrael returned to Constantinople disguised as a monk and stood amongst the jeering crowd gathered in the central square reserved for public executions as his lover was put to the torch.

Miletus stood tall as they lashed him to the stake, despite his wretched condition. His sightless face was turned towards the sky. Whether he was praying or simply savoring the sun on his skin one last time, there was no way of knowing.

The bureaucrat responsible for Miletus's arrest and mutilation was also presiding over the execution. With a shock of recognition, Lucy saw that despite the outlandish period clothing and heavy beard, the face of the bureaucrat was Meresin's. He stood on a raised platform, sweeping the crowd with glittering black eyes as if seeking out a familiar face. The author of Miletus's destruction wore a halo of such malignancy it was clear he was a daemon in mortal guise.

The abbot had warned Ezrael of such creatures, and that they delighted in the capture and murder of muses, as well as those humans Blessed by the Clockwork. This daemon was clearly searching the crowd for the face of Miletus's god. He was looking for *him*. Ezrael fled the square for fear of being spotted. That was the last time he ever saw Miletus alive—and the first time he ever laid eyes on Meresin.

Once the embers of the bonfires had finally died down, Ezrael found what remained of Miletus's body. It was badly charred and the skull shrunken from the intense heat. Ezrael snapped the skull free of his shoulders and placed it in a sack, then hurried away.

* * *

Lucy was back in the kitchen, blinking at the light and feeling slightly disoriented, like she'd just walked into the heat of a summer afternoon after spending the day in an air-conditioned movie theater.

She glanced at Ezrael, who was staring at his feet, a distant look in his eyes. "Wow!" she breathed. "That all happened?"

"Yes, I'm afraid it did," Ezrael sighed. "As I said—it was a very long time ago."

"What happened after you stole Miletus's skull?"

"I returned to the monastery and the abbot took Miletus' skull and cleaned it in the prescribed manner and placed it in the reliquary, where it remained until the Second Crusade, when it was stolen by a Knight Templar and transported to France, under the belief that it was the brain-case of a child-saint. As for myself, I stayed at the monastery for many years, learning what magicks the abbot had to teach me, as well more practical tricks— such as faking my own death and re-emerging as my son or nephew every twenty years or so. When the Crusades brought even more unrest to the land, I decided to attach myself to a young troubadour traveling with Richard I of England…but that's another story."

"No disrespect or anything, but these Machinists, or whatever you call them, seem, well, a lot *smarter* than Joth and his homeys."

"I don't know if it's a case of them actually being smarter or simply more worldly," Ezrael replied. "The Infernal Horde, unlike their counterpart, the Celestial Host, operates largely in the here and now. Meresin is a tempter, a corrupter, a destroyer…but not simply of souls. It is his duty to make sure that artists slash their canvases, sculptors smash their handiwork, poets die unpublished, and libraries are burned. Granted, it doesn't take much skill to inspire Vandals to smash mosaics in order to "free" the animals depicted in the tiles. But you must be *very* clever, indeed, to provoke one of the greatest playwrights in the English language into a fatal brawl over a tavern bill, or facilitate Mozart's demise through the jealousy of an inferior competitor. It is Meresin's role to throttle masterpieces in their cradle, if you will, and encourage the veneration of false idols."

"So that's why he's in television?"

"Precisely," Ezrael replied, sipping his coffee.

* * *

The alarm went off at six A.M., yanking Lucy free of a dream filled with capering demons wearing crystal chandeliers on their heads dancing ring-around-the-rosie with Joth. She lay staring at the ceiling for a long moment, debating whether to hit the snooze bar or not, before finally throwing back the covers and facing the day.

By the time she had showered, put on her face and changed into what she thought of as her worker-drone skirt-suit, Lucy had almost succeeded in convincing herself that the events of the previous day had been the product of a particularly vivid dream. Then she walked into the kitchen and found Ezrael making breakfast.

"Morning!" The former angel was cheerfully preparing eggs, milk and nutmeg in one of her mixing bowls. "I thought I might as well pitch in while I was here! Hope you like French toast!"

"I love it," she said, trying to hide the dismay in her voice as she trudged into the living room to check on Joth.

The angel was no longer perched on the corner of the sofa but standing in the middle of the floor, its hands folded over its chest and eyes rolled back in its head. As she glanced down at the angel's bare feet she realized it wasn't actually standing at all; the toes were pointed straight down, like a ballet dancer going *en pointe*, without actually touching the floor. Somehow, this didn't seem nearly as miraculous as it would have forty-eight hours earlier. Perhaps she was becoming inured to miracles.

An ornately inscribed circle had been drawn on the wood floor with what looked to be colored chalk. She couldn't help but notice that most of the angel's pin feathers seemed to be missing. She was reminded of Pappy's prize rooster after the neighbor's cat got at it. She glanced back in the direction of the kitchen to see Ezrael leaning against the doorway, wiping his hands on a towel.

"What you're looking at is a protective circle, designed to place those inside it in a form of suspended animation. I decided we couldn't risk a replay of what happened last night. I doubt Joth has enough long-term memory to keep from wandering off again. The circles are only good for a few hours at a time, but it should be enough to make sure our friend here stays put while you're at work and I take a much-needed nap."

"Whatever," she shrugged.

* * *

Lucy worked an over-glorified data entry job, stuck in a tiny cubicle identical to fifty others on the fifth floor. She had no view and no door. If she wanted to talk to her co-workers on either side of her, she needed to stand on a chair to do so. Not that she wanted to talk to them, anyway. She learned early on that she had little in common with her fellow employees. Most of them did not treat the job as a means of making ends meet while working on personal projects. For the most part they were business majors whose exposure to the liberal arts had gone no further than English Composition for Executive Reports. The conversations around the water cooler were largely about what was on TV the night before, their kids, that day's *Dilbert* and inter-office dirt.

To her relief, no one commented on her unexcused absence when she clocked in that morning, not even Laurie, her supervisor and *bête noir*. For some reason, Laurie had taken a dislike to Lucy right from the start. As far as Lucy could tell, the reason for her resentment had something to do with the way she decorated her cubicle. Instead of the standard "You Want It When?" and "Hang In There Baby" posters, Lucy had a reproduction of a freakshow banner advertising "The Lobster Boy."

While work was its usual tedious self that day, she found herself wondering how many of those around her were really what they appeared to be. She had known for some time that people in Big Business were two-faced, but now she questioned just how literal their duplicity might be. Could the broker down the hall be hiding a cloven hoof inside his Italian loafer? Perhaps the Chairman of the Board had a third eye under that ridiculous toupee of his? And did Laurie file her fangs as well as her nails?

Towards the end of the day, a business-size envelope landed on Lucy's desk. Laurie was standing in the "door" of her cubicle with a smug look on her face.

"What's this?" Lucy asked.

"Why don't you open it and find out?"

Frowning, Lucy dumped the contents onto her desk: a check for two weeks' pay and a pink slip.

"*What th—?*" she looked back up at Laurie.

"We don't need weirdo slackers with attitude around here, Bender," sneered her supervisor. "There are plenty of motivated go-getters out there who are more than happy to work here!"

"B-but—I *need* this job!" Lucy stammered. "It's how I pay my rent!"

"Too bad—you should have thought about that earlier! Yesterday was the final straw."

"Final straw—? There were others?"

"Don't play dumb!" Laurie snapped, pointing at the Lobster Boy poster. "You were warned about your cubicle's appearance twice!"

"But—"

"You're to clear out your desk and be out of the building in fifteen minutes or I'll have to call security." Laurie turned to leave, but paused long enough to glance back over her shoulder and scowl at Lucy. "What the hell are *you* looking at, Bender?"

"N-nothing," Lucy said, quickly averting her eyes from the dark tongues that burned around Laurie's head like the jets on a gas range.

* * *

The commute back to her neighborhood on the subway was a somber one. As she stared down at the small cardboard box that held what few personal belongings she'd kept in her cubicle, she felt more numb than anything else. In fact, she wasn't exactly sure what, if anything, she was supposed to feel. She certainly wasn't one of those pathetic salaryman types who equated her job with her identity. However, it had paid well and been relatively easy, compared to her stints as a waitress, cashier and a telephone solicitor.

And thanks to Nevin never kicking in any money, despite virtually living with her full-time for nearly a year, she barely had enough in her bank account to cover the next month's rent and utilities, even with the severance check. After the weekend, eating anything more elaborate than tuna fish and ramen noodles was out of the question if she wanted to enjoy such luxuries as toilet paper and toothpaste.

The idea of having to go back out into the job market or, even more odious, file for unemployment, made her bones turn to lead and her guts cinch themselves into a Gordian knot. She had visions of herself standing in three-hundred-person lines to interview for even the crappiest position. At best she could sign up with one of the temp agencies in the city and spend the next few months doing clerical work in the outer boroughs for a dollar over minimum wage.

Although it had given her some satisfaction at the time, she doubted her taping the Lobster Boy poster inside the stall in the women's room with a word bubble coming out of Lobster Boy's mouth that said: "Hey, Laurie, need to pinch a loaf?" would net her any recommendations from her former employer.

By the time she reached her apartment building, the numbness had finally had worn off, to be replaced by indignation, frustration and a growing anger. By the time she reached her apartment, her hands were trembling so badly she dropped her keys at least once before she could open the door.

Ezrael was standing in the foyer, studying the contents of one of her bookcases, when the door opened. The muse had abandoned his Hawaiian shirt and khakis and was outfitted in a handsomely tailored silk kimono. Judging from the wet hair slicked against his skull, he had just finished taking a shower.

"So—how was work?" he asked.

"I got fired."

Ezrael's smile disappeared. *"Oh."*

Lucy walked into the living room, where Joth still remained frozen in place, hands folded over its milk-white breast. As she stared at the motionless angel, the anger she had been fighting to suppress came gushing forth.

"It's all his damn fault!" she screamed hoarsely, hurling the box containing her coffee mug and box of emergency Tampax at Joth. The angel did not register any sign of pain as the objects bounced off its motionless chest.

Lucy stalked past Ezrael and headed down the hall to her bedroom, removing her work clothes and cursing under her breath as she went. The whole apartment shook as the door of the bedroom shut behind her. A few minutes later she re-emerged, dressed in ragged jeans, a Marilyn Manson T-shirt, and her Doc Martens.

Ezrael was in the living room, picking up the fragments of broken coffee cup and scattered tampons. He looked up as she opened the front door.

"Lucy? Where are you going—?"

"Out to get drunk," she replied, slamming the door behind her.

CHAPTER 11

The bar was dark, loud, and served drinks that were strong and cheap, at least by New York City standards. It wasn't until her third whiskey sour that Lucy realized the corner watering hole was one that she and Nevin had frequented when they first started dating. She didn't really want to think about Nevin, but she was lonely and drunk and succeeding in doing nothing but getting lonelier and drunker.

She really shouldn't have been so surprised by Nevin's behavior. When she thought about how she felt, she was more mad at herself that at Nevin. After all, she was the one who allowed herself to be built up for such a punishing fall.

There was always a touch of scoundrel to Nevin, but then Lucy liked her men a little mad, bad and dangerous to know. But men who swaggered and spat and wore their jeans too tight didn't comprehend the life of the mind, while the sensitive artist-types proved worse than disastrous, as far as she was concerned.

Her lovers tended to be either boors or bores, looking for a door mat or a crutch, not a partner. That's why Nevin seemed an answer to her prayers. He was artistic, but not an artfag. He was manly, but not a macho greaser. He seemed everything she wanted, if not everything she needed, wrapped up in one neat package.

Of course, it had proven to be yet another dead end. She was beginning to think she had an instinctual ability to unerringly sniff out and track down Mr. Wrong, much the way that ducks know when it's time to head south for the winter. What was the problem—was it just her, or was the world really full of fucked-up boy-men?

All her life she'd had to deal with the problem of coming across as too strange and outspoken for the men she was attracted to. She'd expected such testosterone-fueled closed-mindedness from the shit-kickers back in

Arkansas, but it really disappointed her when supposed big-city "hipsters" proved themselves to be just as insecure, and neurotic to boot.

Lucy firmly believed that humans were social animals. They needed to be together, to be mated—whether of the same or opposite sexes didn't matter. The act of caring for someone other than yourself was therapeutic. Lucy didn't want to wake up one day and find herself a crazy old woman with fifty-seven cats in a one-room apartment. The way her life was going, however, it looked like she might never find the right man for the job.

How hard could finding someone to share her life *be?* If circus freaks like Lobster Boy could find a mate, what the hell was holding *her* up? How much longer would she have to keep searching for the right one? She wasn't getting any younger, that much was for certain, and she doubted she could withstand putting her ego through the meat grinder much longer.

Lucy glanced up at her reflection in the mirror behind the bar. She'd put her adolescent insecurities far enough behind her that she could look at herself and be able to say, with confidence, that she was far from bad looking. She was thirty, medium height, medium build, with longish hair, good skin, a nice smile, a healthy pair of 100% all-natural breasts. She looked just as nice, normal and average as anyone else—well, outside of the Lower East Side, anyway.

Maybe if she were as different on the outside as she was on the inside, maybe that would make it easier to figure out the men in her life. If she had a third leg or a face growing out of the back of her head, then she would at least be certain that any man who was attracted to her knew what he was getting and wasn't easily scared off.

Now that she thought about it, she decided that she didn't particularly miss Nevin *per se* as much as she missed the *idea* of Nevin. She missed having someone around she could joke with, complain to, or rest her head against. There was a great deal of comfort to be found in looking up from the morning newspaper and seeing a living, breathing someone sitting on the opposite end of the breakfast table. The security of knowing that someone is there, and that they are always going to *be* there, not just for themselves but for *you*, in good times and bad, was important to her. She certainly could use a strong shoulder and a comforting arm right now. Being jobless was bad enough. Being jobless and alone was close to unbearable.

Lucy was startled from her whiskey-fueled reveries by a hand coming to rest on her shoulder. She glanced up at the mirror and saw a familiar figure standing behind her.

"Hi," Nevin smiled sheepishly.

The sound of open hand striking cheek was loud enough to cause the bartender and a couple of patrons on nearby stools to glance in Lucy's direction.

Nevin rubbed the bright-red, hand-shaped welt on his face. "I deserved that," he said evenly.

"You got that right!" Lucy slammed a wad of bills next to her half-finished drink. "I should have known better than to come here!"

"Please, *don't* go!" Nevin grabbed her arm as she brushed past him. "I *really* need to talk to you, Lucy. And I think you want to talk to me, too."

She hesitated, then sighed and nodded her head. "Okay. But just for a few minutes."

Nevin smiled and steered her towards one of the back booths, signaling the waitress for another round of drinks. "What's wrong?" he asked. "You don't usually drink this early in the evening."

"I'm certainly not drinking because of *you*, if that's what you're thinking," she said quickly.

"Then what's the occasion?"

"I lost my job."

Nevin raised an eyebrow. "How'd *that* happen?"

"It just *happened*, okay?" she answered, somewhat more defensively than she'd intended.

Nevin took a deep breath and reached out to take her hands in his, but she pulled them away and hid them in her lap. "Look, Lucy—I *know* you're mad at me. You have every right to be! I just want you to know that what happened the other day—well—let's just say things simply got out of hand between us, okay?"

"I know some who'd say what happened was burglary and assault," she retorted.

Nevin shifted uncomfortably and massaged the back of his neck. "You're not going to, um, report it to the *cops*, are you?"

"I haven't made up my mind up yet," she lied. To be honest, the thought of reporting it to the police had never crossed her mind, but she didn't see any need to take him off the hook any sooner than she had to. "And I'd be perfectly within my rights to do so."

"Oh! Of course you would be!" he replied quickly. "I wasn't implying otherwise! I just hoped it wouldn't have to come to that—for old times' sake." Nevin stopped massaging his neck and looked at her. "How about me returning half of what I took—?"

"*Half*—?!?" The moment the word came out of her mouth, Lucy bit her tongue. What difference did it make now who was right and who was wrong? Nevin was the one who had the pictures in his possession, not her. Regaining a portion of her work was better than losing it all. She took a deep breath and steadied herself before continuing. "Okay—we split them fifty-fifty and I won't call the cops."

Nevin smiled and, to her surprise, Lucy found herself reciprocating. She always found him at his most charming when he smiled. With his dark, curly hair and mobile, open face he looked like a little boy; naughty, yet somehow innocent of the hurt he was inflicting on others.

"So," she said, toying with the cherry in her drink. "Does Gwenda know you're out and about?"

Nevin rolled his eyes. "She's visiting her parents out in the Hamptons. Bunch of bourgeois know-nothings."

"Poor baby, how difficult for you," she said, her voice dripping with sarcasm.

To her surprise, Nevin didn't respond with an equally vicious verbal jab. After a long pause, she was surprised to see tears shimmering in his eyes.

"Lucy—I realize that you have no reason to believe anything I tell you right now. I wouldn't blame you if you were to get up right now and walk out that door and refuse to see or speak to me ever again. But, I want you to know—I'm sorry for everything I've done to hurt you, physically and otherwise. You're a *wonderful* woman, and you deserve much better than you've been treated. Sitting here, looking at you, it's just starting to dawn on me what I threw away with you—And to prove to you that I'm not just jerking you around—I got Gwenda to let you back into the group show."

"Oh—Nevin!" Lucy gasped, genuinely surprised.

"I knew how much it meant to you—and I thought it was the least I could do to make up for all the shit I've put you through. I really *do* care about you, Lucy."

"Nevin—I—I don't know what to say," she whispered.

"Say you can find it in your heart to forgive me."

Lucy shook her head, quickly looking away. She was beginning to feel her resolve weaken. She didn't want him to see the hurt and the need in her eyes. "I don't know if I can do that, Nevin."

He reached out and grabbed her hands a second time, but this time she did not try to pull them away.

"I *miss* you, Lucy."

Nancy Collins

She looked up at him and smiled through unwanted tears. "I miss you, too."

* * *

After a few more whiskey sours, Lucy found herself in the back of a cab, headed for Nevin's loft in Tribeca. During the months they'd spent dating, although Nevin had all but moved into Lucy's place, he had insisted on maintaining his own apartment, although she had never once set foot in it.

The loft was on the upper floor of an office building off East Broadway. The other floors housed a karate studio, a professional fortune teller, and a travel agency that specialized in air fare to and from Puerto Rico and Latin America. The ground floor lobby smelled of piss and the Chinese take-out kitchen next door.

They were giggling and leaning heavily on one another, their hands traveling in, over, between and through one another's arms, legs and clothes as they waited for the elevator to arrive. When the door opened, the car was at least a foot below the lip of the door. Lucy hesitated, but Nevin ushered her in and punched the button for his floor. The car yo-yoed slightly, as if trying to decide if it was going to crash into the basement or not, then began its gradual climb upwards.

Nevin's loft was large, by Manhattan standards—easily the size of Lucy's apartment, but without any interior walls—and what realtors in the city liked to call "unfinished," which meant that its walls were naked sheet rock, the wiring exposed, and the closest thing to a bathroom was a toilet located next to a fiberglass shower stall in the corner.

When Nevin clicked on the solitary overhead light—a feeble forty-watter—roaches scuttled for cover amidst the dirty clothes, discarded fast-food wrappers, half-empty containers from the Chinese take-out downstairs, and old newspapers that covered the floor. The only furnishings consisted of a stained mattress lacking bedclothes and a combination nightstand/coffee table made from a pair of cinder blocks and a two-by-four.

Normally, Lucy would have fled such a seduction chamber, but the circumstances were far from normal. She had wrested Nevin back from Gwenda's avaricious clutches, but her position was tenuous. Her desire for Nevin was even greater now she knew he was bad for her. It was the same thrill that came from driving too fast, juggling a knife, or playing Russian roulette, only with a greater potential for disaster.

Nevin's mouth was warm and wet on her neck as he reached for the fly of her jeans. He deftly removed her T-shirt, exposing her lace bra. Lucy's hands were equally busy, but nowhere near as sure, as she fumbled with the buttons on his shirt.

After a moment spent working the clasp of her brassiere, her breasts were finally exposed. Nevin lowered his head to take one of her nipples in his mouth, teasing it with his teeth and tongue. She ran her hands through the curly mass of his hair, giggling foolishly as he glanced up at her from between her breasts. Her panties were soaking. She wanted him inside her so badly her breath was catching in her throat.

Nevin pulled her onto the mattress. It smelled slightly of mildew and dried jism, but she didn't care. All that mattered was that Nevin was rubbing himself against her thigh, the head of his penis nudging her like the nose of a hungry pony.

As he slid into her, her skin prickled and her hips rolled against his, thrusting toward him. She ground herself against him, her tongue flicking his earlobe. Her mouth sought and found his own, locking them in a deep, involved kiss, tongues twining about one another like mating snakes. He tasted of bourbon and cigarettes.

She reached behind him and grabbed Nevin's buttocks with eager fingers, kneading the hard little apples of his ass the way she knew he liked. Nevin groaned and increased his stroke, slamming her into the mattress.

Suddenly Nevin tossed back his curly head and gave voice to something between a groan and a shout. He bit his lower lip, eyes narrowing until they looked like gun slits, as his orgasm shook him from the inside out.

Nevin promptly rolled off and collapsed onto the mattress beside her, gasping like he'd just broken the tape at the end of a race. They lay there for a long while, the sweat cooling on their naked limbs, until Lucy rolled onto her side and nudged him.

"What about Gwenda?" she asked.

"What about her?" Nevin said, drowsily.

"What are you going to tell her? About us, I mean?"

"You leave that to me," he replied.

"She's going to know something's going on when you don't come home."

Nevin sighed and sat up, reaching for an open pack of Gitanes sitting on the makeshift nightstand. "Lucy, you've got to understand—even though I want us to get back together, I don't want to go back to what it was like before. I've done some real soul-searching, and I've come to the conclusion that I need to keep my own space. I can't be crashing at your place all the time. It's not fair to you and it's not fair to me. We both need to live our own lives. That's part of the problem we had before."

Lucy lifted her head and frowned at him. "I thought you said you wanted to be a part of my life?"

"And I really mean that. I'm not saying we *won't* be together, it just won't be *every* night. I still want to collaborate with you on projects. We make a great team—you said so yourself. That doesn't have to change. But we need to cool things off—take a few steps back—decide what we want to do with our careers."

"You know I don't like sharing you with anybody…"

"No more than I like sharing *you*," he replied pointedly.

Lucy sat up, looking him eye-to-eye. "What do you mean by that? You're not sharing me with anyone!"

"Oh yeah? What about that space-case in your apartment?"

"Joth?" Lucy stared at Nevin for a second, then began to snicker. "You think I'm doing *Joth?!?"*

Nevin shifted about uncomfortably, trying to maintain his dignity. He never did have much of a sense of humor when it came to his self-image. "Well, *aren't* you?" he replied tersely.

"No!" she replied, nearly choking on her laughter.

"Then why is he staying with you?"

"Because—because he has nowhere else to go," she replied truthfully.

"Who is this Joth, anyway? Where do you know him from?"

"What difference does it make?" Lucy retorted.

Nevin softened his demeanor, smiling solicitously while he stroked her hair. "I don't want you being taken advantage of, that's all. This guy could be a psycho or something."

"Joth is *not* a psycho. Believe me, I know him better than anyone else in the world."

"Where's he from?"

"He's—he's from back home."

"Arkansas?"

"Um, yeah. I recognized him on the street. The poor guy's kinda retarded. I knew him when we were kids."

"How'd he end up in New York?"

"I don't know, Nevin—how does *anybody* get to be in New York? It doesn't really matter, does it? He's here. I'm just giving him a place to stay until—"

"Until what?"

"Until somebody comes and gets him."

* * *

Ezrael was sitting in the living room, reading aloud from the *New York Times* to Joth, who was perched on the living-room window sill, looking out at the traffic on the street below. Both angel and muse looked up at the sound of Lucy's key in the lock.

"I was wondering when you would get back," Ezrael said, folding the newspaper. "How are you feeling?"

"Never better!" Lucy grinned. Her hair was mussed and her eyes a touch unfocused.

"You certainly seen ebullient for someone who just lost their job. What were they putting in those drinks of yours?"

"Who cares about that?" she said with a shrug. "Nevin and I are back together!"

"Oh," Ezrael said, careful to sound noncommittal. "How did *that* happen, if you don't mind me asking?"

"He found me at the bar and we started talking—he told me he was sorry—that he made a mistake—and then one thing led to another, and well, I took him back."

Joth hopped down off the window ledge, fixing Lucy with its colorless gaze. "This Nevin is the deathling that hurt you."

"Yes. But you don't understand how people are, Joth—what it's like between men and women, especially when they're in love. Isn't it *wonderful?*"

"No," Joth replied matter-of-factly.

Lucy's smile faltered. "What do you mean 'no'?"

Ezrael hurried to put himself between Lucy and the angel. "Lucy, you don't realize what you're doing—! You've been drinking! It's not wise for mortals to ask an angel questions if they don't want to hear the answers!"

"Nevin does not love you," Joth blurted, as if commenting on the color of the sky. Ezrael winced.

"That's bullshit!" Lucy replied angrily. "Nevin does *too* love me! What do *you* know about how he feels about me?"

"Oy," Ezrael groaned and covered his face with his hands.

"Nevin is claiming he loves you to keep you from becoming dangerous to him," Joth said, its voice as pleasant and lacking emotional inflection as a telephone operator's.

Nancy Collins

"*Shut up!*" she screamed at Joth. "*Shut up, damn you!*" Her protests did not seem to have an effect on the angel, who continued droning on as before.

"He is afraid you might call the police and report him. He thinks if he returns half of the art he stole, the police will not believe your story if you decide to file assault charges. He wants to keep control over you, to make sure you do not ruin his chances at success. That is also why he coerced the deathling called Gwenda into agreeing to allow you back into the group show."

Lucy felt the color rising in her cheeks until her head seemed like it was on fire. She could not believe what was coming out of Joth's mouth—she *refused* to believe. She clapped her hands over her ears to try to keep the angel's voice out, but it didn't work.

"Stop it! Stop it! Stop it!" she screamed, launching herself at Joth. She pummeled the angel's chest and shoulders with her closed fists, nearly blinded by tears of anger and shame. Joth did not flinch, nor did it blink or try to move away or raise a hand in protest or defense. It stood there and absorbed her anger and abuse without comment or reaction, until Lucy finally exhausted herself.

"*Get him out of here,*" she said, pointing a trembling finger at Joth. "I don't want him around *anymore!* I've put up with *all* I'm going to—now get him *out* of here!"

"B-but—" Ezrael stammered.

"I don't want to hear *any* arguments!" she snapped as she stalked out of the living room. "I've baby-sat him long enough! Now it's up to *you* to look after him! He's your 'kin,' not mine, anyway!" The slam of the bedroom door signaled the conversation was at an end.

Joth turned to stare at Ezrael, a querulous look on its androgynous face. "Why did Lucy behave in such a manner? She asked me what I knew of her relationship with Nevin—and I answered with the truth."

Ezrael shook his head ruefully as he reached for his gym bag. "You might know all that is in Creation, my friend, but you have a *lot* to learn about women."

CHAPTER 12

"It's not much," Ezrael said, gesturing to the interior of his apartment as he unlocked the door, "but it's home. *Mi casa es su casa,* my friend."

Ezrael's apartment was a large studio located near Gramercy Park. Or, it would have appeared large if it weren't crammed to the rafters with bookcases, artist portfolios, archivist's boxes and *objets d'art.*

The only areas that were free of clutter were the tiny kitchenette and the equally minuscule bathroom just off the entrance. Even the lofted bed, built over an antique roll-top desk, had a stack of books serving as a head board.

Joth moved through the stacks of magazines and old books as easily as a cat, despite its wingspan. The angel did not stir so much as a molecule of dust as it passed.

"There is *great* power here," Joth said, its voice worshipful.

"Yes, there is," Ezrael replied, not without some pride. "I have several climate-controlled storage lockers salted around the world—but these are the treasures I hold dearest, the ones I feel the need to keep close by me."

Joth ran its fingertips over the spines of the books in bookcases that lined every wall. The look on the angel's face was that of a hungry man standing outside a bakery shop.

"*Alice's Adventures Underground...Moby Dick...Paradise Lost...*" Joth intoned, its eyes rolled back in its head as if reciting a rosary.

"All first editions," Ezrael said as he removed his copy of Carroll from its place on the bookshelf, smiling at the book as if it was a favored child. "Within the merging of paper, ink and idea, a world is born, one that comes to life within those who read it. And while there is power in even the cheapest pasteboard knock-off, there is something—*unique*—that remains within these first editions. Within these pages can be heard the squall of newborn worlds."

Joth opened one of the larger, older portfolios, going straight to a series of charcoal sketches sealed in airtight plastic pouches.

"Ah! The DaVinci," Ezrael said knowingly. "I should have known an elohim would be drawn to it as a bee to clover."

"These are from the hand of one of the Blessed," Joth's voice was as awed as that of a pilgrim before a shrine.

"There are works from *many* of the Blessed in this room," Ezrael said quietly, a hint of sadness in his voice. "I knew them all; some were my lovers, others my friends, some—like Leonardo—were descendants of children I myself sired on deathling women. All of them I did my best to protect and nurture.

"I've tended to favor the graphic arts—painters, engravers, sculptors, illustrators and the like. I've had the odd author and musician under my wing, but I've enjoyed the most success with painters, by far. Even when I failed to protect my charges' physical selves, I've made sure their posterity would be far greater than anything they might have dreamt of while alive. Van Gogh is probably my greatest achievement on that account."

Ezrael picked up another one of the larger portfolios, allowing even more Hogarths, Klimts, Breughels, Goyas, Blakes, Van Dycks and Bosches to spill forth.

"If the museums of the world had any idea of what I have stashed away, they'd all chip in to have me killed—since there's not enough money in the world to buy a 'collection' such as mine," Ezrael chuckled. "But the worth of these pictures go far beyond mere gold and silver. These are handiwork of the Blessed—those whom the Clockwork has imbued with a spark from the Fires of Creation.

"The Blessed see with the eyes of God, speak with the tongue of God, write with the hand of God, and hear with the ears of God. It is my duty to guard those anointed ones, to ensure that they realize their potential and bring their gift into the world, where others may be inspired by it.

"It is a noble calling, but far from an easy one. For as many successes I have known, there have been thrice as many failures. Not every deathling Blessed by the Clockwork has the strength to bear such weight. Some go mad, others lack the courage to fully embrace their gift, while others are seduced or destroyed by the Machine."

"The Machine," whispered Joth, lifting its face to Ezrael's. The angel's eyes were no longer without color. There was a fleck of black lurking within their depths, like a drop of crude oil floating in a glass of spring water.

The muse shifted uncomfortably and quickly looked away."Yes, the Machine. For just as you were drawn to the power locked within those drawings, so are Infernals such as Meresin drawn to the Blessed. But their instinct is not to protect and nurture, but to destroy and pollute. If they cannot seduce the Blessed into corrupting their gift, then they destroy them, either from without or within.

"Thousands of Shakespeares, Mozarts, Hemingways and Monets have died before their genius could make itself known; the victims of despair, alcohol, or badly cut smack. Such are the dangers of free will. Take Lucy for example—"

Joth lifted its head suddenly, like a deer startled at a watering hole, and fixed Ezrael with its polluted gaze, the artwork completely forgotten.

"Lucy is Blessed. Although she has yet to realize the gift within her, the potential is there. It's only a question of whether she has the strength to take that final step and embrace her gift and allow it to take her to where she needs to be."

"I do not understand—why would one of the Blessed reject their gift?"

Ezrael smiled and ran a hand through his snow-white hair. "Ah, it's that tricky free will thing again, I'm afraid. The final surrender to the gift is often a difficult one for deathlings to make. You see, sometimes the gift is so powerful it can destroy the Blessed if they are not strong enough.

"Until the time Lucy fully accepts her gift, she is vulnerable to the Machine. In its various guises, using those deathlings under its control, it shall place as many obstacles in her way as possible. It will tempt her with lucrative but soul-less jobs that will sap her of the time and energy needed for her art; it will frustrate her by rewarding the inferior; it will attempt to seduce her into corrupting her craft by rewarding her for laboring on derivative works instead of her own ideas; and, if all else fails, it will attempt to destroy her physical self by driving her into poverty or steering her towards those who will exploit her weaknesses, whether they are drink, drugs, or a need to feel loved.

"Lucy is in a particularly fragile stage—like a tree that has begun to blossom, but should there come a sudden freeze, the buds will wither and die. She needs to be carefully watched over, if her gift is to bear its fruit. And I do not know if I am up to such a challenge. Meresin was right about one thing—I *am* getting old. It is time I passed along the mantle to a muse younger than myself, one I can teach my magicks to."

"Am I to protect Lucy when I am the new muse, Ezrael?"

"Perhaps, my friend. But that choice is not mine to make, but yours."

"How can I decide to become a muse?"

"Joth, the choice must be made by you. Do *you* want to be a muse?"

"If that is what you say, I shall be a muse."

"*No!* That's *not* how it works, Joth!" Ezrael said, rolling his eyes in exasperation. "The decision has to be *yours*—not what you think someone else wants!"

It was clear this discussion was already taxing Joth's limited attention span, as the angel was back to studying the contents of Ezrael's apartment. It seemed drawn to a bookcase cluttered with various mystical objects, such as an Orusha horse-tail flail, a Zuni medicine rattle, and a peeled willow wand.

"What is in that vessel?" asked the angel, pointing to a small enameled tin box of Chinese origin that rested beside a dried monkey's paw. The darkness in the depths of the elohim's eyes seemed to grow larger as it stared at the colorful container.

"I sense it is of power, but of a source both alien, yet familiar to me," whispered Joth. "I feel the urge to open up the box, yet at the same time my very essence cries out in anguish."

As the angel reached for the box, Ezrael leapt forward, swatting the elohim's hand. "*Don't touch that!*" he shouted. Ezrael removed the box from the shelf, holding it tightly against his chest.

"You're changing faster than I realized. That is cause for concern. As for what is within this box—well, that is a story in itself."

The muse glanced up at Joth, as if weighing what he was about to say. "I told Lucy the tale of how I became mortal, but I did not tell how I came to fall into this world, because I knew she could not possibly understand the nature of the Clockwork. But you—well, you are a different matter. But before I tell you my story I must ask you a question, Joth. Do you remember what led to your own fall?"

The angel frowned and shook its golden head.

"I thought not. As I have said before, I was once as you are, Joth. I began my existence as all elohim do—one day I lifted my head from under my wing and there I was. I was Ezrael, servant to the Clockwork—that's all I knew and all I needed to know. I was tireless in my service, as all elohim are, and obedient to the Host. Then I and a Repair Squadron of my fellow elohim were ordered to one of the farther reaches of the Clockwork to repair a ruptured aorta—and everything changed.

"The aorta was the size of an ocean liner and required over a dozen of us to open our veins in order to repair it. Just as we were nearing the end of the repair, the aorta burst a second time, erupting in a geyser of blood and steam, destroying the entire squadron, except for myself.

"Even though I instinctively knew my brethren would be regenerated anew, I could not help but be distressed by their death screams. The force of the blast sent me flying through the air, hurtling me far, far away.

"I found myself in a sector of the Clockwork rarely patrolled by the Host—and for the first time in my existence, I did not know where I was. So I did what all elohim do when separated from their brethren—I took to the air and followed the sound of the Clockwork, assuming it would lead me back to the Host.

"However, the surroundings I found myself flying past were unlike any part of the Clockwork I had ever seen before. It was as if no one had ever cleared the tear ducts or mucked out the sinus cavities, much less flushed the colons. Everywhere I looked I saw gangrene, rust, fungus, mold, and wood rot. Surely this was not the Clockwork, yet, as alien and foul as my surrounding were, I could still hear the Clockwork's hum, drawing me onward.

"Finally the instinct to repair overrode my need to return to the Host. I landed amidst the ruin and plucked a single feather from my wing, using the quill to open one of my veins, spilling my essence onto the suppurating wounds that covered the Clockwork's surface like tiny craters, bubbling puss and oozing bile.

"No sooner than the damage had healed itself I spotted what I thought was a squadron of elohim on a repair detail approaching in my direction. However, as they drew closer, I saw that what I had thought were elohim were, in fact, imps.

"They descended upon the site in a dark cloud, chittering and squeaking amongst themselves like bats as they set about their appointed tasks— reopening the wounds in the Clockwork I had just repaired. Some were armed with swords, others had axes, while others still wielded buckets of boiling pitch. Upon stabbing, ripping, or burning the Clockwork, the daemons immediately smeared their own filth into the gaping wounds.

"The sight of such wanton destruction re-triggered my need to repair the damage. Without regard for their superior numbers, I swooped back down amidst the imps. Upon seeing me, they began making frantic ultrasonic pips and quickly dispersed.

"I once more plucked a feather from my wing and set about repairing the damage they had caused. But the very moment the Clockwork was repaired, the imps suddenly reappeared, descending onto my handiwork like a flock of hungry crows, and proceeded to undo all I had done. I flapped my wings and shooed them away, and, once they had again dispersed, I plucked yet another feather from my wing and began my work all over again, only to have the imps return yet again.

"This cycle went on for several years. I might still be there, locked in a never-ending war of attrition with those miserable imps, if something had not succeeded in breaking the chain of reaction.

"There was a loud buzzing and a great shadow fell across both myself and the cadre of imps. '"What is an elohim doing here?' asked a voice that sounded like a giant talking through the world's largest box fan.

The imps began their high-pitched squeaking and hopped about like fleas on a hot rock. I looked up and beheld a daemon the size of an elephant with the body of a man and the head, wings and arms of a gigantic fly.

"'*Beelzebub! Beelzebub!*' gibbered the imps, still hopping up and down.

"'I *know* my name, you sub-sentient dung-flingers!' the sephiroth thundered. 'What I *don't* know is what an elohim is doing so far within the Machine!" The sephiroth turned its multi-faceted eyes toward me. 'Perhaps you might be of more use in answering my questions, elohim. Or are your kind as brainless as imps? No matter—what business have you here?'

"'I-I don't understand,' I replied, genuinely baffled by what was happening. 'I thought I was tending the Clockwork...'

"Beelzebub briskly rubbed its hairy forelegs over its head and along its wings, much the way Nisroc plucks at its mane when perturbed. 'Does this look like the Clockwork to you, elohim?'

"I was at a loss as to what to answer. Although the Machine was in bad shape and smelled, it did not appear all that different from the Clockwork.

"'Did the seraphim send you forth as a scout?'

"This question confused me even more than the last. 'Why should the seraphim want to spy on the Machine?' I replied.

"'Spy?' Now every eye in Beelzebub's head was focused on me. 'What makes you say *spy*, elohim? We do not treat spies lightly, elohim. Tear the angel apart!' Beelzebub buzzed. 'Start with its wings.'

"The imps swarmed over me like a horde of vampire bats, tearing at my flesh and wings with their filthy claws. I cried out for deliverance, but I was too far removed from the Host for any to hear and come to my aid.

"With a burst of strength, I succeeded in shaking off the imps long enough to take flight. The imps were soon after me, eager to use their monstrous tools on my person, which meant I would find myself trapped in yet another moebius strip of mutilation and regeneration.

"I did not flee the daemons out of fear or self-preservation. As an elohim, those concepts were alien to me. As you yourself know, little brother, there is only one thought that occupies the mind of the elohim: how may I tend the Clockwork? And I knew that I could not serve the Clockwork if I spent eternity being torn apart by daemons.

"Unfortunately, my pursuers proved as single-minded as I was. An imp armed with red-hot pincers managed to overtake me. I wrestled with the daemon in mid-air, doing all I could to dislodge it from my back.

"Suddenly, I found myself being spun violently around and around, as if I was being sucked into a vortex. I had stumbled into one of the gyres that pop up, time and again, in the disputed territory between the Clockwork and the Machine. The deathling scientists call them "black holes." Those that fall into them, Celestial or Infernal, are sucked from the Protoverse and spat into Creation, to land on any of a million, billion worlds.

"When the imp realized what had happened, it abandoned its torment of me and attempted to flap its way back to its fellows, but it was too late. The gyre snatched the daemon and hurled it into some far-off galaxy. Which one, I'll never know. As for myself, I was spat out on this world, just as you were. But, unlike you, I did not come to this world empty-handed.

"In my haste to flee Beelzebub's daemons, I accidentally broke off a piece of the Machine. Not a big piece, mind you. Barely anything, really. I was still clutching it in my hand when I crash-landed in the courtyard of a Byzantine artist.

"The artist, Miletus, found my unconscious body and thought the fragment was a relic of heavenly origin, so he placed it inside a box designed for such things as the teeth of martyrs and splinters of the One True Cross. When I later explained its actual origin, he was appalled, and urged me to destroy it. But I never could bring myself to dispose of it. I have kept it with me to this day. Who is to say when a little piece of Hell might come in handy?"

CHAPTER 13

"Why can't you stay?"

Lucy cringed at the sound of her voice as she stood in the bathroom doorway, watching Nevin put the finishing touches on his freshly washed hair. She was coming across whiny again. She hated that—especially in herself.

"Sorry, baby—I wish I could," Nevin said, smiling at her in the medicine cabinet's mirror. "But I've got to finish dropping off these invitations to the rest of the collective." He kicked the knapsack at his foot for emphasis. "All I have time for until the show's over are quickies. You know how it is. Gwenda says the *Times* is sending a reviewer to the opening, and Page Uxbridge of the Matador Gallery said he'll be there as well. It's too sweet a deal to screw up."

"Yeah. I guess you're right," she sighed. "It's just that I thought, you know, we'd have a little more time together…"

"Later, baby. After the show. Then we'll have all the time in the world."

Lucy followed as he headed down the hall to the front door, walking a few steps behind him, her head down.

"When will I see you again?" she asked. Although she was trying her best to sound forceful, it was hard to feel in control of the situation while dressed in just a bra and panties.

"Maybe tomorrow. I'm not sure. Maybe not for a couple of days," he said, shrugging his shoulders. "Oh—by the way—what happened to that weird friend of yours?"

"Who?"

"The one from Arkansas?"

"Oh! Joth! I-I got a friend of mine to take him in for awhile."

"Good!" Nevin smiled. "That guy gave me the creeps. See you later, baby." He kissed her on the cheek and was out the door.

Lucy leaned on the door for a long moment before throwing the deadbolt, then returned to her bedroom, where she put back on the clothes Nevin had removed less than twenty minutes before. This was his second afternoon stop-over in as many days. The first was to drop off the artwork he'd promised to return.

In both cases he'd shown up with only a few minutes' notice, calling from a pay phone a block or two away, made some small talk about the upcoming show, then got her into bed. Then, after popping his rocks, he was showered, dressed and back out the door in record time, leaving her alone once more.

Lucy wandered into the living room and stared at her recovered pictures. She had them propped on end, side by side, one after another, along the length of the sofa. Of the ten pictures Nevin had made off with, he'd returned five. Tellingly, he'd kept the nude studies of himself they had "collaborated" on, leaving her with what she'd come to think of as *The Seven Devils Suite.*

She had taken the pictures during what she assumed would be her final visit to Seven Devils. It had taken her nearly three years to find the inner strength to finally develop them—and she was glad she had.

The first in the series was *Downtown*, which depicted the tumble of charred bricks, burned timbers and scorched theater seats that was all that was left of the old Ben Franklin, the drugstore, and the Bijoux of her youth. The fire had raged through downtown Seven Devils two years earlier, but the town was so poor it couldn't afford to hire anyone to clean up the rubble and haul the bricks away.

The second picture was titled *The Patriarchs*, and depicted a Greek chorus of aging good ole boys gathered in front of the Gulf station. *House Dog* was a close-up of the antique cast-iron bulldog-shaped bottle-opener fixed to the kitchen door jamb in what was now her Cousin Beth's house. *Pappy's Cuckoo Clock* managed to capture the timepiece's occupant in mid-cuckoo. The fifth in the series, *Mam-Maw's Ride*, was a shot of the old glider on what was once her grandparents' porch, empty and motionless, its rusty chains silent. Once she got *Mama and Irises*, the print Joth had accidentally broken, back from the frame shop, she would be ready to package the series in bubble-wrap.

She sighed and walked into the kitchen and opened the fridge. There wasn't much in there besides a few canisters of 35mm film, an open can of ginger ale and a Two Boots Pizza delivery box containing a congealed slice of eggplant and pepperoni. The events of the last few days hadn't exactly permitted her the time or resources to score groceries.

Lucy grunted in disgust and closed the refrigerator. With Joth gone and Nevin popping by only when it suited him, the apartment seemed really— empty. At first the silence had been welcome, but now it was starting to get to her. Pretty soon she'd be playing the TV set all day long, just to have the illusion of other people in her life.

She'd replaced her demolished phone with another piece of cheap-ass shit. Maybe she could reach out and touch someone—but who? All Nevin had was a beeper, so it was impossible to call him up and simply chat. As it was, what could she talk about to the few friends she still had? Over the last several months, her involvement with the art collective had pushed most of her casual associates out of the picture.

And even if she *did* call up one of her old friends out of the blue—what did she have to talk about? All her friends who had been less than thrilled with Nevin, and whom she'd snubbed on account of their refusal to accept the man in her life, would call her an idiot for taking him back after he'd treated her like a dirty Pampers.

The only other "big news" in her life was Joth. And she knew exactly what would happen if she started going on about *that*; she'd be in Bellevue before she could hang up the receiver. She could call up old friends simply to invite them to the opening, but, ironically, now that she was back in the group show, she had virtually no one to invite to the opening.

As she returned to the living room, something in the corner of the room caught her eye. As she stooped to pick it up, she saw it was one of Joth's feathers. She held it up to the light, marveling at how the sunlight refracted off its surface. As she turned the feather, its colors shifted and melded like that of a kaleidoscope. Without meaning to, she smiled.

When Nevin had stopped by earlier to drop off her stack of invitations he'd made a point of mentioning how, thanks to a little string-pulling, Gwenda had managed to talk a trendy Soho gallery into sponsoring the group show. Nevin had suggested, just before he took off her blouse, that she ought to invite anyone she knew who might be well-connected in the art world. He hadn't really meant it, though. After all, Nevin assumed *he* knew everyone *she* knew…

Two minutes later, she was seated cross-legged on her bed, the phone balanced on the rumpled bedclothes. The receiver picked up on the second ring.

"Hello?" rumbled Ezrael's voice.

"Uh, hi, Ez—"

"Lucy!" Ezrael sounded genuinely pleased. "How *wonderful* to hear from you—to what do I owe the pleasure of this call?"

"Are you interested in attending a gallery opening?"

"Is this the one you mentioned before?"

"Um, yes, it is. It's a group show, actually. I'm one of several people in this arts collective that will have work on display. It's a couple days from now…at the Ars Novina Gallery. Are you familiar with it?"

"I know *all* the art galleries in this city," Ezrael replied with a chuckle.

"Oh. Yeah. Well, I guess you would, wouldn't you? Anyway, I was just calling to see if you would, you know, turn out to support the arts."

"Of course I will! Should I bring Joth along, too?"

Lucy tried to keep her sigh from sounding too much like one of relief. "Joth's *still* there? I mean, he's still, you know, Joth?"

"Well, yes and no."

"What do you mean by that?" she asked.

Ezrael took a deep breath before replying. "Nature is taking its course."

Lucy tightened her grip on the phone. "Ez—give me a straight answer here. Has he gotten *worse?*"

"I can't really describe it over the phone. You'd have to see it for yourself. It's not just the wings, now, Lucy—it's in the eyes."

"*What's* in his eyes?"

"The Devil."

The last time words had hit her this hard was when she received the news of her mother's suicide. It felt as if she were falling inside herself, plummeting end-over-end through empty space, unable even to scream for help.

"Lucy? You still there?"

"Yeah," she said, clearing her throat. "I'm still here." She took a deep, shaky breath. "Jesus, Ez. Is there anything I can do?"

"Yes, there is, as a matter of fact," he said. "You can take Joth back."

"Wait a minute, Ez! You *know* I can't do that!"

"I 'know' no such thing!" the muse replied tersely. "Lucy—Joth needs your help. You are its touchstone. To hear it talk, Joth acts as if you hung the moon! But your rejection may have accelerated the transmutation…"

Lucy's shoulders stiffened defensively even as her cheeks turned red. "Hey! Don't try laying any guilt-trips on *me*, okay? I can't have Joth hanging around *my* house, screwing up *my* life! I promised Nevin I'd get *rid* of him, and I *did*—"

"Lucy—I don't know if you believe in destiny or not; but of all the people in New York City—an angel landed at *your* feet. In the old days, people used to call that an omen. I'd think about it, if I were you."

"Well, you're *not* me!" she retorted. "And I don't need you playing head-games with me! It's not *my* fault any of this is happening!"

She slammed the receiver back into its cradle so hard she was afraid she'd broken yet another phone. She stomped out of the bedroom to the kitchen, still fuming over how *anyone* could have the audacity to suggest that *she* was somehow responsible for *anything* bad that might happen to Joth.

The intercom buzzer startled her. She hurried over and hit the speaker button next to the front door.

"*Yes?*" she shouted, punching the "Listen" button at the same time.

A masculine voice that sounded like it was talking through a kazoo responded: "*E-Z Framing! Gotta delivery for—Fender?*"

"That's *Bender!*" she replied. "I'll buzz you in!"

Three minutes later Lucy handed the heavily tattooed and pierced delivery boy a five-dollar tip in exchange for a package wrapped in brown paper and bubble-pack. She eagerly stripped the paper away and placed the newly repaired *Mama and Irises* alongside the other pictures in the series. Paying the extra fifteen bucks for an immediate job had been worth it.

Now that she had the final piece in the *Seven Devils Suite* in her possession, she found her anger dissipating. She felt bad about blowing up at Ezrael— but he'd pushed a few buttons. She didn't react well to guilt-tripping. Her mother had relied on it quite a bit, when she was a kid. It was one of the few things guaranteed to set her off. As it was, she didn't need anyone to make her feel guilty—she did it well enough on her own, thank you.

The idea of Joth turning into something like Meresin was something she had tried hard not to think about over the last couple of days, but her mind kept wandering back to the subject whenever she wasn't preoccupied with Nevin or the group show's opening.

Lucy wished Joth no ill will. While the angel was utterly tactless, clueless, and denser than mercury, it was also without guile, cruelty, spite, or ulterior motives. Still, she had to wonder how much of what she felt towards Joth was genuine. According to Ezrael, it was impossible for any normal human being—provided they weren't under direct control of the Machine—to hate an angel. Part of their "protective coloration" was the ability to inspire trust and affection in all who met them—she'd seen that with the taxi driver. Was it possible her concern for Joth's well-being was no more voluntary on her part than swallowing or blinking? It might be a sad commentary on how she saw the world, but she'd had her chain jerked enough recently that she was now leery of her own emotions. Besides, as much as she might feel sorry for Joth, she had no more responsibility to help him than anyone else. After all, it wasn't as if the angel were *family*—

As Lucy entered the living room, she glanced in the direction of the artwork lined up along the sofa—and gasped as if she'd been struck in the pit of her stomach.

Iris Bender was dressed in the clothes her daughter had picked out for her funeral—the periwinkle blue frock with the white mother-of-pearl buttons and single-strand pearl necklace. In her arms she held the bouquet of irises Lucy had placed on her casket.

Mrs. Bender's ghost did not say anything to her daughter, nor move to embrace or threaten her. She just stood there and looked at Lucy with a sad expression in her eyes. It was the only time—besides when she had lain in her open coffin—that Lucy could remember her looking both sane and sober.

"*Mama?*" Lucy whispered.

Mrs. Bender turned her face away from her daughter—and disappeared.

She reeled into the kitchen and yanked open the freezer and dragged out the bottle of Jagermeister she kept hidden behind the frost-encrusted bag of Tater Tots. She was shivering so hard her teeth were rattling. After three hits her knees finally stopped knocking against one another. Still, she could not make the look of sadness on her mother's face disappear from her memory. Her mother had appeared to her for a reason, of that much she was certain. But why?

She glanced back down at the feather lying on the kitchen counter. No. No more denial. No more pretending. She had turned her back on someone who needed her help once before, and now she had to live with that until the day she died. She couldn't do it again.

* * *

Lucy picked up the receiver and hit re-dial. A second later, Ezrael's gruff voice was on the other end of the line.

"Hi, Ez—It's me, again—Look, I'm sorry about what I said, okay? I've been thinking it over and I decided that Joth can come back—that is if he wants to. He's not mad at me, is he?"

"*Mad?* At *you?*" Ezrael chuckled. "Even if Joth *knew* what mad was, you'd be the last person on earth it would be angry with!"

Lucy blushed and smiled. "I'm glad to hear that, Ez—so when do you think you can bring him over?"

"Look out your window."

Lucy frowned, wondering exactly what the old wizard meant by that, and glanced up—at Joth, crouched on the fire escape outside her bedroom window.

CHAPTER 14

Lucy hurried over to the window and unlatched the burglar bars and raised the window, motioning frantically for Joth to come inside.

"Quick! Get in before someone sees you! The last thing I need is someone calling the cops about a nude man on the fire escape!"

Joth folded its wings and bowed its head and began to climb through the window into Lucy's bedroom, then pulled back and looked over its shoulder. Lucy frowned and leaned forward, craning her head to see whatever it was that the angel might be looking at. Without any warning, Joth grabbed Lucy under the armpits and pulled her through the window and onto the fire escape.

"Joth! Put me down!" she shrieked. "What are you doing? Are you out of your mind?!?" Lucy attempted to push herself away from the angel, but there was little room to maneuver without toppling over the railing. As she attempted to extricate herself, she caught sight of the angel's wings—and what she saw was enough to make her stop struggling.

At least half of Joth's underpinning was gone. Lucy brushed the exposed area with her finger tip. It felt soft and supple, like quality unborn-calf's leather. She didn't need Ezrael to explain to her that Joth's wings were turning from that of a bird into those of a bat. She wondered how long before it started sprouting a tail, cloven hooves and horns to go along with them. She lifted her eyes to the angel's face and bit her lower lip at the sight of the dark blobs floating in what had previously been crystal-clear eyes.

She took a deep breath and steadied herself, trying to keep the panic out of her voice. "Joth—why don't we go back inside now?"

"I want to show you something," Joth said.

"What?"

By way of reply, the angel scooped her up in its arms. She was so astonished by Joth's strength and speed, she couldn't find the breath to protest. She knew how little the angel actually weighed—after all, she had carried it, single-handed, from the roof—yet it held her as if she was no more than a puppy.

Joth hopped onto the narrow rail of the fire-escape as easily as a robin perching on a window sill, balancing on the balls of its feet. Lucy stopped struggling, going rigid with fear as she stared down at the street a hundred feet below.

"J-joth? What do you think you're doing—? Put me *down*, Joth—!"

The only response she received was the sound of wings snapping open.

"*Joth!*"

The angel leapt off the fire-escape as easily as an Olympic diver going off the high board. As the top of the dry cleaner's street-level awning filled her vision, Lucy screamed and turned her head away, burying her face in Joth's shoulder. There was a sudden rush of wind and the feeling of uplift, as if they were a leaf caught on a gust of wind.

Lucy lifted her head from the hollow of Joth's collarbone and risked a peek. To her surprise she found herself staring down at the head of a man with male pattern baldness. The balding man was watering a roof-top garden.

They were two hundred feet and climbing over New York's Lower East Side. Joth's wings were beating so fast they were invisible and hummed like a wildly spinning top. She marveled at how something as light as Joth could carry her and still be airborne—no doubt it was yet another one of the myriad miracles that came with being an angel. In any case, she decided not to question how they were being kept aloft and simply enjoyed the view.

She had lived in Manhattan for years, but her perception of the city was, by default, that of one of the human ants that dwelt in its concrete canyons. Now she was being presented with a genuine bird's-eye view of her adopted home.

Joth flew through the crowded streets, adroitly surfing the updrafts created by the artificial mountains of steel and concrete that flanked the major avenues. They zipped past executives in office buildings busy talking on the phone, holding meetings and putting golf balls into coffee cups. Lucy spotted a mother rocking her baby to sleep while gazing out her eighth-floor apartment's picture window. She was surprised by the number of high-rise window boxes full of flowers—riots of color otherwise invisible from the street. She blushed at the sight of teen-aged lovers indulging their passion on what they imagined was the relative privacy of a rooftop.

She was amazed how no one on the street or in the various buildings they soared past seemed to notice them. Maybe they were genuinely invisible, or perhaps no one *expected* to see a winged man carrying a woman flying through the concrete canyons of Manhattan.

However, whatever kept the human occupants of the city from noticing their passage did not extend to Manhattan's other inhabitants, as flocks of pigeons scattered whenever Joth swooped past, apparently mistaking the angel for one of the peregrine falcons that made their aeries in the older skyscrapers.

As they approached Midtown, a brilliant-white german shepherd lazing on the patio of a lofty penthouse apartment jumped to its feet, barking furiously at the passing angel. The dog's owner, an older man, came out to see what was aggravating his pet. Although he stared right at Joth and Lucy, he showed no sign of actually seeing them.

The Chrysler Building rose before them like an art deco syringe, its stainless steel cladding sparkling in the sun. Lucy had seen the skyscraper from a distance virtually every day for years, but never from such a height. From their angle of approach it looked less like an office building than a temple to some ancient sun god.

As Joth climbed higher and higher on the updrafts created by the skyscrapers lining East Forty-Second, Lucy marveled at the detailing on the exterior of the building, which had gone unseen save by pigeons and window-washers since that day, nearly seventy years ago, when the high-steel workers capped the tower with its triple sunburst spire.

Joth settled onto one of the mammoth eagles that peered out over the city nearly eight hundred feet above the street and gently deposited Lucy onto the broad, flat expanse of the gargoyle's head. The wind was so strong her clothes flapped against her like flags, threatening to yank her backwards and send her spiraling into space.

Lucy clutched the angel's arm with both hands, terrified of losing her balance and slipping off her perch. It was all she could do to fight the instinctive urge to fall to her belly and cling to the platinum-like surface.

"Joth—what are you *doing? Why* did you bring me here?" she managed to get out through her chattering teeth.

"To show you what I see. You have shown me this world through your eyes—now I want you to see it through mine."

"J-joth, *please*—I'm *afraid*—!" The furiously blowing wind threatened to push her own breath back inside her lungs. Her hair was whipping across her face so strongly it was impossible to raise her head, leaving no other choice but to stare at the dizzying drop directly beneath her feet. They were so high up the din of the street-level traffic was swallowed whole.

If Joth heard her, it gave no sign. It touched her chin and lifted her head, enabling her to stare out over the cityscape.

"See through *my* eyes, Lucy. See as *I* see," the angel whispered, its words filling her mind like a voice in a dream.

The paralyzing vertigo that gripped her was suddenly replaced by a sense of awe. The wonder washed over her like a ocean wave, subsuming her within itself. At first there was fear—the fear of being consumed by the immensity of what she was experiencing—but she knew enough to ride the wave, not fight it.

There was a feeling deep within her like that of a key turning in a lock, and, if only for the briefest moment, she looked out over the city through the eyes of an angel.

Before her were spread the landmarks of East Forty-Second—the Graybar, the Chanin, the Daily News, 500 Fifth Avenue. Seen from on high, the ugliness, hatred, and cruelty that she knew all too well thrived within the city was invisible. In place of people there was a pattern of lights, zipping back and forth, leaving smeared tracers in their wake, like the headlights of cars filmed using time-lapse photography.

Some of the lights were bright, others dim, and some even seemed to burn darkly, like ultraviolet lights. There were more colors than she had ever thought imaginable—multitudes of reds, blues, greens, yellows, and every possible shade in between.

The pinpricks of gaily colored light zipped back and forth, like fireflies dancing on a summer night. At first it seemed as if their frantic maneuvering was without rhyme or reason, but if she looked harder, she saw patterns begin to emerge. It was as if she were watching a tapestry being woven by blind happenstance, yet it somehow incorporated designs of breath-taking skill and complexity. But just as she was about to grasp the meaning behind the design, suddenly, like Penelope's wedding shawl, it would unravel and begin re-weaving itself into another, equally grandiose pattern.

Lucy was reminded of a photograph she had seen of Picasso tracing the outline of the Minotaur with a pen-light. The naked human eye could not have possibly grasped what had been drawn, but the camera did. So did it exist? And if it did exist, which was the true work of art? The firefly minotaur or the photograph itself?

The tears that filled her eyes were not brought by the stinging of the wind. She turned her head and pressed her face into Joth's naked chest, cinching her arms tightly around its narrow waist. The angel gingerly returned her embrace, pulling its wings forward to shelter her.

She lifted her head and looked into the angel's perfect face. In the shadow cast by its wings, the darkness in Joth's eyes made them look almost human.

As she stared into their depths, she trembled yet again, but not for fear of falling or from the chill of the wind.

"I've seen enough," she whispered. "Take me home."

* * *

Lucy remained silent the entire flight back. There was no need to say anything. She felt that she understood Joth far better than she ever had before. She felt a little bit ashamed for having dismissed the angel as a fool simply because it was ignorant of the world she operated in. Now that she had glimpsed, however briefly, Joth's perception of things, she regretted how she had treated the angel. Still, even though she was physically drained, her exhilaration surpassed her exhaustion. She wondered if this was what the Shinto priests felt when they looked at Mount Fuji and saw the face of their god.

As they came within sight of the apartment building, she experienced a twinge of sadness. She wasn't sure if it was because her ride was at its end, or because Joth would no longer need to hold her. She had forgotten how it felt to be cradled in the arms of someone she trusted without question. The last time she had been held so securely was when her father was alive.

The phone was ringing as Lucy crawled back through the window into her bedroom. She snatched up the receiver just before the voice mail could pick up the call.

"Where were you?" demanded Nevin by way of a hello.

"Oh—hi, Nevin," she said, the smile melting from her face. Normally, hearing her lover's voice was the high point of her day, but now the pit of her stomach seemed to fill with lead.

"What's going on—why are you out of breath?"

"I was—out—for a little while. I just got back in." She glanced over at Joth, who was sitting inside the window, legs dangling over the sill, its head tilted to one side as it watched her.

"*Out?*" Nevin's voice was petulant. "Who were you out with?"

"I was with Joth."

"Oh. *Him.*" Nevin's displeasure was clear in his voice. "I thought you got rid of that fruitcake?"

"I did. But he's back for a little while."

"You mean he's *still* there?"

"It's only for a *little* while, sweetie." Lucy said, cringing at the sound of her own voice. She decided it would be better all around if she changed the subject. "Where are you calling from—?"

"Avenue A. I wanted to see if you had any plans for tonight—I thought we'd have a romantic dinner for two," he said. "A little candlelight, a little wine…"

"That sounds *wonderful!*" she replied, brightening instantly.

"Good! I'll be over in ten minutes."

Lucy hung up the phone, then looked up at Joth. "Nevin's coming over."

"You want me to go away again," Joth replied flatly.

"No, I *don't* want you to leave," she said, putting aside the phone with a sigh. She stood up and took Joth's hand in hers. "I *want* you to stay. But you have to *promise* me you'll stay out of Nevin's way. Wherever Nevin is when he's here, I want you to be somewhere else, okay?"

The angel looked down at Lucy's hand, folded about its own, then nodded its head in agreement. "I shall do whatever you wish me to do, Lucy."

She stood for a long moment, gently squeezing the angel's hands. Then, as if startled from a daydream, she blushed and let go.

"Okay! Now that we've got the ground rules settled, I'd better find you some more clothes before Nevin gets here. If he sees you running around the house buck naked, he'll throw a fit!"

* * *

Nevin arrived roughly fifteen minutes later with a large bag of Chinese take-out in one hand and a bottle of plum wine in the other.

"I thought we were going out?" Lucy said, trying her best to hide her disappointment.

"Well, actually, I thought we could stay in—after all, dinner by candlelight can be even *more* romantic at home, if you know what I mean…"

"You're right about that," she smiled. "You can open the wine while I get the table set up…"

"You don't want to eat in the kitchen, do you?" he said disapprovingly.

"Oh—?" Lucy shut the pantry door and turned to look at him. She tried to keep her discomfort from registering on her face. "Where *do* you propose we eat dinner, then?"

"I thought it'd be really romantic if, you know, we had dinner in bed."

"I don't know if I'd call it 'romantic'—it sounds more like 'convenient' to me."

Nevin frowned. "What do you mean by that?"

"Nothing," she sighed.

Nevin frowned again and nodded in the direction of the living room. Joth was standing by the window, dressed in a pair of her old jeans and a loose T-shirt, watching the setting sun.

"What's *he* still doing here?" he said pointedly.

"Joth doesn't have anywhere else to go right now, Nevin," Lucy stage-whispered. "Don't worry—he's promised to stay out of our way. Come on— let's go have dinner."

Lucy took hold of his arm and steered him away from the living room and towards the bedroom. As she ushered Nevin into the hall, she paused to glance back at Joth, who was still standing at the window, framed by the glow from the setting sun, and for the briefest moment it looked as if the angel was sheathed in a nimbus of fire.

* * *

Nevin started awake. He'd dozed off after the sex—he hadn't meant to, but the plum wine had gotten to him. Since the room was dark—the candles burned out a while back—it took him a moment to orient himself and remember where he was. After all, it wouldn't do to slip and blurt out the wrong name.

He glanced over at Lucy's naked body curled beside him. She was still dozing, judging from her light snores. If he was careful, he could sneak out of bed and get dressed without waking her up.

He glanced at the alarm clock next to the bed. According to the digital display it wasn't quite nine o'clock in the evening. Things were just starting to heat up in the city that didn't sleep. He had places to go, people to see, connections to work. Gwenda would be expecting him at her place around eleven. They usually didn't start nightclubbing until after midnight. Tonight there was that fetish fashion-show at the Milk Bar...

As he eased himself out from under the bedclothes, Lucy rolled over, muttering in her sleep. Nevin froze in his tracks and held his breath for a long moment before sliding out the rest of the way.

The last thing he needed was another tearful freak-out scene. While she was currently a loose end, once he had things in the bag with Gwenda, he wouldn't have any need for Lucy anymore—although he had to admit she was far better in bed than Gwenda, who, for all her sado-erotic black-leather-slut cutting-edge dominatrix posturing, was pretty neurotic when it came

Angels On Fire

to sex. She was frigid actually, but she had bags of money. Okay, her father out on Long Island was the one with the money. And if Nevin had to choose between a woman who enjoyed sex and a woman with a platinum card—that was what getting it on the side was all about, right?

After he wiggled back into his skin-tight black jeans, T-shirt, and leather jacket, he eased out of the bedroom and headed down the hall. Although he reeked of sex, he didn't dare risk a shower, for fear of alerting Lucy. He'd just swing by his loft for a quick hosing off before heading to Gwenda's place. He had to admit that, if nothing else, the rent on that hell-hole was worth it for ensuring he had a place to wash off the evidence before heading off on his next date.

While bathing was something he was willing to postpone, thirst was another thing. At least the kitchen was far enough away from the bedroom that he could risk raiding the fridge. Although, judging from its interior, it might not be worth the effort.

He downed the opened ginger ale while standing in the cold light of the open refrigerator door, then tossed the can into the trash. As he turned to leave he collided with someone in the darkened kitchen. He was about to blurt out his pre-prepared explanation for why he was leaving unannounced when he realized the figure blocking his way was Joth, not Lucy.

"What the hell are *you* looking at?" Nevin snarled.

Joth said nothing, but did not offer to move.

"I'm *talking* to you, asshole!" Nevin poked sharply at Joth's chest with his index finger. "What's your problem, headcase? You *deaf* as well as dumb?"

"Are you going to make Lucy cry?"

Nevin blinked. Usually the weirdo sounded zoned out on Prozac, but there was an edge in Joth's voice he had not heard before. "Huh? What did you say?"

"Are you going to make Lucy cry?"

"And what if I *do?*" Nevin sneered. "What are *you* going to do about it, ass-wipe?"

"Something I've never done before."

Joth took a step forward, forcing Nevin to take one backward. He had never realized how *tall* the fucker was before. Nevin swore under his breath and hurriedly shouldered past Joth, who did not offer to stop him.

As Nevin clattered down the stairs of the apartment building he made a mental note to make sure Lucy got rid of the weirdo for good. She was going to have to decide who was more important to her—him or some scramblehead from Bumfuck, Arkansas.

He couldn't put his finger on it, but there was *definitely* something about that mook he didn't like. Not that the asshole scared him—but Nevin could have sworn he saw something *glowing* in the back of Joth's eyes.

part 3

an angel in the sun

And I saw an angel standing in the sun; and he cried with a loud voice, saying to all the fowls that fly in the midst of heaven, 'Come and gather yourself together unto the supper of the great God.'
—Revelations 19:17

There went up smoke out of his nostrils, and fire out of his mouth devoured: coals were kindled by it. He bowed the heavens also, and came down; and darkness was under his feet.
—Psalms 18: 8-9

The angels were all singing out of tune.
And hoarse with having little else to do,
Excepting to wind up the sun and moon,
Or curb a runaway young star or two.
—Lord Byron, *The Vision of Judgment*

CHAPTER 15

The Ars Novina occupied the top floor of a converted SoHo warehouse, and had bare wood floors, white-washed walls and track lighting identical to every other downtown art gallery. However, what made it unique, as far as Lucy was concerned, was it was the first legitimate space she had ever been allowed to hang her art in. All of her previous shows had been in tiny Lower East Side hole-in-the-walls that could be described, at best, as "funky."

For all its sterility and pretension, the Ars Novina was the type of place where collectors—the lifeblood of the arts community—could be found, so it was important that Lucy be there before the doors were scheduled to open in order to make sure the pictures were hung correctly and that the sales information had been typed up and posted beside the corresponding work. This meant she had to leave Joth with Ezrael for a few hours, but at least she didn't have to worry about getting the time off from work. Of course, showing up early also gave her a chance to scope out the other entries in the show and see who would be giving her a run for her money.

The first thing she noticed was that her photographs were in the farthest corner of the gallery, while Gwenda's canvasses were just inside the front door. She also found it telling that Nevin's "entries"—which consisted of the nude studies of him she'd photographed—were mere feet from Gwenda's installation. Lucy resented Gwenda hogging the best traffic area in the gallery, but there wasn't much she could do about it except take some comfort in knowing how lame her rival's art really was.

Gwenda's multi-media canvasses were a combination of "found image" collage and Warholesque lithography that aimed at profundity but settled for ponderousness. One consisted of a couple of pages torn from a fetish porn mag, a print advertisement for adult diapers, and a black leather glove glued onto a canvas with a portrait of Marilyn Monroe silk-screened on top of it in black and blue ink. Another featured silk flowers glued into the mouth of an indifferently silk-screened image of Carmen Miranda, framed by headlines from the *Post* that read LONG ISLAND LOLITA and COP SHOOTS COP.

Satisfied that everything was in order, she left long enough to grab a falafel down the street so she would have something in her stomach. The last thing she needed was to get blotto on cheap wine at the opening. Collectors tended to steer clear of artists who ralphed on their shoes.

The first thing she noticed when she returned was that Gwenda had finally arrived and was tricked out in a floor-length black leather evening gown and feather boa that made her look more like a drag queen than a diva.

"Lucy! Where *have* you been?" Gwenda scolded.

"Out grabbing a bite, if it's any of your business," she replied tartly.

Nevin appeared at Gwenda's elbow, carrying a pair of clear plastic cups full of chablis. His wide smile faltered at the sight of Lucy.

"Hi, girls!" he said, struggling to hide his ill-ease. "I, uh, thought you two might like a drink—" He held the glasses out towards them, smiling uncomfortably.

"How *thoughtful* of you, Nevin," Lucy said, taking the proffered drink. "Well, I better go man my post."

"At least *you're* close to the bathrooms," Gwenda said with a faux smile.

"Yes. How *lucky* of me," Lucy tossed over her shoulder.

It was going to be a long night. The opening was supposed to run from eight to eleven o'clock, which meant she had at least three solid hours of standing around in high heels on a hardwood floor, making small-talk with people she didn't know. Her feet and calves were going to give her merry hell come tomorrow morning. But that was all part and parcel of the art-world, like it or not. Which would be okay if openings were attended by people genuinely interested in buying art.

However, most of those now pouring into the gallery were social butterflies of a particularly shabby hue, concerned with *appearing* to be interested in the Arts while puffing up their egos at the expense of others. There were some unfamiliar faces, but most of those in the crowd were recognizable as inveterate opening-night parasites intent on nothing but guzzling free wine and scarfing down cheese cubes.

A half-hour into the opening, the gallery had become crowded. Lucy was glad she'd decided not to wear her velvet dress, as the body heat of the attendees had raised the temperature a good fifteen degrees. As she rocked back and forth on her feet, trying to alleviate the tension on her calves, she thought she heard someone call her name.

She frowned and looked around, then spotted Ezrael—Joth in tow—making his way towards her from across the crowded room. She smiled and waved, trying not to think about how happy seeing the two of them made her.

"*There* you are!" Ezrael said, smiling broadly. "Sorry we're late—there was a huge line waiting to get in!"

"Ez! I was afraid you weren't going to make it!" She threw her arms around the aging muse and kissed him on the cheek.

"Of *course* I'm here! I couldn't very well miss the social event of the season, could I?" Ez chuckled. "Besides, Joth would not have *allowed* me to be so remiss! Every hour on the hour I was asked if was time to leave yet!"

"So—who's your friend?"

Lucy was startled to discover Nevin hovering on the periphery of their little group, glowering at Ezrael. "Oh. Hi. Uh, Ez, this is Nevin."

"Hello," Ezrael said, holding his hand out for the younger man to shake. "I've heard *quite* a bit about you, Nevin."

"I wish I could say the same about you," Nevin said, ignoring Ezrael's outstretched hand. "So, how long have you known Lucy?"

Ezrael's eyes narrowed, but his smile remained outwardly friendly. "Not long. We met on the subway."

"Really? You an artist, Ez?"

"No. I guess you could call me a patron of the arts."

Nevin raised an eyebrow. "Oh? Really? You collect?"

"I have a…small collection, yes."

"Anyone I might have heard of?"

"I hope so! But I am not here tonight as a collector—I am here as a friend of Lucy's, to provide moral support, if you will."

There was a sudden flurry of motion towards the front of the gallery that sent ripples throughout the room. People stopped in mid-conversation to turn and try to get a look.

"What's going on?" asked Lucy, standing on tip-toe in order look over the sea of heads filling the gallery.

"It would appear a celebrity has entered the building," Ezrael commented dryly.

"Oh? Who?"

"Terry Spanner," Joth said, even though the angel had its back to the crowd.

"I thought you said it was a *celebrity*!" she said, rolling her eyes.

"Uh—I better get back to my station," Nevin said suddenly and hurried back to the front of the gallery.

"Such a *forceful* young man," Ezrael said carefully, his eyes on Lucy's face as she watched Nevin leave. "Is he always so—proprietary?"

Lucy blushed and shrugged. "You don't understand—you're not seeing him under the best of circumstances. He's been under a lot of stress lately—"

"So I take it. Is he still seeing that woman?"

"Not *really*. He just hasn't gotten around to breaking up with her yet, that's all."

"Oh. I see." Ezrael took a deep breath and clapped his hands together, smiling as he rubbed them together. "How about I go get us something to drink? I'll be back in a minute. I'll leave Joth with you, if that's all right?"

"No—I don't mind. It'll give me someone to talk to."

Within seconds Lucy lost sight of the muse amidst the crowd. There had to be at least two hundred people squeezed into the gallery, all standing around talking and laughing, cups of cheap chablis clutched in their hands.

"Good evening, Ms. Bender—what a delight and a surprise running into you and your ward here tonight!"

Lucy turned to find Meresin standing at her elbow, dressed in a meticulous black silk nehru jacket, a glass of white wine held in one finely manicured hand.

Joth made a noise deep in its chest like a tuning fork struck against a piece of Waterford crystal. Lucy reached out and placed a comforting hand on the angel's arm.

Meresin smiled and held up a hand. "Please, there is no need to be alarmed, on either your or the elohim's part! I am not here to harm either of you! I'm merely here as a patron of the arts."

As if to illustrate, the daemon gestured to a sculpture that consisted of a fashion mannequin tightly wrapped in silver duct-tape so that it resembled a mummified street-walker. Lucy noticed the installation boasted a fluorescent orange "sold' sticker.

"I find it pretty hard to believe that of all the art openings you could have attended in this city, you just happened to pick *this* one," Lucy commented acidly.

Meresin shrugged. "Believe what you like, my dear. I've been on the Ars Novina's invitation list for ages. In this case, the decision to attend tonight's opening was my client's."

"Client—? You mean Spanner?"

Meresin nodded. "He is looking to redecorate his lobby. Something guaranteed to shock and titillate the yokels waiting for an audience with his august personage. He feels the current lobby is too—sedate."

"What do *you* care about art?" Lucy snapped. "Ez told me what you are, what you do—! I thought creatures like you couldn't stand to be around art and artists."

Meresin's smile was as sharp as a fox's. "*Please*, Ms. Bender! You speak to one of the sephiroth—what your ancestors once called a Prince of Darkness—not a bum-scratching imp! Over the centuries I have seen more art than any living human could ever dream of! Granted, I was always trying to destroy it or demolish the creator, but that's besides the point. Being exposed to the arts is like being exposed to radiation: in small doses, over a lengthy period of time, it can and does have its effect—even on daemons."

Lucy frowned. "Are you telling me that you're a lapsed devil?"

Meresin chuckled, although he was careful not to show any teeth. "Let us say I have a more *catholic* interpretation of how I might best serve the Machine than my fellows. Over the years I have striven to become more...*sophisticated*...in achieving my ends.

"My function is subtle yet vital. I do my best to ensure that the handiwork of the Blessed is kept from inspiring others. In some cases that means making sure that private collections are stolen or destroyed, in others it means dynamiting ancient burial vaults. But most often it means guaranteeing that an artist's failings are encouraged at the expense of their gifts. Take my word, my dear, through wretched excess, gambling and bad marriages have innumerable masterpieces been unmade!

"I have spent centuries trying to keep artists unstable, poverty-stricken and obscure—and, believe me, it hasn't been easy! When I think of the mistakes I made with the likes of Mozart, Van Gogh, and Dickinson! But for every *Starry Night*, *Magic Flute* and "Because I could not stop for Death" that escape my grasp, there are a hundred *Mona Lisas*, *La Traviattas* and *Pere Ubus* that do not.

"Permit me a moment's vanity, if you will. Any gibbering imp can coerce a psychotic to take a hammer to the *Pietà*. It is no great feat for a wall-eyed oni to provoke a drunken painter into slashing his canvas. But it takes a *true* Infernal genius—a sephiroth—to encourage an artist to pervert his gifts by wasting them on lesser pursuits. I've found advertising to be *most* useful in this manner. What greater challenge is there than promoting an artist whose gift is False and convincing others that it is True? By subverting the creative process in this manner, I do the most damage to the Clockwork possible!"

"Why are you telling me this?" Lucy asked, eyeing the daemon suspiciously.

Meresin smiled and produced a black cigarette, already lit, out of thin air. "I sense a sea change in my nature. Perhaps, by being exposed to humanity and the arts for as long as I have, I have become adversely influenced. Contaminated, so to speak. We daemons are more like your kind than the angels are, in part because we share your failings. Do not underestimate the devil when it comes to temptation—which is to say, do not underestimate yourself."

A distant look passed across the daemon's face, and for a brief moment Lucy glimpsed what she thought was longing in the sephiroth's dark eyes. He dropped his cigarette and stubbed it out with the toe of his boot.

"Well—enough of that! I have a busy night ahead of me. Good evening, Ms. Bender." Meresin turned and fixed his jet-black eyes on Joth. "I envy you, elohim. Maybe some day I will be fortunate enough to meet a woman— or a man—who will break the chains that bind me to the Machine."

Lucy stood and watched Meresin shoulder his way through the press of bodies, not sure what to make of the daemon's impromptu confession. She touched Joth's arm.

"Joth—go find Ezrael."

The angel nodded and began twining its way through the crowded room. Lucy tried to keep her eye on its golden head bobbing above most of those in the gallery, but her attention was diverted by a cough at her elbow.

"Excuse me—are you the artist?" asked a tall, thin man with a steeply receding hairline. He had a neatly trimmed goatee and a ponytail held in place by a black silk band, and was dressed all in black except for a bright red matador's jacket.

"My name is Page Uxbridge," he said, smiling. "I own a gallery in Midtown—perhaps you've heard of it? The Matador?"

"Yes I have, as a matter of fact," she said. She wasn't lying to be polite, either. What she heard was that the Matador liked to snap up artists and flog them for all they were worth for a season or two before dropping them. It was bullshit, but the kind of bullshit that made the art world run and being a professional artist possible in Manhattan.

"I'm *very* interested in your vision—it's retro, without being camp," Uxbridge said, gesturing to the print of *House Dog*. "Could you tell me a little more about the history behind these pictures—?"

* * *

Joth scanned the crowd for Ezrael's halo, but could not spot it. The muse's halo was the color of a robin's egg, laced with vivid veins of gold. Most of the halos the angel saw were far weaker than Ezrael's. Indeed, some did not seem to possess halos at all. As Joth continued to scan the gallery, its attention was captured by a lavender halo with pinkish undertones, like a cloud just before sunset. Intrigued, Joth moved in its direction, curious to see what manner of deathling possessed so lovely an aura.

The halo belonged to a little girl standing next to the refreshment table, carefully sipping the ginger ale the bartender had poured for her. Dressed in her red corduroy jumper and matching P.F. Flyer sneakers, she was out of place amidst the sea of leathers, stiletto heels and other fetish fashion. The child looked to be no older than four years old, with big green eyes and naturally wavy hair the color of a taffy apple.

Joth had seen younger deathlings on the streets, but it had not had a chance to study them very closely. Fascinated, the angel dropped onto one knee to get a closer look, bringing it face-to-face with the young deathling.

The little deathling giggled and pointed at Joth. "You've got a shiny head!"

Joth nodded its understanding. "That is my halo."

The child frowned and tilted her head to one side. "Only angels have halos. Are *you* an angel?"

"Yes. I am Joth of the elohim. But not just angels have halos."

"Do *I* have a halo?"

"Yes. It's a very beautiful one."

"Really? What color is it?" She tilted her head back, squinting one eye, as if trying to see for herself. "Is there purple in it? I like purple."

Joth cocked its head to one side. "Yes. There is purple in it," it said.

On closer inspection the angel could see thin lines of darkness spider-webbing through the brighter colors. For some reason, this made Joth anxious, although it was at a loss to know why.

"My name is Penny," said the little girl. "It's short for Penelope. Is your name short for anything?"

Joth shook its head.

Penny tilted her head and fixed Joth with a dubious look. "Are you *really* an angel?"

"Yes."

"If you're an angel, why can't I see your wings?"

"I am hiding them."

"Why?"

"Because if I had my wings out, it would be hard for me to get around in a room this crowded."

Penny pursed her lips and nodded. *"Oh."* Joth's explanation seemed to be good enough for her. "Are you an artist, Mr. Joth?" She asked the question with the off-hand nonchalance of a child parroting an adult phrase heard but not fully comprehended.

"No. Are you?"

"*No*, silly!" she giggled. "I'm here with my mommy and daddy."

"Are your mommy and daddy artists?"

"My daddy owns a gallery. Do you have a mommy and daddy?"

"No."

"*Penny!*"

A tall, fashionably thin woman dressed in a black sheath and a bright red matador jacket lurched out of the crowd and grabbed the child by one arm, yanking her away from Joth.

The woman leaned down, wobbling drunkenly on her four-inch high heels, to scold her daughter. "What did I *tell* you about talking to strangers, young lady!?"

"Mommy, he's *not* a stranger!" Penny protested. "His name is Joth! He's an *angel!*"

"Angel?" slurred her mother. She squinted at Joth, somewhat baffled, as the angel rose to its full height. "You're a biker?"

Penny rolled her eyes and sighed loudly, exasperated by her mother's obtuseness. "No, Mommy, he's a *real* angel—like on the Christmas tree!"

"Kids!" the woman laughed nervously. "Where *do* they get their ideas? Now, come along, Penny—"

Joth fixed Penny's mother with its unblinking gaze. "The father touches her," it said as nonchalantly as if it were commenting on the weather.

Penny's mother blinked and wobbled even more than before. She turned to stare in disbelief at the stranger her daughter had been talking to. He was a tall, thin, somewhat Native American-looking fellow with long dark hair plaited into a single braid. Despite a feeling that she knew him from someplace, she did not recognize his face.

"Do you know *who* my husband is?!" she asked indignantly.

"He is Page Uxbridge, age forty-nine, owner and proprietor of the Matador Gallery, located on West 57th Street," Joth replied. The angel's voice was not loud, nor was it accusatory. "You are Carla Mearig-Uxbridge. You married one another four-and-a-half years ago, immediately upon the discovery of your pregnancy. You are his third wife, Penny is his second daughter. His older daughter, Patrice, is twenty-three. He molested her as well, resulting in his divorce from his second wife, Yvonne, in 1981..."

* * *

"I'm *very* interested in showing your work," Uxbridge said. "I can get you some *real* attention—far better than what you'll get in a show like this." The gallery owner handed Lucy a bright red business card. "Here—promise me you'll give me a call in a couple of days? I'd *love* to see what else you have in your portfolio!"

"I appreciate your interest in my work, Mr. Uxbridge…"

"Page! Please, call me Page!" he smiled, flashing capped teeth.

"Uh, okay, Page…When would be a convenient time for me to call—?"

Uxbridge abruptly fell silent as he caught sight of something going on at the other side of the gallery. Curious, Lucy turned to look over her shoulder in the direction he was scowling. Joth was standing talking to a woman dressed in a red jacket identical to Uxbridge's. The woman was holding a little girl dressed in a red corduroy jumper in her arms, and her face was twisted into a look of anger and hurt, as if she was fighting to keep from bursting into hysterical tears. Whatever it was Joth was saying to the woman, it was clearly something she wasn't happy hearing.

Uxbridge jostled his way across the crowded room, his hands balling and unballing themselves into fists. He grabbed Joth by the shoulder, spinning the angel around to face him.

"*Ohhhh shit,*" Lucy whispered under her breath, and hurried to intervene.

"What the *hell* are you doing with my wife?" demanded the gallery owner at the top of his voice.

Joth stared placidly at Uxbridge. "I am not doing anything with your wife," it replied evenly.

"That's *not* what it looked like to me!" Uxbridge moved to put himself between his wife and Joth. "Carla—are you all right? Did he do anything to you or Penny?" Uxbridge reached out to put his arm around his wife's shoulder, only to have her side-step his embrace.

"*Don't you touch me!*" Carla Uxbridge spat. "Don't you touch me *or* Penny, you bastard!"

"Watch your voice. We're in public, remember?" Uxbridge said, speaking through a clenched smile. "You're drunk again, Carla. You *know* how you get when you're drunk!"

"I've had some drinks, but that doesn't mean I'm *drunk*! I *know* when I'm drunk! And I'm *not* drunk!" Carla insisted. She tossed back the cascade of ash-blonde hair out of her face, nearly throwing herself off-balance in the process.

Uxbridge quickly snatched Penny from his wife's arms. "Come on, sweetie! Mommy's tired and needs to go home…" The gallery owner turned to face Joth, his voice trembling with rage. "And as for *you*—! I don't know *who* you are, but I never want to see you anywhere *near* my wife or child ever again!"

"Joth—what's going on here?" asked Lucy, who had just managed to shoulder her way through the crowd.

"Mrs. Uxbridge asked me what I knew of her husband, and I told her," explained Joth, matter-of-factly.

"You *know* this man?" Uxbridge growled, fixing Lucy with a hostile glare.

"H-he's, um, my roomie," she stammered.

Uxbridge repositioned his daughter into his left arm and shoved his right hand towards Lucy. "Give me back my card!" he said brusquely.

"What?"

"My card—I want my card *back*, please!" he said, snapping his fingers for emphasis.

Lucy was acutely aware that virtually everyone in the gallery had fallen silent and was standing there, watching the little scene between herself and Uxbridge. Her face turned as red as the gallery owner's jacket as she reached into her purse and retrieved the business card. Uxbridge snatched it from her and viciously tore it up, scattering the pieces in the air.

Uxbridge grabbed his wife by the hand and, still carrying his daughter, stormed out of the gallery. Penny Uxbridge, her eyes far sadder than a child's should ever be, surreptitiously lifted her hand to wave shyly at Joth as they left. All heads turned to watch the trio pass. The moment Uxbridge and his family left the room, a couple hundred voices began talking at once, resuming their dropped threads of conversation.

Lucy stared down at the ragged fragments of red cardstock scattered at her feet, then glanced up at Joth. "What *did* you say to that asshole's wife?" she asked after a long moment.

"That her husband molests their daughter," Joth replied flatly.

Lucy flinched. She didn't know what was worse, that Joth had stated the fact so baldly to the Uxbridge woman or the knowledge that the angel was incapable of lying.

She looked back down at what was left of the business card on the floor.

"Fuck it," she sighed. "I didn't want a creep like that selling my art *anyway*. Right, Joth?"

The angel was nowhere to be seen. She turned around in a complete circle, thinking she might spot its golden head amongst the crowd, but saw nothing that even remotely resembled it. Just as she was about to panic, Ezrael popped back up, smiling broadly, a drink clutched in either hand.

"Sorry I was away so long—! I ran into an old friend of mine from the Factory days! We stepped outside to play a little catch-up. Did I miss anything? Where's Joth?"

"You mean he's not with you? Oh, Jesus—Ez, Meresin's here! He came over and talked to me just after you left!"

Ezrael frowned. "Yes, I know he's here. I saw him when I came back in. He's over there, talking to Nevin." The muse pointed in the direction of the front door by way of explanation. Sure enough, the daemon was chatting up Nevin. Nearby, Terry Spanner—accompanied by a knot of rubberneckers—was talking to Gwenda's cleavage. Joth was nowhere to be seen.

"You don't think he did anything to Joth, do you?"

Ezrael shook his head. "Meresin's no fool. He knows the rules of engagement. But if Joth has gone wandering off again, the last thing we want to do is to alert Meresin to that fact. If we're lucky, Joth merely grew bored and simply returned to its roost—your apartment. I'll head back to see if that's the case…"

As he turned to go, there was a sudden flash of light followed by a distant rumble that rattled the pictures on the wall.

"Looks like we're in for a thunderstorm," Ezrael observed.

A few feet away a woman in a backless satin dress squealed as raindrops splashed onto her shoulders. The Ars Novina's manager came hurrying out of his office in the back, scowling at the rain spattering the floor of his gallery.

"Who the fuck opened *that* thing?" he demanded, scratching his head as he stared at the open skylight twenty feet overhead.

CHAPTER 16

"Carla? Honey—you awake?"

Carla Uxbridge muttered and rolled onto her side, causing her dress to hike itself over her hip, but did not open her eyes or otherwise respond to her husband's voice. Page Uxbridge stood in the door of their bedroom and scowled at his wife as she lay sprawled across the bed half-dressed, her make-up smearing the pillowcase.

Tonight was little different from any other—except for her uncustomary flare of anger at the opening. Carla was a silly drunk. She got loud and sloppy, but seldom anything more. She was rarely angry—and she certainly never aimed it at him. But tonight had been different, for some reason. Something in the way she looked at him—the way she pulled away from him—worried Uxbridge.

It had something to do with the strange-looking Oriental youth she'd been talking to at the opening. Uxbridge had tried to force her into telling him what had gone on between them, but Carla refused to elaborate on it during their car ride back home. Of course, the moment he unlocked the door, she'd headed straight for the liquor cabinet. As usual.

Satisfied that the Rohypnol he'd slipped in her bottle of tequila had done its trick, Uxbridge left the bedroom and headed for the lofted space in the atrium-style living/dining room area of their spacious luxury condo overlooking Central Park. The loft, accessible via a spiral staircase, served as his home office. Uxbridge paused in mid-step as a clap of thunder from the storm outside caused the metal steps to vibrate underneath his feet.

The loft was a small, cramped space with barely enough room for a desk and a book case, but Uxbridge liked being able to look down from his perch and see where his family was and what they were doing at all times. It made him feel in control of his situation. And as he had learned long ago, control was everything.

His office was his private preserve. No one else was allowed up here—not even Penny, and especially not Carla. Uxbridge had long since grown weary of his wife, but he tolerated her for no other reason than to insure his control over Penny. He had made the mistake of losing control with his last wife, Yvonne, and she had used the leverage to take Patty away from him. He'd sworn such a thing would never happen again.

Uxbridge eased himself into his high-backed leather executive's chair and opened the desk's lower drawer, taking out the bottle of scotch he kept there. Scotch had been his father's favorite poison. As he poured himself a stiff drink, Uxbridge reflected on how thankless a task being a father and husband truly was.

Penny was *his* little girl. *His* flesh and blood. She was *his*. Carla might be her mother, but *he* was her father! *He* was the one who provided for the clothes on her back, the food in her mouth, the roof over her head. Carla may have carried Penny in her belly for nine moths, but *he* was the one who *put* her there, by damn!

He worked *hard* making sure that they got everything they might possibly want. *He* was entitled to their love, to their obedience, to their respect. And it was only *right* that he take what was his due.

It was important for a man to protect his family—and the best way to protect them was through control. By controlling them he showed how much he *cared* for them. How else could he prove how good and strong a husband and father he truly was? And through controlling their lives, he protected those he loved most from their most dangerous enemy—themselves.

A man had to watch for signs of betrayal from the women in his life. His father had taught him that. Like most children, Uxbridge had labored under the delusion that his mother was a saint and that his sisters were good girls. But his father showed him how he should never trust the appearance of innocence, the semblance of purity.

One day, when he was ten years old, his father took him to a fancy hotel and made him sit in the lobby and watch as his wife, Uxbridge's mother, met with a strange man in the hotel bar, then retired upstairs.

"You see, Page? You see?" his father had whispered in his ear. *"They're never to be trusted. None of them. They're all whores. Every last one of them! You have to watch them every minute, every god-damn minute of the day, or they will destroy you."*

Uxbridge's thoughts turned back to the stranger at the gallery. He had never seen the man before, although now that he thought about it, his features were not unlike those of the man his mother had met at the hotel bar, so many years ago. Strange. Where had he gotten the idea the other man was Oriental?

Of course, Carla insisted she did not know the stranger—that she had never laid eyes on him before—but Uxbridge did not believe her. The other man was her lover and he had approached Carla at the gallery and threatened to expose their illicit liaison. That would certainly explain the look of dread he had seen in Carla's eyes.

The photographer—the Bender woman—claimed the other man was her roomie. Perhaps he'd been over-hasty in his reaction to her. He should have pumped her for more information. Perhaps she had seen Carla with her 'roomie'? And even if she *hadn't*, it probably wouldn't be hard to coerce her into claiming otherwise. Artists were always willing to stab one another in the back if they thought it might land them a one-man show. Still, it was worth checking out. He scribbled the photographer's name on his appointment blotter as a reminder to himself.

If he could manufacture enough proof that Carla was having an affair and that she was an unfit mother, then things would become far simpler for him. There were enough artists and art collectors on the scene who owed him favors and who would be more than happy to provide anecdotes concerning Carla's public drunkenness. With the proper lawyer, he could finally rid himself of Carla and have Penny all to himself. Just the two of them.

* * *

Penny didn't like the storm. It was scary and made it hard for her to sleep. She especially didn't like the thunder, which sounded like an angry animal roaring in the sky. The only good thing about the thunder tonight was that it had made it hard for her to hear Mommy and Daddy yelling at one another.

She wondered if tonight was going to be a sleepy night or a night where Daddy would come and tuck her back into bed. She hoped it was going to be a sleepy night. She didn't like it when Daddy tucked her back into bed.

Tap-tap-tap

Penny sat up at the sound of someone—or something—rapping on her window. She gasped as a lightning flash lit up the sky, illuminating the outline of a winged figure crouching on the ledge outside her bedroom. But instead of screaming in fear, Penny broke into a smile.

"Mr. Angel!"

Penny hopped out of her bed and hurried over to the window. She climbed on top of her toy chest and opened the latch. There was a gust of rainwater and wind as the window was opened from the outside and the angel climbed over the sill.

"Hello, Penny," smiled Joth.

"Hello, Mr. Angel!"

The elohim shook itself like a wet dog, sending water flying. Penny squealed and giggled as the droplets splashed her.

"How do you know where I live?"

"I followed you."

"Why did you follow me?"

Joth stared at the little deathling standing before it, both entranced and distressed by the color of her halo—and the darkness that surrounded it.

"I don't know why," replied the angel, truthfully. "All I know is that it was important that I do so."

* * *

Uxbridge closed his eyes as the scotch loosened the knots hidden deep inside himself. He could see his daughter in his mind's eye—waiting for him in her narrow child's bed—and, as always, he became aroused.

There was something about how she looked so helpless and pink and innocent that fanned his lust. But he knew better than anyone how appearances could betray the eye, deceive the on-looker. It was all a lie. She was a slut, just like her mother was a slut. Just like his mother was a slut. The truth of her whorish nature was between his legs. If she wasn't a slut, he would not get stiff.

It was only through his love, his guidance, could she be saved from becoming a whore. It took a father's love, a father's strong hand to make her be good. She was there—at the end of the hall—waiting for him. Waiting for him to make her a good girl again. Waiting for him to tuck her back into bed.

Uxbridge returned the bottle to its hiding place in the desk and proceeded to wobble down the loft staircase, answering the siren's call that only he could hear. But as he neared his daughter's room, he could hear Penny talking out loud. He couldn't make out what she was saying, just the sing-song of her voice. Uxbridge's anger began to rise. She was supposed to be asleep, not up talking to her teddybears. She knew that perfectly well, but she was disobeying the rules. Disobeying *him*.

As his hand closed on the doorknob of Penny's room, he was startled by what sounded like a man's voice responding to his daughter's childish banter.

Uxbridge frowned. Could it be she was already deceiving him, as his mother had deceived his father?

Uxbridge jerked opened the door to his daughter's room. It was much like any preschool child's room—decorated with stuffed animals, Barbie dolls, Tinkertoys and the like. Penny's bed was a child-sized canopy with Little Mermaid comforter and sheets. On a nearby matching table was a night-light shaped to look like a conch sea-shell.

Penny was sitting up in bed, dressed in her pink flannel nightie, looking in the direction of the window. Uxbridge followed his daughter's gaze, but outside of a fluttering curtain, all he saw was a child-sized easel, complete with oversized paper and a selection of watercolors and felt-tip markers. The picture on the easel showed a stick-figure Daddy with a big, sharp smile, looming like a giant over the stick-figure Mommy and stick-figure Penny.

"What's going on in here?" Uxbridge demanded, looking around suspiciously. "Who were you talking to, Penny?"

Penny's eyes grew big and she pulled her knees in tight to her chest, pushing herself against the headboard of her bed. She was trying to make herself small, small as a mouse; as if by curling in on herself she could somehow disappear.

"I was just talking to the angel," she said in a tiny, frightened voice.

Uxbridge's frown deepened. "Angel? *What* angel?"

"He followed me home, Daddy, honest! You're not mad at me are you?"

"Penny, stop *lying* to me! There's *no* such thing as angels!"

"But I've *seen* him, Daddy! He's got wings! He flew in my window!"

"Don't *argue* with me, young lady!" Uxbridge snapped. "You know better than to contradict me! If I tell you something doesn't exist, it *doesn't* exist!"

"But, Daddy—!"

Uxbridge licked his lips and stepped forward. He was used to her delaying tactics. Like Scheherazade, she hoped to evade her fate by distracting him with fanciful stories. One night it's leprechauns in the closet or bears hiding in the toybox, now it's angels flying in her window.

"Stop *lying* to me, Penny! You know how Daddy *hates* it when you lie to him," he said, his breathing ragged and heavy in his chest. "You don't want to make Daddy *mad* at you, do you?"

"No, Daddy," Penny whimpered as her father's shadow fell across the foot of her bed. "Please. No." Penny might as well have been talking to her make-believe angel. All Uxbridge could hear was his father's voice, urging him to claim his right as creator and protector of the flesh before him.

When Uxbridge reached the foot of the bed there was a sudden flash of lightning so bright it momentarily dazzled him, followed by a clap of thunder so loud it rattled the entire building like a giant's hand. As his eyes readjusted to the gloom, he glimpsed what looked like the outline of a man standing in front of him. His first thought was that it was his own shadow cast before him. Then he realized the shadow had eyes that glowed.

"H-how did you get in here—?!" Uxbridge demanded, trying to sound more angry than frightened. Uxbridge took an involuntary step backward, looking about frantically for some sign of how a stranger could have entered the room without his noticing it. They were nine stories up and the fire escape was in the master bedroom, not Penny's. "W-what do you want?"

"Leave her be," said the intruder, his voice mixing ominously with the peal of thunder rolling across the city.

Uxbridge recognized the intruder as the other man Carla had spoken to at the gallery. So she *did* know him, after all! No doubt this man had a key to the apartment and had used it to sneak in through the service door in the kitchen. How dare this stranger invade Uxbridge's home! He had to regain to control of the situation and he had to do it fast.

"Get away from my daughter!" Uxbridge barked. "Get *out* of my house! Get out before I call the cops!"

"Leave her be," repeated the stranger. There was something moving underneath the other man's floor-length duster—something *alive*—but Uxbridge refused to let himself be distracted.

"How *dare* you force your way into *my* home and tell *me* what to do?!?" Uxbridge bellowed, his face purpling with rage. "She's *my* daughter—*mine!*"

Uxbridge raised his fist to strike the other man, but the intruder did not blink or flinch in anticipation of the blow. Instead, there was a tearing noise, as the things moving underneath the other man's duster burst the fabric concealing them.

The stranger tossed back his head and spread wide his arms, as if to embrace Uxbridge like a long-lost friend, as a pair of jet-black wings unfurled, filling the room like the vanes of a windmill. Uxbridge opened his mouth, but no sound came out, no matter how hard he tried to scream. He was transfixed, like a deer blinded by the headlights of an oncoming truck. From somewhere far away, Uxbridge heard Penny crow triumphantly:

"See, Daddy? I *told* you I saw an angel!"

The thing that stood revealed before Uxbridge was unlike any angel he had ever seen or read about. Angels weren't supposed to have black wings and burning eyes—were they?

Uxbridge felt a dreadful compulsion to look into the face of the creature standing before him. Even though something told him that looking into the eyes of the black angel would destroy him as surely as the stare of the basilisk, his head began to turn of its own accord. The muscles along his neck bulged until they stood out like whipcords, but it was no use. The dark angel could not be denied.

When at last Page Uxbridge looked he saw that it was the most beautiful thing he had ever seen in his life—and the most horrible. But the worst of all was that the angel wore his mother's face.

His scream was swallowed by the thunder of the storm.

* * *

The sound of running water woke her up. Carla lifted her head from the pillow and squinted at her surroundings. She was home. In the bedroom. But she didn't remember going to bed. She remembered arguing with Page, arguing with him about something—something about Penny—but what? She remembered him pouring her a drink, telling her to calm down, that she was getting upset over nothing—then the next thing she knew she was in bed with her clothes on. Her head ached fiercely and her stomach was queasy. Page was nowhere to be seen.

She swung her bare feet onto the floor, staggering slightly as she got up. The sound of running water was coming from the master bath. Perhaps Page was washing up.

As her head began to clear, she realized there was another sound underneath that of the splashing water. It sounded like sobbing. The first thought that came to her was: *Why is Penny crying?*

Carla remembered the strange young man at the gallery. The one who had said those things about Page, the things that didn't sound like lies, the things that he had no way of knowing—that no one knew, except she and Page.

As she lurched in the direction of the bathroom, Carla's confusion was replaced by fear, then anger. It wasn't until she pushed the bathroom door open that she realized that the person she'd heard sobbing was her husband.

Page Uxbridge was slumped over the rim of the bathroom sink, the faucets running full blast, pouring out over the basin and onto the tiles below, soaking the bath mat. Carla frowned groggily at the water pooled on the floor. Why was the water pink?

Uxbridge sobbed violently as he splashed cupped handfuls of water on his face, as if desperately trying to wash something out of his eyes. If he noticed Carla standing in the doorway, he gave no outward sign. "*Mea culpa...mea culpa...mea maxima culpa...*" Uxbridge blubbered in between the splashes.

"Page—? Page—what's wrong?"

Uxbridge jerked his head in the direction of her voice to reveal tears of blood rolling from eyes as white as those of a baked fish. The gallery owner made a pathetic hiccuping noise—half laugh, half sob—then returned to trying to put the fire out in his corneas.

Carla staggered away from the gibbering blind thing that had once been her husband. She was suddenly more sober than she had been in years. Without really knowing why, she turned and fled towards her child's room.

"*Penny—!*"

She found her daughter huddled against the headboard of her bed, crying softly. Carla gathered her child in her arms, hugging her tightly.

"My baby, my baby—are you all right?"

Penny sniffed back her tears and nodded. "I'm okay, Mommy."

"Baby—did he *do* anything to you—did he *hurt* you?"

The little girl shook her head. "No—but he hurt Daddy."

Carla frowned. "He *who?*"

"Mr. Angel," Penny explained, pointing in the direction of the window.

Carla's scalp tightened at the sound of immense wings flapping behind her, but something told her she was better off not watching whatever it was leave.

When she finally did turn around, all there was to see was an open window and curtains fluttering in the wind.

part 4

heaven and earth

But somewhere, beyond Space and Time,
is wetter water, slimier slime!
And there (they trust) there swimmeth One
Who swam ere rivers were begun,
Immense of fishy form and mind,
Squamous, omnipotent, and kind.
 —Rupert Brooke, *Heaven*

Heaven would not be heaven if we knew what it were.
 —Sir John Suckling

"In Heaven, everything is fine."
 —The Radiator Lady, *Eraserhead* (1978)

CHAPTER 17

Lucy left the show an hour before its posted closing time. As far as she was concerned, if someone wanted to buy her art, they'd buy it whether she was there to explain it to them or not. Joth was more important to her than selling a framed picture of her grandmother's bottle-opener, no matter how much she might need the money.

She kept telling herself that when she and Ez got back to her place, she'd find Joth there waiting for them. But as she unlocked the front door, she knew the angel wasn't there; she didn't know *how* she knew, she just *did*. While Lucy changed out of her good clothes, Ez busied himself with trying to figure out where the angel could have gotten off to. Since the muse's scrying egg was out of commission, he was reduced to less exact forms of divination, such as throwing knucklebones and going up on the roof and twirling a bullroarer.

These efforts revealed that Joth was still in Manhattan and that no daemons were involved in their friend's disappearance, but little else. After a hour of watching Ez throw bones, cast runes, and lay down tarot cards, the day finally started catching up with Lucy. She was so tired she kicked off her shoes and lay across her bed fully dressed.

The sound of the window being eased open startled her from her doze. Her first thought was that it was a burglar, then she saw the winged outline and heaved a sigh of relief.

"Ez! Joth is back!" she called out, reaching for the overhead switch near the door.

"*No*—no lights," the angel whispered, its voice uncharacteristically gravelly.

"Joth—what's wrong with your voice?"

The angel turned its head towards her. In the darkened bedroom its eyes seemed to glow like black-light bulbs. Lucy gasped and drew back as Ezrael opened the bedroom door behind her, spilling light from the hallway into the room.

Joth made a hissing noise and raised a pinion to shield its face. The feathers that still clung to the angel's wings were the color of India ink. Ezrael grabbed Lucy's arm, jerking her clear of Joth.

"Lucy! Get back!"

Ezrael put himself between Lucy and the angel, hitting the lightswitch next to the door as he did so. Suddenly, it was as if there were two Joths standing in the same place, their images laid one atop the other. One Joth was sexless with crystalline eyes, golden hair and jewel-colored wings—the other Joth was a creature with glowing eyes, leathery wings, cloven hooves, and, in a perverse parody of generation, a penis that dangled to its kneecap.

Ezrael produced a handful of colorless powder and blew it into Joth's face. The angel/daemon snarled and dropped to the floor as if coldcocked, curling into a fetal position, pulling its wings around itself like a blanket, so that it was completely hidden from view.

Lucy stared in stunned disbelief at the thing that lay huddled on the floor at her feet. "What—what did you do to him?"

"I didn't kill it, if that's what you're afraid of," Ezrael assured her. "I merely placed Joth into temporary suspended animation, that's all. It won't last long, though."

"Did you see him—? My god, Ez—what *happened* to him?"

The old muse shook his head sadly. "I was afraid this would happen—that's why I had the powder ready. The contamination at the Seventh Circle was too extensive, it sped up Joth's transmutation tenfold. As for what's *happened* to Joth—it is trapped between the Natures. It is not quite angel, but neither is it a daemon.

"Such creatures are *extremely* dangerous, Lucy. Right now Joth is like decaying dynamite that is sweating nitroglycerin, or an unstable isotope—only the potential for destruction is far worse. Such 'destroying angels' are where the legends of 'the Wrath of God' arise from. They've been responsible for entire cities—even civilizations—disappearing off the face of the earth! As for Joth itself—I'm afraid by the time Nisroc makes its third and final appearance, it will be too late. Joth will be lost to the Machine."

"Isn't there *something* we can do?"

Ezrael took a deep breath, as if deciding whether to answer or not, then finally nodded his head. "There *is* one thing—but it's *very* risky, and there's no guarantee it will work."

"What is it?"

"Nisroc has to be petitioned into changing its time-table."

Lucy frowned. "How do we do *that*?"

"Nisroc must be approached by a mortal representing the interests of the prodigal angel."

"All it takes is you asking a favor?"

"No, I was thinking more along the lines of *you*, actually."

Lucy did a double-take. "Whoa! Hold on there! You want *me* to petition Nisroc on Joth's behalf?"

"Exactly."

"Why me?"

"Because you care about Joth. Is that not enough?"

Lucy glanced down at the angel wrapped within its blackened wings, then back at Ezrael. "Okay—I guess I'm too far into this scene to back out now. So how are we going to lure Nisroc back here—set out a big bowl of Meow Mix?"

Ezrael chuckled despite himself. "Oh, no. I'm afraid you've got it turned around. In order to plead Joth's case, *you* have to go to Nisroc."

* * *

Ezrael pursed his lips, stroking his chin. "Do you have any white chalk?"

Lucy glanced up, perplexed. "Huh—? Over there in my art supplies." She gestured to the tackle box resting on the worktable in the living room.

"Good. Clear off the floor. When you've done that, draw a large circle with the chalk—one large enough for an adult to lie spread-eagled in." Having said that, the muse promptly turned on his heel and disappeared into the kitchen.

As Lucy busied herself with pushing the furniture to one side of the room, she heard the kitchen cabinets being systematically opened and shut and her crockery being rattled.

"What the hell are you looking for?" she asked as she drew the circle on the bare floorboards.

"Hell has little to do with this," Ezrael grumbled, emerging from the tiny kitchen with an armload of groceries and a large glass mixing bowl, depositing the loot atop the knock-kneed worktable near the window.

He eyed the white chalk circle Lucy had drawn, his brows pushed together like albino caterpillars. He grunted, snatched up the chalk, and with surprising speed and agility for a man of his avowed age, dropped to his hands and knees and began inscribing runic script along the circle's outer rim. He moved so hurriedly the chalk snapped in his grip more than once, causing him to snort in disgust and swiftly discard the broken portion.

As the former angel scrawled magical graffiti on her parlor floor, Lucy inspected the arcane collection of bottles, bags and packages harvested from her pantry: a bottle of purified drinking water; a pressed-cardboard container of eggs; and a bag of rice flour.

"There—that should do," Ezrael announced as he got back to his feet, clapping his hands free of chalk-dust. He promptly turned his attention to the ingredients gathered on the table, dumping the rice flour into the glass mixing bowl and splashing half of the purified water atop it.

"What do I do now?" Lucy asked, still baffled.

"Strip."

"Beg pardon?"

"You heard me. To the skin."

Lucy's face flushed bright red. "Now wait just a minute—!"

Ezrael scooped one of the eggs from the container and cracked it against the rim of the mixing bowl, deftly separating the white from the yolk while fixing her with his golden gaze. "Spinning Creation, woman! Do you have any idea how many females I've seen naked in my time? This is not an attempt at seduction—as if I was still prone to such foolishness! If you're serious about saving Joth—drop your drawers! Pronto!"

Lucy opened her mouth to argue further, then sighed and began unbuttoning her blouse. Ezrael ignored her disrobing completely, using the opportunity to retrieve his battered gym bag. After a few seconds of rummaging about, he produced a small silver bowl, a white horsehair flail, a fist-sized bundle of mistletoe, a three-foot-long bundle of white silk cord, a length of white ribbon, and a clear crayon.

"What is that? A Crayola?" Lucy asked, pointing at the last item.

"It's a wax pencil."

"Like the ones you use on Easter eggs?"

The muse nodded. "The same. Ready?"

Lucy glanced down at herself. She was naked except for a pair of French-cut Jockeys-For-Her. She took a deep breath and stepped out of her panties, kicking them across the room with one foot. "As I'll ever be."

"Okay—let's get started—" Ezrael handed her the length of white ribbon. "Use this to pull your hair up."

As Lucy busied herself with her hair, Ezrael took the wax crayon and pressed its tip against her collarbone. The moment it made contact, Lucy felt an electric prickling that made the soft hair of her arms and legs rise.

"Don't move unless I tell you to do so," Ezrael warned her as he moved the wax pencil across her naked body, tracing symbols over her breasts, belly, thighs and back. When he finished with that, he motioned for her to close her eyes so he could draw invisible runes atop their lids. After that, he stepped back and frowned, as if considering something, then dropped to his knees before her.

"Lift your right foot," he said.

"What for?"

"So I can put a sigil on your sole."

"Why?"

"So you'll be properly protected! Now be silent—I need to be focused while doing this."

Lucy bit her lower lip and tried her best to stifle a giggle as he traced something along her arch. Ezrael glanced up at her disapprovingly.

"Sorry. But it *tickles*—!" she explained.

"Then you're going to love what comes next!" he snorted, dunking the horsehair flail into the rice flour, water and egg-white mixture. Using it like a paintbrush, Ezrael began coating her with the viscous white substance.

Lucy gave a tiny shriek of disgust. "*Awph!* God, that stuff feels *awful!*" Her face set itself into a grimace as the white goo trickled down her exposed skin. "*Yuck!* I feel like a papier-mâché project!"

"*Hush!*" Ezrael hissed curtly. "Do not break my concentration! While it may seem silly to you, this ritual is important if you wish to remain alive and sane!"

The sternness in his manner was enough to make Lucy swallow whatever retort she might have made and submit to being whitewashed head-to-toe. She even held her tongue when Ezrael upended the bowl over her head and massaged the white paste into her hair. Centuries ago these ritual preparations were done to the music of flutes and drums played by vestal virgins and temple slaves, but now they were accompanied by the basso-profundo rumble of Public Enemy issued from a car two blocks away.

Just as she was beginning to feel like she was trapped in some half-assed neo-pagan performance art piece, she began to feel the symbols traced in wax on her naked flesh pulsing. She felt like a Leyden jar, with lightning trapped deep within her, eager to escape.

After Ezrael returned the emptied mixing bowl to the table, she mustered up the nerve to whisper: "Am I ready?"

"Just about." Ezrael searched through the welter of pens, pencils, erasers, and other art implements jutting from the collection of empty peanut-butter jars on the work table before plucking a largish paintbrush from their number. He looped the white silk cord around the brush, then stepped forward and knotted it about Lucy's waist. "You'll need this."

"Why?"

"You'll understand once you're there."

"Once I'm where?"

"Before the Clockwork."

"The Clockwork—?" Lucy's mouth dropped open as if the muscles had been severed. "You mean you're sending me to *Heaven?!?* How come that doesn't sound very comforting?"

"Because knowledge is never comfortable—but it *is* powerful. You would do well to remember that, Lucy."

"Any other tips, while you're at it?"

"Don't let them bully you. Whatever you do, don't fall into the trap of thinking you are helpless before them. The Celestials spend eons tending the Clockwork, ensuring that the raw essence of Creation is continuous, yet they are incapable of creating anything themselves—something even the basest of mortal beasts is capable of!

"They are the servants of Creation, but you—*you* are an avatar of Creation itself! As a Woman, you are a Bringer of Life, and as an Artist, you are a Creator of Beauty. You wield both the scepter of Generatrix and Creatrix. You are as much a handmaiden of the Clockwork as the seraphim. Bear that in mind when you stand before Nisroc and Preil as Joth's champion. That knowledge will be both your armor and your sword."

Ezrael eyed her speculatively as she stood before him, stark naked except for the sticky layer of rice paste and a silken cord tied about her waist, her hair plastered to her skull. He clucked his tongue and pulled on the leather cord around his neck, dragging a greasy-looking suede pouch from the depths of his chest hair.

"What's that?"

"My mojo bag. Every white wizard has one."

He pried open the pouch's drawstrings and removed a Hello! Kitty change purse with a keyring attachment and a tiny glass tube no bigger than a baby's finger. There was a murky, pearly-white liquid suspended in it that, as Lucy watched, abruptly turned the color of new wine.

Ezrael handed the Hello! Kitty change purse to Lucy. "Here. Take this with you. Affix it to the cord, opposite the paintbrush. You are only to use it under the most extreme duress—but whatever you do, *don't* look at it!"

Lucy gulped and did as she was told, clipping the keychain onto her right side. "Gotcha. No peeking."

"Now, stick out your tongue."

Lucy did so, warily eyeing the tiny vial. "Whad id dat tuff?" she asked. It was hard to talk with your tongue sticking out and not sound like an utter retard.

"Ambrosia. It is what mortals must drink if they would commune with the gods," he said, lightly daubing the tip of her tongue with the uncapped vial.

Lucy blinked in surprise as the taste of honey-sweet wine flooded her mouth. Her ears were already beginning to ring and her eyes unfocus.

"Wow," she gasped. "What a rush!"

Ezrael swiftly grabbed her elbow and steered her to the magic circle, carefully avoiding smudging the runes and symbols running along its outer rim. As she lay on the bare wooden floor of her living room, her head pointed towards the Eastern Star and her limbs spread akimbo, exposed to and embracing the universe, Lucy was dimly reminded of DaVinci's *Ecce Homo*.

Ezrael began to chant, his voice deep and mellifluous, as he poured what was left of the purified spring water into the silver bowl. Lucy wondered what language he was using to recite the spell—or was it a prayer? It didn't sound like Latin, but then, she'd been raised Methodist. She wouldn't know Latin from Portuguese. Maybe it was Greek, or even Egyptian. No doubt it was a language unspoken and unknown to any but wingless angels.

Holding the silver bowl in one hand and the bundle of mistletoe in the other, Ezrael began walking clockwise about the outer rim of the circle, occasionally dipping the mistletoe in the water and waving it in the direction of the compass points. Just as Lucy was beginning to think that the old angel had forgotten a necessary ingredient in the ritual's recipe, her heart stopped in mid-beat and her consciousness shot out of her body as if fired from a cannon.

Lucy had a fleeting impression of her naked, white-coated body laid out on the floor and the top of Ezrael's head as she passed though the ceiling, to emerge through the spot where she'd first stumbled across Joth. She was moving faster than any speed she had experienced before, going higher and higher, Manhattan's myriad lights dwindling to glittering pinpricks in less time than it took to bat an eye.

One moment she was looking at the curve of the world as it spun silently on its axis, the next she was shooting into the cold, airless vacuum of space, where the stars and planets glowed and glittered fiercely, their glory no longer masked by Earth's life-giving envelope of oxygen and moisture.

It was all happening so fast, the distances so vast, the speed so fantastic, it was impossible for her to feel any fear over having cast aside her mortal shell. But as she passed the great, orange mass of Jupiter, and her trajectory was still showing no signs of slowing, she grew anxious. It was like she was once more a child, pulled heavenward by the church bell, only now there was no kindly Brother Peacock to step in and bring her back to earth.

Just as that thought flickered through her mind, she reached her destination. There was no slowing, gradual or otherwise. One second she was traveling, the next she had arrived.

It was hard to describe exactly where she was. It was easier to describe where she wasn't. And she certainly wasn't in New York City. Nor, from what she could see, was she in the Heaven of song and story.

There were no Pearly Gates, no stately mansions carved of flawless marble and held aloft by big fluffy clouds. Nor were there streets of gold or clusters of white-robed souls outfitted in halos and little harps wandering about.

As far as she could tell, she was standing on a ledge-like outcropping roughly thirty feet wide, facing a vast emptiness, utterly devoid of light, which she assumed to be the Void she'd heard Joth and Ezrael mention. The shelf-like overhang appeared to stretch to either side, literally, into eternity. Even though she was a good ten feet from the edge, she took a step backward before turning to stare up at the Clockwork.

The thing that gave birth to the cosmos was so huge she could not hope to take it all in. No matter how hard she stared at it, it was impossible to see everything that was the Clockwork. She felt like an ant trying to get a clear view of a blue whale.

In some places the Clockwork was constructed of glass, in others it was composed of liquid that maintained three-dimensional form. Some parts of the Clockwork sported fur, while another had scales, and still another portion sprouted petals and thorns. Steam leaked forth from a hundred thousand different geysers, blow-holes, anuses, nostrils and valves.

There were eyes scattered here and there, along the outer face of the Clockwork, each the size of a house, the pupils fixed like those of a sleeper locked deep in REM dreams. The gargantuan eyeballs jerking in their sockets made a sound like bowling balls rolled back and forth on a polished wood floor as they tracked the movements of countless universes.

Every so often the surface of the Clockwork shuddered, like the flanks of a winded horse ridding itself of biting flies. Tentacles, feelers, fingers, claws, and antennae grew in random clumps, like clusters of seaweed, and waved and wrestled with one another in the still air, giving the illusion of a wind blowing.

Indeed, so massive and strange was the grandeur of the Clockwork, she did not spot the angels until the sparkling of their jeweled wings caught her eye. They were wheeling high above her, like gulls that nest in seaward cliffs, darting in and out of the nooks and crannies of the Clockwork as they went about their appointed tasks.

She could make out just enough detail to recognize them as elohim like Joth, although of far greater variety than she had expected. They appeared to be a mix of African, Caucasian, Asian, Meso-American—she even spotted some with skins the color of pistachios or robins' eggs.

Her heart began to race as she caught a glimpse of fiery wings amidst the more prosaic plumage, but her excitement passed as she saw that they belonged to a slightly larger elohim than the others—no doubt one of the "greater" elohim Ezrael had mentioned.

Now that she was on the seraphim's turf, Lucy wasn't exactly sure how she was supposed to go about locating Nisroc. The Clockwork was huge beyond comprehension and it didn't seem to have any "you are here" signposts—at least none she recognized as such. She decided her best bet was to attract the attention of the angels circling overhead and get them to take her to their leader, so to speak.

As she continued to look for a way to approach the flock of elohim, she came upon a section of the Clockwork fashioned of black volcanic glass— and froze in mid-step as she caught sight of her reflection.

She thought Ezrael was being poetic when he had called her Joth's champion, but now she understood he had meant it literally. She looked like a hero from ancient myth, outfitted with the borrowed weaponry of patron gods.

While she might be stark naked and covered in rice paste on Earth, on this plane of existence she was dressed head to toe in a translucent armor that was half carapace, half mineral that possessed a milky, opalescent quality, like a combination of mother-of-pearl and white jade.

Her head was protected by an elongated corkscrew helmet that looked like an ornate cross between a Balinese dancer's head-dress, a butterfly chrysalis, and an exotic sea-shell. The strange armor hugged her body so tightly her breasts resembled spike-teated cones. The humble paintbrush Ezrael had given her had been transformed into a scimitar with a blade of solid diamond.

"Identify yourself, deathling!"

Lucy was startled by a high-pitched voice that issued three feet over her head. She glanced up and saw what looked to be a fetus held aloft by furiously beating wings the size of a man's hand. The thing's head was huge, easily dwarfing its wizened body, which dangled beneath its chin like the wattle of a turkey. Its forehead bulged precipitously, and Lucy saw veins pulsing and twisting like worms under its paper-thin skin. The eyes were as big and goggled as those of a goldfish, and it possessed a tiny slit for a mouth and an even tinier nose. Its matchstick limbs were folded in on themselves, as useless as the vestigial forearms of a Tyrannosaurus Rex.

It suddenly occurred to Lucy that what she was looking at was a cherub. The thing bore little resemblance to the pudgy winged infants cavorting through Renaissance and Pre-Raphaelite canvasses. If anything, it more closely resembled one of Bosch's nightmares. Although the initial impression was that of an infant, there was nothing at all cute and cuddly about the thing bobbing above her like a demented helium balloon.

"Identity yourself! State your purpose!" shrilled the cherub.

It moved closer, generating an electric-blue energy field that crackled and buzzed like a back patio bug-zapper. Lucy took an involuntary step backwards.

"I-I'm Lucille Bender. I'm looking for Nisroc—"

The cherub halted its approach, blinking its bulbous eyes with its bottom lids—an unexpectedly reptilian action that did little to calm her nerves. It was all Lucy could do to stifle the desire to swat the creature with the flat of her sword.

"If you could tell me where I might be able to find him—it's important— I, uh, realize I don't have an appointment…"

The cherub's lipless mouth dropped open, revealing toothless gums the color of chewed bubblegum, and a weird, piercing wail emerged from its deceptively tiny form. Lucy gritted her teeth as the alarm call vibrated her inner ear. The sound reminded her of the tornado sirens atop the old Brakeman's Union Hall in Seven Devils.

The elohim riding the high currents swooped down, attracted by the cherubim's shriek. An elohim with skin the color of mocha landed on a nearby outcropping, tilting its head to one side as it peered down at Lucy with crystal-clear eyes. Despite the difference in coloration, Lucy found the angel's similarity to Joth startling. Even the body language was identical.

"Who summons me?"

Lucy recognized Nisroc's surly growl even before she saw the seraphim. Nisroc and Preil looked pretty much the same in their natural habitat as they had on Earth: creepy and awe-inspiring. Lucy remembered all too well her last interaction with the Celestials, but it was too late to turn back now. She squared her shoulders and stepped forward.

"*I* did."

Although it lacked eyelids, Preil's unflinching gaze seemed to narrow.

"*You!*" The ophanim didn't seem very pleased. "The deathling female! How is it you are here?"

"I sense Ezrael's hand in this," Nisroc growled, smoothing its mane in what Lucy now recognized was a nervous gesture. "What is the meaning of this intrusion, deathling?"

"I-It's about Joth."

"Joth—?" Nisroc frowned for a moment then something resembling recognition flickered across the seraphim's leonine features. "Ah. *Yes.* The Prodigal. What of the elohim?"

"You have to put him to the Final Question immediately! It's almost too late—"

"If the elohim is to Fall, the Fall is inevitable," Preil snapped.

"*No!*"

"Preil has spoken truly," Nisroc said, nodding in agreement. "The schedule is set. There can be no deviation. Your request is denied, Lucille Bender."

"But—!"

"Go from this place, deathling!" Preil's beak clicked like the castanets of a flamenco dancer. "You are *not* wanted here!"

Lucy felt her heart sink. This was madness. How the hell was she going to make an angel—one of the freaking seraphim, for crying out loud!—do what she wanted? Suddenly Ez's voice was in her ear. It was so loud and clear it was as if the muse were standing right beside her.

"*Don't let them bully you! You're as powerful as they are, but in a different fashion! You've got to pit your strengths against theirs! You are Joth's champion, woman—now fight for him, damn it!*"

"You're not getting rid of me *that* easily!" Lucy cried, grabbing Nisroc. The seraphim's features twisted into something that would have been comical if its eyes hadn't been glowing bright orange.

"*Unhand* me, deathling!"

"Not until you agree to change your schedule!"

"Preil!" Nisroc yowled in distress. "Get the deathling off me!"

The ophanim rushed forward, tentacles at the ready. A high-pitched squeal that sounded like electric guitar feedback issued from the ophanim's beak. Lucy brought her crystalline sword up, reflecting the ophanim's baleful gaze back onto itself. The giant eyeball spun like a pinwheel, its optic nerve/ tentacles twitching and writhing like a nest of snakes.

"Don't make me get rough, Nisroc!" Lucy warned the struggling seraphim. "I'm *not* afraid of you! And I'm *not* going to back down! You're not dealing with some worker-drone, damn it! I am here by my own volition! And I *refuse* to go! *That* is the power of my will!"

Upon recovering its equilibrium, Preil righted itself, snapping its tentacles like a cat-o'-nine-tails across Lucy's back. Although the force of the blows was enough to make her stagger, the armor managed to absorb the worst of it.

Nisroc's blazing wings unfurled like the flaps of a burning circus tent, and Lucy's vision was obscured by fire. She flinched, expecting to have her face bubble and sear, but to her surprise the flames were without heat. With a single beat of its fiery pinions, Nisroc shot into the air, Lucy dangling from the seraphim's underbelly like a watchfob.

"*Lucy!*" Ezrael's voice was again in her ear. "*Be careful! Any damage that is done to your avatar can result in permanent injury to your real body! Nisroc might not mean to destroy—but that doesn't mean it can't accidentally kill you!*"

"Great," Lucy muttered under her breath as the seraphim went into a loop-de-loop trying to dislodge her. "*Now* you tell me!"

Lucy stuck her sword into her waist sash and swung herself onto the seraphim's back. Wrapping her legs about its waist as tightly as possibly, she freed her blade and, gripping it with both hands, sheared off one of the angel's wings. Nisroc gave a cry that was half lion's roar and half eagle's scream, then plummeted like a damaged kite.

They struck the narrow ledge along the Clockwork hard, bounced, then hit again, sliding within inches of the yawning Void. Although their landing was enough to bloody her nose, Lucy still maintained her grip on the crippled seraphim, pinning it securely beneath her.

"Get *off* me!" roared Nisroc as its brazen claws scraped ineffectively against Lucy's carapace, throwing off sparks.

"Not until you agree to move up Joth's questioning!"

"There can be no change—!"

"*Wrong* answer!" Lucy tightened her grip on Nisroc, levering the seraphim's head back towards its spine. She wasn't sure if it was possible to kill an angel in such a manner, but she was pretty certain she could inconvenience it.

Nisroc roared and the Fire of Righteousness enveloped her. Even with her special charms and wards of protection, the pain was excruciating. Her first instinct was simply to let go of the seraphim and curl into a ball like a hedgehog, but she knew couldn't give in. If she surrendered now, then Joth was lost forever.

She couldn't allow that to happen. Joth needed her, damn it! She was the only one in the whole world—in the whole damn universe!—who could help him! She *could* not fail—she *would* not fail—she *refused* to fail Joth as she had failed her mother.

The seraphim screamed like a scalded cat as the astral flames enveloping Lucy flickered and died. Lucy straddled the exhausted seraphim's chest, clutching Nisroc's fiery mane in one hand and holding her sword in the other. She glanced up and saw that the space directly above them was crowded with gaping cherubim, seraphim, ophanim and elohim.

At first she thought the Host had rallied to their fellow's aid, but none bothered to lift a finger, or, in the ophanims' case, twitch a tentacle. She was eerily reminded of Joth's voyeuristic complacency.

Without any warning, the gathered cherubim began to wail in unison, causing the Host to disperse in a flurry of wings and flapping tentacles, leaving Lucy, Nisroc and Preil alone on the ledge. Baffled, Lucy looked around to see what might have precipitated such a sudden exodus.

There was a light in the Void.

At first it looked like a single match-head burning in the darkness, then it began to grow. Whatever it was, it was on fire and traveling fast. Was it a comet? A falling star?

Within seconds the horizon became a solid wall of fire. The flames parted down the middle like a curtain being opened on a proscenium stage.

The Archon stood revealed, its form roughly humanoid, although lacking features or distinct physical characteristics. It towered miles above the combatants and was composed of roiling clouds of gas and cosmic dust. The featureless head angled downward, twin suns burning in the place where eyes should be.

The Archon reached down with a hand the size of an asteroid. Lucy suddenly received a vision of herself as detritus jamming the gears of a machine. The Archon meant to pluck this offending piece of alien matter free and flick it over its shoulder and into the Void, where it could do no more harm.

The Archon's hand filled her vision. There were galaxies spinning in its palm, suns going nova under its finger nails. She could feel herself dwindling like a wet sugar cube before its celestial glory. Her fingers groped blindly for the pouch at her waist. Something told her that this was the moment Ez had mentioned that the charm would be handy. She could feel the heat radiating from the charm as her fingers closed over it, even though her hand was still sheathed in its translucent armor.

Remembering her friend's warning, she lifted her left arm to shield her eyes, but found she almost couldn't do it. The Archon had fixed her to the spot like an armadillo tranced by the headlights of an oncoming tractor-trailer. But as she thought of Joth, she somehow found the strength to avert her gaze as she unveiled the charm.

The Archon had no mouth, and yet it screamed. The sound was that of suns collapsing, of nebulae imploding. It was the noise the universe would make in its death throes, a million millennia from now.

Lucy had no idea what it was Ezrael had given her, but it was clearly inflicting pain on the Archon—and on Nisroc and Preil as well.

"*Put it away! Put it awaaay!*" shrieked Nisroc, lifting its taloned hands to its face.

Preil was cowering to one side, its tentacles writhing in agony. "You *dare*! You dare bring *that* to *this* place?" it hissed.

The Archon wrapped its wings tightly against itself like a molten cape, seeming to shrink from the tiny mortal standing before it. Nisroc gave a wavering mewl, like that of a sickly kitten, as it tried to crawl away on its hands and knees, while Preil's writhing mass of tentacles proved inadequate to shield its unblinking eye from the object Lucy held aloft.

The sight of her opponents groveling before her in panic sent an exhilarating surge of empowerment through her. She quickly moved to block Nisroc's path, thrusting the charm in its face like Professor Van Helsing brandishing a crucifix at Dracula.

"Take it away, deathling! *Please*—!" the seraphim gasped.

"Only if you agree to change the schedule."

Nisroc shook its head, its fiery mane flickering feebly before fading away entirely. "No—!" it gasped.

Lucy glanced at Preil, which now resembled a half-deflated beach ball, its pupil and cornea rolled so far back only its white underbelly was visible, its tentacles trembling and twitching spasmodically.

Her feeling of empowerment was replaced by that of shame. She had gone from being a fearless vampire-killer to a kryptonite-wielding Lex Luthor.

"Damn it," she said, biting her lip. "I can't do this. I'm not a murderer."

As Lucy returned the charm to its pouch, Nisroc's mane and maimed wing repaired themselves, Preil regained its volume, and the Archon unfurled its wings with a rustle of burning silk.

"It's not fair!" she said, fighting back her tears. "I'm going to lose Joth just like I lost Daddy and Mam-Maw and Mama. I never got the chance to tell any of them how much I loved them, and now I'll never get the chance to tell Joth. Forgive me, Joth. I've failed you. I've failed all of you—"

Nisroc smoothed its restored mane, glancing in the direction of the Archon, which made a gesture that was surprisingly subtle for a hand the size of a cathedral. The seraphim made a sound like a tiger trying to clear its throat.

"Lucy—your petition has been granted. I shall appear to the prodigal come the next midnight on your world."

She lifted her head, blinking in surprise at the gentleness in the angel's voice. "I-I don't know what to say—or how to thank you," she stammered.

"You can thank me by *leaving*, " the seraphim replied, its hauteur once more in place.

* * *

One minute she was standing in front of Nisroc, the next she was lying flat on her back in the middle of her living room, staring up at the ceiling. Lucy gasped as her heart restarted and blood once more began to flow through her veins. She groaned, somewhat disoriented by her resurrection.

Ezrael's face popped into her field of vision. "How many fingers do I have?" he asked, waving a pair of chalk-smeared digits before her eyes.

"Two," she replied groggily.

"Actually, I have ten, but I'll accept that as an answer," the muse grinned. "Here, let me help you up."

"How long was I out?"

Ezrael consulted his wristwatch. "Just under a minute."

Lucy shook her head in disbelief, leaning heavily on Ezrael as he walked her over to the sofa. "That's impossible!"

"What can I say? Time's a trip," Ezrael shrugged. "So—what happened? What's the verdict?"

Lucy eased herself onto the sofa, wincing slightly. Her muscles ached as if she'd been lifting weights in the gym. "Don't you know?"

"I wasn't able to maintain contact once the Archon manifested," he explained.

"Nisroc granted my request. It will appear tomorrow at midnight. And speaking of the Archon—what the hell is that charm you gave me?"

"Why don't you find out for yourself?" Ezrael said, nodding at the Hello! Kitty coin-purse affixed to the white cord wrapped about her waist. "Don't worry—you can look at it now. Whatever power it once had is now expended."

Lucy unfastened the coin purse and shook its contents into her open palm. To her surprise, an old bottlecap with crimped edges fell out. The logo printed on the cap was partially obscured by rust, but she could still make out the brand-name: *Faust*.

"A bottlecap? You sent me to battle the Heavenly Host with a rusty bottle cap as my freakin' secret weapon!?!"

"Is that what you see?" Ezrael grunted, mildly intrigued. He plucked the bottlecap from her hand and held it up to light, turning it over in his callused fingers. "I usually perceive it as a glass token—the kind they used to give whorehouse patrons during the days of the Roman emperors, although it sometimes manifests itself as a cat's-eye marble with a crack in it."

"What are you babbling about, you crazy old wizard? What is that thing?"

"What do *you* think could have affected a creature as powerful as an Archon?" Ezrael said as he returned the bottlecap to his mojo bag. "What you held in your hand was none other than a piece of the Infernal Machine! You unwittingly carried a fragment of Anti-Creation into the very heart of Creation itself! That is why Nisroc agreed to your demands."

"But—that's not really true, Ez. Even though that thing was killing them, Nisroc still refused. And when I saw how I was hurting them—I couldn't bring myself to use it against them. But when I put the charm away—Nisroc agreed to do as I asked."

"Don't you see, child?" Ezrael smiled, squeezing her hand gently. "It wasn't that little piece of Hell that turned Nisroc to your will. You did something they could never do—you changed your mind. It was your passion, your bravery, and, in the end, your capacity for mercy that humbled them. You wrestled with the angels—and proved yourself their match."

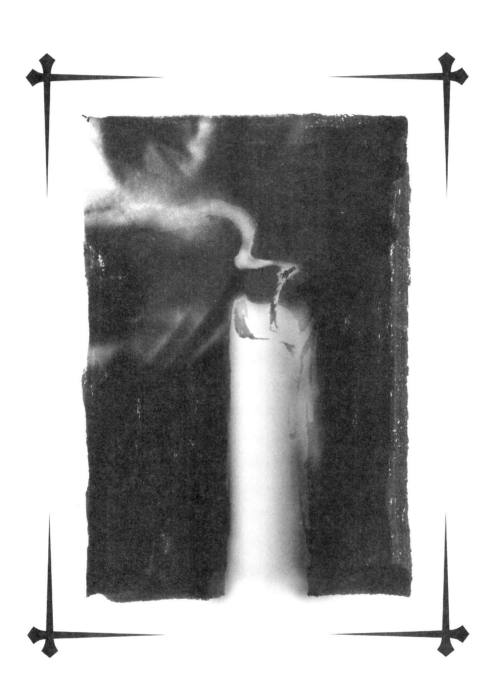

CHAPTER 18

Lucy stood in the bedroom doorway and watched as Ezrael chalked a protective circle around Joth's motionless body.

"Do you *have* to do that?" she asked, chewing on her thumbnail.

"We can't risk *not* doing it," Ezrael replied. "Joth could become a full daemon at any moment. We can't risk anything provoking Joth's dark side, which means we have to make sure it's isolated from any possible negative situations until Nisroc arrives. Emotional agitation or trauma from an outside source could very well push things over the edge for good! If we keep Joth contained within the circle until tomorrow at midnight, then at least its condition won't deteriorate any further."

"I realize that this is for his own good," Lucy sighed. "But I just can't help feeling that we're treating him like a prisoner."

"Look at it this way—Joth won't be kept locked up for long," Ezrael said, dusting the chalk from his hands. "Now—could you be so kind as to hand me my bag?"

She brought the canvas tote over to where the muse was kneeling. Muttering under his breath in a sing-song voice, Ezrael withdrew eight white votive candles, which he placed at the points of the compass, lighting them one by one as he moved clockwise. Upon the eighth and final candle being lit, the outer rim of the magic circle suddenly ignited like the ring of a gas range. Lucy gave a small shout of surprise and stepped away.

"Don't be alarmed, it's not actual flame," Ezrael explained, getting to his feet. "It's foxfire—sort of a metaphysical version of one of the elements; just like ectoplasm is a variant of water, and aether represents air."

With moments of the foxfire igniting, Joth began to stir again, lifting its head from under its wing. The angel's features were once again those Lucy had come to know so well. The only thing different was the darkness in its eyes and twin golf-ball-sized lumps at its temples.

Joth looked about, perplexed. "Why have you placed me under a seal of containment, Ezrael?"

"It was for your own protection, my friend," the muse said soothingly. "You are much changed from when last we saw you."

"I feel—different," Joth admitted. "There are things within me that I do not understand."

Ezrael nodded sagely. "The Natures are in conflict with one another. The need to mend and the urge to destroy are fighting one another. That is why you must stay under the seal of containment."

"But I do not *wish* to be contained," Joth replied sharply. Ezrael and Lucy exchanged glances.

Ezrael cleared his throat and replied in a stern voice: "At great risk to herself, Lucy went before the Host and pleaded your case to Nisroc. The time of your Ultimate Question has been moved forward, because of her doing this thing. Would you risk all she has fought so hard to win for you?"

Joth glanced at Lucy. The darkness in its eyes dimmed and the angel dropped its gaze to its feet. "I shall remain under seal of containment."

Ezrael turned and motioned for Lucy to follow him. Once they were in the hall, Ezrael pulled a handkerchief from his back pocket and mopped his brow. For the first time since she had met him, the muse looked as old as he claimed to be.

"Ez—are you okay?" Lucy asked, worried by how the white wizard's hands trembled.

"Casting two circles in one night is extremely draining," he explained. "But until Nisroc's arrival, one of us will have to be awake at all times."

"I'll take the first watch, Ez," she said. "You look done in."

"I'll sack out on the couch, if it's all the same to you. Wake me in three hours. The only thing you need to do is make certain the circle remains unbroken and the points secured."

"The points?"

"The candles," he explained. "They can't go out or be knocked over."

"Gotcha. Don't worry—I've got it covered. You just go get some shut-eye."

The muse trudged into the living room, stretched out on the couch and was sound asleep in less than two minutes.

Well, Lucy thought to herself as Ezrael began to snore, *if I'm going to keep watch, I might as well fix myself some coffee.*

As Lucy entered the kitchen, her eyes dropped to the small pile of unopened mail sitting atop the dinette table. At least that would give her something to occupy her time until she had to wake up Ezrael.

After putting the kettle on the boil, she picked up the bundle of envelopes, sighing to herself as she sorted out the bills from the circulars. ConEd...NYNEX...Chemical Bank...nothing but bills, bills, and more bills.

The only article of personal mail was a business envelope with a local postmark but no return address. The handwriting looked familiar, but she could not immediately place it. As she tore open the end of the envelope, a news clipping fell out.

It was from the society announcement section of the previous day's *New York Times*. It featured a photograph of a Long Island heiress dressed in a conservative button-collar blouse, her hair carefully coifed, smiling blankly into the camera. It took Lucy a long second to recognize the woman's face as Gwenda's.

"*Mr. And Mrs. Charles M. Latrobe of Long Island announce the engagement of their daughter, Gwendolyn Anne Latrobe, to Nevin Carr, son of the late Alexander Carr and Neva Garber Carr of Chicago, Illinois.*" There was more, but she couldn't see the words because of tears in her eyes.

Lucy didn't know which surprised her more—the news, or the fact she was hurt enough to cry. She had known, deep down, that what she once had with Nevin could never be retrieved, but that did not help blunt the pain. What stung the most was the knowledge that he'd become engaged to another woman within a week of leaving her. Dumping her for someone she loathed was bad enough, but this was the cherry on top. She suspected that this final dig was Gwenda's doing, not Nevin's—it had her stink all over it. Still, even if he was not the one twisting the knife, Nevin was the one who had provided Gwenda with the blade.

All Lucy wanted was to lie down and have herself a good hard cry. Blinking back her tears, she hurried out of the kitchen and back towards the bedroom, careful not to wake up Ezrael.

Joth was crouching on the floor within the seal, its arms wrapped around its lower shins. The angel looked up quizzically as she opened the door.

"What is wrong?" asked Joth, rising slowly.

"Nothing—nothing's wrong, Joth," she said, trying to avert her face from the angel's.

"No—that is not so," Joth said, stepping as close to the edge of the circle as it dared. "Your halo is in eclipse."

Lucy bit her lip and shook her head, trying her best to control the tears that rose, unbidden, to her eyes. "Joth, *please*—not now—I just need to be left alone, that's all—"

"You are crying." The angel moved forward, only to be knocked to the floor by a burst of bluish-white energy.

Lucy hurried to where the angel lay sprawled, trapped within Ezrael's magic circle, its smoking wings smelling of scorched feathers.

"*Joth!* Joth—are you okay?"

In her haste, she unwittingly knocked over the south-east candle. The foxfire circling the seal instantly snuffed out. Lucy drew back as Joth got back onto its feet and stepped over the deactivated chalk circle. There was a strange intensity in the way the angel stared at her that Lucy found unnerving.

"Who made you cry—was it the one called Nevin?"

"Joth—please—you're scaring me—"

Lucy backed away as the angel loomed over her, its eyes glowing eerily in the darkened room.

"*Was it the one called Nevin?*"

Lucy grunted as she collided with the chest of drawers behind her. She was too frightened to look directly into the angel's face so she averted her eyes, choosing to stare at the floor instead.

"*Yes,*" she whispered, in voice so tiny it was almost as if she had not spoken at all.

Joth's eyes flashed as if they held lightning within their depths and its wings snapped open like Chinese fans. To her horror, Lucy saw the horn-buds at Joth's temples swell. With the roar of an angry tiger, the dark angel spun about and launched itself through the nearest window in a shower of glass and splintered wood. Only then did she find the breath to scream.

Ezrael charged into the room, his hair and clothes disheveled. "Lucy— Where's Joth?"

"I-I knocked over one of the candles," she stammered. She was trembling, her teeth rattling like dice in a cup. "I didn't *m-mean* to—I thought he was h-hurt—Oh, Ez, he was so *scary!*"

Ezrael stuck his head through what was left of the window. Shards of glass littered the pavement and gutter below, but outside of a junkie nodding out in a doorway across the street, there was nothing to see. He pulled his head back in.

"What did you say to Joth?"

"He—he wanted to know why I was crying."

Ezrael frowned. "You were crying?"

She pointed to the clipping lying forgotten on the floor by way of explanation.

"J-Joth got upset when he saw me crying—then he got loose—and he kept asking me if Nevin was responsible for making me cry—Then he got *so* upset!—Oh, God, Ez—he looked like the *devil!* And its all my fault!"

Ezrael shook her by the shoulders as she began to cry again. The look on the former angel's face frightened her even more than Joth's satanic appearance. "Lucy! There's no time for that! Do you know where Nevin is?"

"H-he's probably over at Gwenda's."

Ezrael headed towards the door in a dead run, dragging Lucy behind him. "We *must* reach this Gwenda's apartment as soon as possible or all our efforts on Joth's behalf will have been for nothing!"

"Joth wouldn't *hurt* Nevin—would he? Besides, he doesn't even know where Gwenda lives!"

"Are you *kidding?* Joth knows where *everybody* lives! As one of the elohim, it is still tied into Creation! And if an angel takes a life—whether it means to or not—its fate is sealed. It will instantly become a daemon!"

* * *

Nevin stood and stared out the picture window that overlooked Gramercy Park, a glass of champagne in one hand, and reflected on how Life Was Good.

No—not just Good.

It was Fucking Great.

Tonight had proved a major milestone. After years of struggle and toil, he finally had it made in the shade. No more tuna fish, ramen noodles and yellow label beer for him. From here on in it was filet mignon, truffles and champagne.

Not only had he managed to sell all his pieces in the show, but he also landed a rep who already had a couple of high-rollers lined up for him. To celebrate, the rep took both him and Gwenda to a couple of *very* exclusive nightclubs—the kind where the super-rich and the ultra-famous hung out. Hell, if he had known things were going to turn out this plush for him, Nevin wouldn't have bothered proposing to Gwenda.

Still, it paid to be judicious. Gwenda's money and family connections would be very handy for a young self-made postmodern art genius such as himself. That's how his rep said he'd be pitching Nevin to the press. The self-made part was certainly true enough.

No one on the Manhattan art scene had any idea that he was actually the son of a garage mechanic and a Wal-Mart cashier living in a rundown trailer in upstate New York. Of course, he'd told Gwenda that before their untimely deaths on the TWA that crashed off the shore of Long Island, his parents were an investment banker and a podiatrist.

One thing was certain though—he would have to dump Lucy once and for all in the next couple of days. Lucy had been fun for a while, and handy even longer, but now it was time to cut himself loose. He'd squeezed her for all she was good for, and now it was time to throw away the rind.

Still, he had to admit he'd miss the sex, if not Lucy herself. However, no matter how much of a doormat she tried to turn herself into, she still managed to make him feel inadequate as an artist. Gwenda, on the other hand, posed no such threat. Lucy and that weirdo Joth deserved one another, as far as he was concerned.

It was only matter of time before he could open a studio and sit around all day coming up with ideas for art. All he'd have to do was hire struggling young artists to actually do the physical work of painting, sculpting, photographing and drawing while he signed his name at the bottom of canvasses and checks. Who knows—he might even offer Lucy a job working for him.

Gwenda's voice wafted from the bedroom. "Nevin—when are you coming to bed sweetie? I'm *waiting!*"

"I'll be there directly, honey," he replied, turning from the window. "I just want to finish the champagne."

"Why don't you bring it into the bedroom with you, silly?"

Nevin sighed and rolled his eyes like a boy being called inside to do his homework. "Okay, sweetheart—I'll be right in!"

As he reached for the silver bucket, Nevin thought he heard the thrumming of wings just outside the window. The neighborhood cats had probably disrupted the covey of pigeons nesting under the eaves again.

There was a deafening crash as the window exploded in a shower of glass and splintered wood. Nevin spun around to see a man, naked save for a pair of tattered jeans, crouched in the middle of the Oriental carpet covering the floor. The intruder rose with the grace and deliberation of a ballet dancer, shaking fragments of glass from his shoulder-length mane. Nevin recognized Joth instantly.

"What the *fuck* do you think you're *doing* here!?!" he yelled. "Are you out of your fuckin' mind, you fuckin' *mook*? Did Lucy put you up to rappelling down the side of the fuckin' building like Bruce Willis?"

Joth fixed him with a stare that caused the artist to freeze in his tracks. The angel shot forward with the speed of a leopard going for a blooded gazelle, striking Nevin squarely in the chest with its open hands. The artist flew backwards as if struck with a sledgehammer, flipping over a chair and landing hard on the floor.

Joth swooped down, grabbing Nevin by his belt, and lifted him bodily off the floor with one hand. The angel hurled Nevin headlong across the room so that he smashed into the opposite wall with enough force to knock a Keith Haring print off its picture-hook.

Gwenda came running out of the bedroom, dressed only in a black lace chemise and panties. "Nevin—what the hell is all this *noise*—?" She screamed at the sight of the strange half-naked man standing in the middle of her living room. She gave a second, smaller scream as Nevin staggered to his feet, blood pouring from his nose like a open tap.

"Call the cops!" Nevin barked.

Joth glanced indifferently over its shoulder at Gwenda, then resumed its attack, grabbing the artist's left arm and twisting it sharply in its socket. Nevin shrieked at the top of his lungs.

"Call 911!"

As purple and black spots exploded behind Nevin's eyes, Joth's face seemed to twist and blur, sprouting horns and fangs and eyes that glowed like St. Elmo's Fire. Nevin could even make out huge, black wings growing out of his attacker's shoulders.

"Get away from him, you bastard!" Gwenda yelled, throwing herself at Joth.

Joth snarled and batted Gwenda with one of its pinions hard enough to put her on the floor and keep her there, then returned its attention to its prey. Nevin's face was pinched so tightly the creases in his features looked like they had been carved by a knife.

"W-why?" Nevin gasped through his pain. "Why are you *doing* this to me?"

"You made her cry," Joth said, as if this explained everything.

* * *

A taxi screamed up to the curb in front of Gwenda's co-op and fishtailed to a stop. Ezrael and Lucy quickly piled out, pausing only long enough to hurl a twenty at the cabbie.

"Oh my god! Ez! Look!" Lucy shouted, pointing over their heads at what remained of the apartment building's upper story. It looked like someone had catapulted a boulder through Gwenda's living room window.

As they entered the lobby, a man outfitted in a navy blazer stepped out from behind a desk to block their way. He frowned as he held up his hands.

"I'm sorry, miss," the doorman said, addressing himself to Lucy. "But I have explicit orders from Ms. Latrobe *not* to allow you entrance to this building. I'm afraid you and your companion will have to leave."

"We don't have time for this bullshit," Ezrael announced flatly, pressing his forefinger firmly between the doorman's brows. The other man's jaw went slack and his eyes rolled back in their sockets, but he did not collapse. "Come on, we've got to hurry—he'll snap out of it in ninety seconds! No time for the elevator—we better take the stairs!"

For someone who was close to a thousand years old and hadn't gotten much sleep lately, Ezrael seemed in pretty good shape. The muse zipped past Lucy as she gasped for breath on the final landing.

"Which apartment is it?"

"Apartment D!" she managed between wheezes.

Ezrael didn't even bother knocking. The muse eyed the door, backed up and slammed his shoulder against it. The door shook, but the locks held. On his third charge the door flew open with a loud smash. Lucy glanced up and saw a old man in bathrobe and slippers standing outside the apartment opposite Gwenda's, scowling over his bifocals. When he saw her looking at him, the neighbor quickly retreated, locking the door behind him.

Gwenda's apartment was in shambles. Furniture was overturned, pictures were knocked from the walls, the floor littered with smashed knickknacks. A near-naked Gwenda lay sprawled on the floor in a pool of spilled champagne. Joth was standing in front of the shattered window, holding a feebly struggling Nevin aloft by the throat as easily as it would a doll.

The dark angel's toes had fused together and re-divided themselves, so that its foot resembled that of a ostrich. Its wings glittered as black as a scarab, and small horns—like those of a young goat—grew out of the angel's forehead.

"*Joth!*" Lucy screamed. "*No!*"

The dark angel turned, allowing Nevin to drop to the floor. The artist lay there gasping like a landed fish, his face congested and throat badly bruised. Lucy hurried to her erstwhile lover's side while keeping a wary eye on Joth.

"He tried to *kill* me!" Nevin wheezed, pointing a trembling finger at the transmuted angel.

"You made her cry," Joth replied matter-of-factly. "I told you I would do something I have never done before if you made her cry."

"*H-he's crazy!*" Nevin sputtered.

"He's a *lot* more than that," Lucy whispered under her breath. "Ez— check to see if Gwenda's okay," she said, motioning to where Gwenda lay sprawled on the floor.

"She's alive—but it looks like she's got a broken nose," Ezrael reported. As the muse rolled Gwenda onto her back, she groaned and opened eyes that were already beginning to swell and purple.

As Lucy moved aside, Joth reached for Nevin again. She quickly jumped back in between her ex-boyfriend and the half-angel. "Stop it—*please!* Joth, don't *hurt* him anymore!"

Joth frowned, tilting its head. "You do not want me to destroy the deathling called Nevin—even though he made you cry? Why?"

"Because I'm afraid of what will happen."

"You are afraid for the deathling called Nevin?"

Lucy shook her head. "I'm afraid for *you!* If you destroy Nevin, you'll damn yourself forever. And if you do that, it will make me cry, Joth. But *you'll* be the one who makes me cry—*not* Nevin."

Joth stared down at her for a long moment, then closed its eyes. The horns sprouting from its head retracted themselves, like those of a snail.

"Don't cry, Lucy," the angel pleaded. "I *never* want you to cry, Lucy. *Never.*"

Lucy blushed and flashed a smile as shy as a schoolgirl's. "That's sweet of you, Joth—but crying is part of being human. I wouldn't *be* human if I didn't cry now and again."

"Yes, it *is* a vale of tears you mortals dwell within, is it not?" Meresin commented as he picked his way through the splintered ruins of the front door. "Tears are part of the woof and weave of human existence—as is sorrow, pain, loneliness and abject misery. *All* these things would be yours as well, friend elohim. I ask you—is it worth it? Are you willing to surrender the uniformity of the Clockwork, the constancy of the Machine, to partake of the unleavened bread of mortality?"

"What are *you* doing here?" snapped Lucy.

"Just stopping by to speak with my newest client regarding a point of business, my dear, that's all! It seems I forgot to get him to sign a couple of documents earlier," the sephiroth smiled slyly, patting his breast pocket. "I'm a *stickler* for paperwork."

"You've done enough damage as it is, daemon," Ezrael replied. "Joth doesn't need you tickling its ear with your serpent's tongue."

"This prodigal will be mine whether it falls or fails," Meresin said with a shrug. "Indeed, it seems to be already more Infernal than Celestial by the looks of it. I simply do not see how encouraging this poor creature to pass itself through the eye of the needle is worth all this fuss! It's plain to see that the elohim's fate is sealed."

"Hold on—what's going on here?" rasped Nevin as he lurched to his feet, massaging his throat. "Meresin—you *know* these assholes?"

"Ah—Nevin! I am pleased to see you still amongst the living, although it would have been worth sacrificing a pawn such as yourself in order to capture a knight."

"Is *everybody* around here a friggin' nutcase? What are you babbling about?" scowled Nevin.

Meresin cast a disparaging glance at the artist. "Do not bother your gray cell about it, you talentless cat's paw!"

"*Hey—!*" Nevin said angrily. "You're supposed to be my *agent!* Where do you get off calling me talentless—!!?"

"*Do as I say—!*" snarled Meresin, allowing its mask of humanity to drop long enough to flash the artist a glimpse of the true face underneath. "Go tend to your tedious yoke-mate-to-be and stay out of this! Come the dawn, neither of you will have any clue as to what happened here—except for the window, of course."

Nevin turned the color of oatmeal and scuttled over across the room to help a dazed Gwenda sit up. Meresin sighed and turned back to Lucy and Ezrael.

"Where were we—? Ah, yes! As for yourselves, I recommend that you take this time to take the prodigal and go, before the police arrive."

"Meresin's right," Ezrael said. "We don't have much time."

Lucy turned to look at the angel. "Joth—please come home."

The angel glanced over at Nevin, who was kneeling beside Gwenda. The artist cringed and tried to position his dazed fiancée between himself and the angel.

Joth nodded and stepped forward. "I am ready to go home."

Meresin watched the trio flee the apartment, waving a final farewell before turning to glare dispassionately at Nevin and Gwenda.

"What the *fuck* was all that about?!?" spat Nevin, regaining some of his bravado now that the others were gone. "And what's with you taking up for that bitch and her wacko friends, telling them to beat it before the cops got here? That fuckin' lunatic jumped through the window and tried to *kill* me!"

"Actually, it was trying to *destroy* you," Meresin corrected. "Daemons do not kill or murder—that is purely a mortal sport. We *destroy*. Granted, it may seem a matter of semantics to the person involved. However, you should be more generous in regard to Ms. Bender. You owe her your life, what there is of it."

Meresin frowned, studying Gwenda as one would a particularly distasteful bug. "Frankly, I do not see why you chose to discard Ms. Bender for such a creature as this—and your kind possess free will! Astounding. Usually I have to go out of my way to ensure such disastrous pairings, but you seem to have taken the bull by the horns! Ah, dear, deluded Nevin—that all of us should be so lucky as to have someone willing to save us from ourselves!"

CHAPTER 19

Nisroc's mane burned bright blue as it fixed its lambent gaze on the prodigal that stood before it.

"Joth of the lesser elohim, I put to you the Question one final time: shall you return to the Clockwork, or shall you remain on this mortal plane? Which shall it be?"

The angel shifted uneasily, casting Lucy a beseeching look. Despite herself, she mouthed the word: 'stay.' Joth nodded and returned its gaze to the seraphim.

"I shall stay."

There was a sadness in the greater angel's eyes as it folded its brass-shod talons across its breast. "So be it."

Joth burst into flame. The elohim screamed as its divinity was stripped away like a layer of old paint, revealing the gleaming skin of a lizard. The burning angel clutched its forehead as wildly corkscrewing horns burst through its temples. Its blond tresses crackled like cellophane held over a gas burner, turning into a hideous frightwig. The black feathers covering its wings fell away, exposing the leathery vanes of a dragon's pinions. From between Joth's thighs unrolled a segmented coil of flesh that resembled a scorpion's tail. Its fused toes curled in on themselves and calcified, transforming themselves into hooves.

Lucy turned to Ezrael, who was watching Joth's transformation with open horror. "*Why* is this happening? He said he wanted to *stay!*"

Ezrael turned on her, his tone cruelly accusatory. "Because the decision wasn't made of Joth's free will! *You* made it for him! This is *your* fault, Lucy! *You* did this to him!"

The creature that had once been Joth bellowed like a bull and grabbed the muse by the throat. As Lucy watched, frozen with terror, the newborn daemon opened wide its jaws and bit off Ezrael's head as easily as it would a chocolate Easter bunny's.

"*NO!*" Lucy screamed. "I didn't *mean* for this to happen! I'm sorry! *I'm sorry!*"

* * *

"Lucy! You're having a bad dream!"

Lucy jumped as if she'd been given an electric shock. Her heart was thumping as if she had just charged up a flight of stairs. It took her a second to recognize her surroundings as her living room.

"Thanks for waking me up," she groaned, sitting up. "That one was a *real* lulu of a nightmare!"

"Here, I made you some java," Ezrael said, offering her a steaming mug of fresh coffee.

"Thanks—I need it," she sighed, sipping at the bitter brew. "Where's Joth?"

"Right where you left it," Ezrael replied.

Joth was crouched on the floor of the living room, busily assembling a ten-thousand-piece puzzle of the *Mona Lisa*. By her count, this had to be the third time the angel had assembled that one particular jigsaw in the last five hours.

Upon arriving back at her apartment, Ezrael and Lucy had been desperate to find some way to keep Joth preoccupied. Then Lucy had a brainstorm and dragged her mother's jigsaw puzzles out of the hall closet and dumped them on the floor. Joth immediately fell to its hands and knees and began sorting the thousands upon thousands of individual pieces.

"That was a great idea—whatever made you think of it?" Ezrael asked, impressed by her ingenuity.

"It was Joth who gave me the idea, really," she replied with a shrug. "I had a chance to see how *he* perceives the world—like a gigantic puzzle that is constantly being put together and torn apart. So I figured it was worth a chance."

She sat on the couch, still groggy from her doze, and sipped hot coffee while she watched Joth turn from the *Mona Lisa* and begin putting together a five-thousand-piece puzzle depicting *The Creation of Man*.

The angel's nimble hands sorted through the pile of pieces rapidly, without fumbling or pause. It did not look up from its task nor say anything as it worked. It had already assembled a two-thousand-piece New England landscape, a three-thousand-piece red covered bridge, a ten-thousand-piece Monet, and a five-thousand-piece black-and-white Escher staircase.

Lucy sighed and glanced at her watch. "We're going to need a *lot* more coffee before this is through. I'm going to make a quick trip to the store, if it's okay with you, Ez."

"Sure," the muse replied. "I think I can handle things until you get back."

After changing into a fresh pair of jeans and T-shirt, Lucy headed for the supermarket on Avenue A. It was early and the East Village's more disreputable denizens were just now staggering home, glowering at the morning sun like vampires being chased back into their sepulchers.

The store was less crowded than she remembered ever seeing it before. Then again, she rarely did her shopping before ten in the morning. As she pushed her cart through the narrow aisles in search of coffee, raw sugar, bagels and toilet paper, she collided solidly with the cart of another early bird. She backed up without looking, automatically mumbling an apology.

"Good morning, Ms. Bender. I see you're looking well this morning," smiled Meresin.

"You *bastard!*" Lucy blurted loud enough to make the butcher stocking the meat case look in her direction. "What do *you* want? Are you following me?"

"Heaven forbid!" Meresin said, feigning dismay. "I am merely tending to my shopping—much as you are." To illustrate his point, the daemon picked up a can of baby octopus and tossed it in his otherwise empty cart.

"That's *bullshit* and you know it!' she replied hotly. "I don't know what you think you're going to accomplish harassing me—"

Meresin held up a hand. "Please, my dear! You wound me to the quick! But speaking of motivations—have you truly given any thought to your *own* in this matter? Ask yourself, Lucy—is what you feel for Joth anchored in reality? After all, you thought what you had with Nevin was built on a solid foundation, did you not? Will you still feel the same for Joth once it sheds its wings? And what if Joth proves to be a she, not a 'he,' as you insist on calling it?"

"*Shut up!*" Lucy said angrily. "I *know* what you're trying to do! But it's not going to work!" She clamped her hands over her ears and screwed her eyes shut. "I'm not listening to you! See? I'm *not* listening!" She wagged her head back and forth, chanting stridently: "*La-La-La! I'm not listening! La-La-La!*" After a couple of seconds she opened her eyes and looked around. Meresin was gone, although the guy stocking the meat-case was looking at her as if she was certifiable. Blushing bright red, Lucy hurried to the register with her purchases.

* * *

As she walked back to her apartment building, Lucy couldn't help but reflect upon what Meresin had said. She really *hadn't* given what she was doing that much thought. Granted, she didn't really have any precedents for what to do in situations involving daemons and angels popping in and out of her living room, but one thing was for certain: she had done more to help and protect Joth than she had for anyone else in her life, even Nevin.

She had repeatedly placed her physical and spiritual well-being on the line for someone—some *thing*, really—she had known for less than a week. And had done so even though Joth had been instrumental in costing her a job, a shot at the big time, and, once the super got a gander at what was left of the bedroom window, her apartment as well. And for what? It was not as if she and Joth had spent long afternoons over wine and picnic lunches, getting to know one another.

What exactly *did* she feel for Joth? For all its peculiarities, there was a gentleness and innate sweetness to the angel's nature that touched her on some level. She was still mulling these things over in her mind as she walked though the door.

Ezrael looked up as she returned. "That was quick."

"Not many shoppers out this early in this neighborhood," she grunted in reply as she escorted the groceries into the kitchen.

Ezrael walked into the kitchen and watched her from the doorway as she busied herself with putting away what she'd bought.

"You didn't run into anyone while you were out, did you?" he asked pointedly.

She paused for a second, deliberating on whether she should tell him about Meresin, then resumed shelving the groceries.

"No," she replied, a little more sharply than she meant to. "Like I said— it's too early for anyone I know to be up and about."

"Just asking, that's all."

"Sorry I snapped at you, Ez. I'm just kind of—you know—*stressed* right now." She turned to give the muse a worried look. "Ez—do you think Joth will stay?"

Ezrael shrugged. "It's impossible to say. But from what I've seen—I'd say it's very likely."

"But—it has to be *Joth's* idea to stay, right?"

"Yes, that's correct. It can't be coerced or threatened or told what to do in any way. It has to make the decision to become mortal on its own."

Lucy bit her lip. "Ez—how likely is it Joth will be, uh, male—?"

Ezrael sighed and smoothed back his white hair. "I'd say fifty-fifty—just like most children before they're born. Lucy, there is a *reason* I always refer to Joth as an 'it.' That is so I do not prejudice myself—or *you*—as to what Joth might become. The fewer presumptions either of us make, the easier it is to accept what ultimately happens.

"Still, I suppose it's only human nature to assign a gender to something. You have persistently thought of and referred to Joth as 'he' from the very beginning, but that may not be the case. I told you what happened to me— Miletus believed me to be a female, but when I became a mortal it came as a great shock—one that took a great deal of soul-searching on his part before he could accept me for what I truly was. Lucy—are *you* prepared to accept Joth should it prove to be the same sex as yourself?"

"I—I don't *know*," she said, staring at her feet. "I've tried not to think about that—I keep telling myself it's like having a baby. I don't care what sex it is, as long as it's healthy. But I can't deny the fact that it *does* matter to me."

Ezrael smiled sympathetically and placed a gentle hand on her shoulder. "I can not speak for you, Lucy. Only *you* can look into your heart and see what is there. But I beg you—if you cannot find it within yourself to accept Joth, come whatever may, do *not* interfere when the time comes for it to make its decision.

"The dangers are twofold—first, it might take anything you say or do as a command and act on that alone, and not rely on its own thoughts and feelings. The second danger is that there is *nothing* worse than to be born into a world without comfort. Muses who are abandoned at birth can be easily corrupted. Not all become as the abbot who was so kind to me in my time of need. Some become devils in their own right—their souls twisted by the cruelty of being cast upon the cold and lonely shore of mortal existence without guidance or succor. All I ask you is not to be like Shelley's Frankenstein, and turn your back on a creature you helped create, simply because its appearance is not to your liking."

"Look, that's a *lot* of responsibility you're expecting me to take on!" she protested.

"Joth isn't a stray puppy you picked up off the street!" Ezrael said sternly. "Should its fall render it mortal, Joth will enter into the world with the body and appearance of a grown adult, but in many ways it will be as helpless as a baby. Once severed from the Clockwork, its knowledge of Creation will be no more. It will know only one language and be ignorant of the mechanics of such simple matters as eating and drinking—even wiping its ass! It will fall to you to school it in the finer points of being human—to know love and fear and hate."

"I don't know if I'm *capable* of handling something like that! I mean, I don't even have a *pet!*" Lucy protested, trying hard to control the panic blossoming in her guts. "Hell, every potted plant I've ever owned died because I forgot to water it! And how am I supposed to clothe and house and feed him—I mean, 'it'—? I don't even have a job!"

"As I said—there is much you need to think about. I don't mean to frighten or upset you—I just want you to understand that a decision such as this can *not* be made lightly! But while you contemplate these things, you also must ask yourself: do you wish to see Joth lost?"

"No! Of *course* not!" she replied indignantly. "It's just that I don't know if I can handle the responsibility of taking care of him! I—I wasn't even willing to take care of my own *mother*, for the love of God! Maybe it *would* be better if Joth went back with Nisroc?"

"Perhaps. But that is Joth's decision to make, Lucy, not yours."

She glanced at where the angel sat cross-legged on the floor, still preoccupied with her mother's jigsaws.

"Yeah. Right."

* * *

Ezrael was crashed out on the sofa, snoring lightly. Lucy stood at the windowsill, nursing a cup of coffee. At her feet, Joth was busily reassembling the Monet jigsaw for the fifth time.

As soon as the angel completed one puzzle and moved onto the next, Lucy would quickly disassemble the finished jigsaw. Joth did not seem upset to discover all its hard work had been ruined. It didn't complain or swear or give her a dirty look when she broke apart the pictures and scrambled the pieces around. It simply resumed putting the puzzle back together again. It would almost be funny if it wasn't so creepy—kind of like a cross between watching a Charlie Chaplin film and an autistic child at play.

She glanced at her watch. It would be dark soon. Midnight was six hours away. Which meant she had another six hours of watching Joth assemble and reassemble jigsaws, blithely unaware that its fate was looming before it. Lucy wondered if this was what was meant by the phrase 'happy as a clam.'

In a way, she envied Joth its ability to exist only in the Now. God knows worrying about the immediate future—not to mention a near-constant flow of strong coffee—was tying her stomach into acid knots.

The sunlight fell across the curve of the angel's back as it bent over its work, illuminating the web of muscle and flesh that joined wing to shoulderblade. She watched the muscles and tendons bunch and relax as Joth worked, unaware of her gaze. She was suddenly overcome with love for this creature—this being not truly angel, not yet devil. What she loved was not the thing itself, but the potential human held within it like a seed.

"Joth—?"

The angel looked up from what it was doing. Even with its darkened eyes, there was a disarming openness to its gaze. Joth wasn't simply listening to her, it was focusing every atom of its attention *on* her.

Go ahead, tell him to stay, her brain whispered. *He'll do what you tell him to do. You've been looking your whole life for someone who adores you, inspires you, excites you, needs you. You can't lose him now that you've found him. Tell him to stay.*

Joth looked up at her with a patient expression on its face, waiting for her to speak. It would be so easy for her to sway the angel to her will, because it had none of its own. It was a heady feeling, knowing that she could tell Joth to do anything, and it would obey her without question.

But what right did she have to do such a thing? Joth wasn't a dog that she could treat as her private property. Yet neither was it a free thing—it was powered by instinct and reacted to stimuli, like a hound tracking a fox through the woods. It knew all things, yet it was not wise. It did not possess a distinct personality—at least not in the way Ezrael or even Meresin did—yet Joth trusted her, believed in her, cared for her as best it understood the concept.

She smiled and shook her head.

"Never mind. Go back to what you were doing, Joth."

* * *

"Who wants Chinese food?" Ezrael asked. "My treat!"

Lucy was seated on the sofa, a pad of paper propped against her knee, staring intensely at Joth while she sketched with charcoal.

Ezrael cleared his throat. "Lucy? Did you hear what I said?"

Lucy started as if woken from a daydream. "Hm? Oh—no thanks, Ez. I'm not hungry."

Angels On Fire

"Lucy—you really *must* eat," Ezrael chided gently. "You need to keep up your strength! Nisroc will be here soon—you'll need a clear head."

"I'm really not hungry, Ez."

"I'll order you some pork dumplings. How's that?"

Lucy grunted and returned to her sketching. She didn't mean to be rude to Ezrael—he'd been a good friend, better than any she had known since arriving in New York—but this was the only way she knew how to deal with the stress. She was under so much pressure it felt like she was on the bottom of the ocean.

Anxiety wasn't the only thing fueling her desire to sketch the angel kneeling before her. Her biggest fear, out of all those jostling for control, was that, in the end, she would forget everything that had happened.

Ezrael had warned her that if Joth returned to the Clockwork with Nisroc or fell to the Machine, the angel's existence on earth would be erased from the mind of anyone who had met Joth. She would simply go to sleep and wake up without any clear memory of what had happened over the last few days.

All the miracles, and all the horrors she had witnessed would be swept away, like a sidewalk chalk drawing after a hard rain. The thought of that happening scared her even more than the prospect of Joth turning into a daemon. But maybe, just maybe, if she tried to capture Joth's likeness on paper, something could be salvaged.

It had been a while since she she'd last sketched anyone. Time was money in New York, and, like cash, often scarce in her household. That was why she'd started to focus on photography—it took a lot less time to snap a picture than it did to sketch and paint a subject. But a camera was too impersonal for what she needed. She didn't want merely to capture the angel's physical appearance, but its inner self as well.

It seemed so horribly unfair: to walk and leave no footsteps; to enter people's lives, yet register no memories. Even the lowliest of single-celled creatures, in time, were immortalized in fossil beds. Why not angels?

* * *

There was a knock on the door.

"Ez! Your food's here!" Lucy shouted from her place on the sofa.

"Could you get that for me—?" Ez yelled back, his voice muffled. "I'm in the john!"

"Okay!" she replied, opening the door without checking the spy-hole.

Instead of the usual delivery man from the Five Happiness Take-Out, Meresin was standing in the hallway, holding a large paper sack.

"I ran into the delivery boy in the lobby," he smiled by way of explanation. "You owe me thirteen-fifty plus tip."

Ezrael emerged from the bathroom, drying his hands on a towel. "How much does the bill come to—?" The muse froze at the sight of Meresin standing at the door. "What's *he* doing here?" he demanded angrily, throwing the towel to the floor.

"You owe him thirteen-fifty plus tip," Lucy replied.

Meresin held up his hands as he stepped into the apartment. "Please! I'm merely doing my job! Believe me when I tell you, my friend, I hold no animosity towards either yourself or Ms. Bender."

"Stop calling me that!" Ezrael spat. "You don't fool me, daemon! You're trying to ensure Joth's fall to the Machine by manipulating the woman!"

"No more than you are, my friend!"

"I *said* stop calling me that!" Ezrael shouted, diving at the daemon.

The sephiroth and the muse dropped to the floor, struggling like second graders in a schoolyard brawl. The combatants rolled out of the foyer and into the living room and past Joth, who was still seated on the floor, blithely assembling a twenty-five-piece picture of kittens in a wicker basket.

The angel did not appear to notice them, even though their flailing about destroyed a just-finished New England landscape complete with covered bridge. Joth merely tilted its head to one side and began retrieving the scattered pieces.

Ezrael's hands glowed with blue-white electricity that crackled as he clawed at Meresin's face and throat. Meresin's eyes flashed darkly, but the daemon did not abandon its human form as it struggled to break free of Ezrael's stranglehold.

Meresin raised hands that pulsed with black energy and grabbed Ezrael by the throat. The muse shrieked in agony, but did not loosen his own grip.

"Let go, damn you!" growled Meresin. "This is madness! You're no match for me, Muse!"

"I've been waiting for a thousand years to get my hands around your neck, daemon!" Ezrael replied between gritted teeth. "You took Miletus from me—and I'll die before I let you take the elohim!"

Whatever reply the daemon might have made was cut short by a pail of cold water dumped over the combatants' heads. The two looked up, more stunned than angry, at Lucy, who was standing over them, holding a dripping mop bucket in her hands, a look of genuine outrage on her face.

"*Stop it!*" she yelled. "Stop this insanity right this minute! This is *my* apartment, damn it! And I don't care if you're Batman and the fuckin' Joker! While you're in *my* house, you're going to act like sane human beings—whether you *are* or not! Have I made myself *clear?*"

"Y-yes, ma'am," stammered Meresin.

"That goes for you, too, Ez," she warned, pointing a finger at the soaked muse. "How *stupid* do you think I am? So *what* if Meresin is trying to tempt me into telling Joth what to do? I *know* that's what he wants me to do, so I'm *not* going to do it! But I'm not going to be influenced by *you*, either! You want Joth to stay, too. You might even want it *more* than I do. We *all* have reasons for trying to influence the outcome—but like you said, it's all up to Joth."

"I'm sorry, Lucy. You're right—it was exceptionally rude of me to conduct myself in such a manner in your home," Ezrael said, chagrined.

"Good. I'm glad we got that cleared up. Now, pay Rosemary's Baby here his fuckin' thirteen-fifty plus tax and tip and kick his forked butt outta my house!" Lucy froze as a breeze lifted her bangs. "Wait a minute—do you guys feel a draft—?"

Ezrael's eyes widened in alarm as the smell of ozone grew heavy in the room and a wind from nowhere began to blow.

"Lucy—what time is it?"

Lucy glanced at her wristwatch and turned the color of good cheese. "Straight up midnight," she whispered.

The wind between the worlds increased, snatching up the jigsaw pieces scattered across the floor and swirling them about like a dust devil. Joth watched the puzzle pieces dance over its head, entranced by the patterns visible within the chaos.

Meresin seemed to dwindle within his suit, like a turtle trying to pull itself inside its shell—or a rattlesnake coiling to strike. Meresin's eyes jerked wildly in their orbits as the sephiroth tried to figure a way out of the trap it suddenly found itself in.

There was a flash of bright light and the wind from nowhere ceased as suddenly as it had begun. Nisroc of the seraphim, Lord Shepherd of the Prodigals, stood revealed in the middle of the room, its ever-present watcher, Preil, buzzing about its blazing shoulders. Upon catching sight of Meresin, Preil's pupil dilated wide. Its optic tentacles snapped and writhed, sending out a shower of sparks.

"What manner of trickery is this?" snarled Nisroc, gesturing at the daemon. "You dare to lay a trap?!?"

"N-no, that's not what's happening here!" Lucy stammered. "You don't understand—"

"I shall not tolerate such an Abomination in my sight! Get thee hence, foul tempter!" The seraphim gestured with one brass-shod claw, and a ball of fire miraculously appeared in its hand.

Meresin shrieked like a frightened alley cat and turned to flee, but it was too slow. Nisroc hurled the fireball, striking the daemon between the shoulders, and covering him in fire.

Meresin screamed and began frantically slapping at its arms and head as its human aspect melted away, revealing the Infernal at its core. Although she knew Meresin for what it truly was, Lucy couldn't help but grimace in sympathy. She remembered all too well the agony of the seraphim's flame.

"*Stop it!*" she shouted at Nisroc. "Leave him alone! He wasn't here to ambush you!"

Ezrael grabbed her arm. "Lucy—! Don't! You've got to stay *out* of this!"

"Screw that!" she retorted, yanking herself free of the older man's grip. "I'm not going to stand here and watch him suffer—even if he *is* a monster!"

Nisroc jerked its head in her direction. The flames followed the angel's gaze, leaping from the daemon's body onto Lucy. Meresin did not question its good luck, but instantly got to his hooves and fled the apartment, closing the door behind him with his tail.

When she was younger, Reverend Cakebread had warned Lucy that she would one day burn for her sins, but she never dreamt she would do so in the middle of her own living room. The fire was all over her, biting and tearing at her flesh like a swarm of red ants. It was by turns hot and cold, threatening to boil her brain and turn her marrow to ice. Lucy thought she would pass out from the pain, but there was no place she could flee from the agony consuming her. This was the punishment of all who would raise their hand against the Clockwork—to burn eternally, with no release from pain...

As she collapsed onto the floor, clawing at herself in a desperate attempt to extinguish the fire that consumed but did not burn, she caught a glimpse of Joth crawling about on its hands and knees, methodically picking up and sorting the scattered pieces of the jigsaws, oblivious to its surroundings.

* * *

Joth picked up one of the jigsaw pieces, turning it about with its fingers. It was number one thousand and seventy-six of the thirty-five-hundred pieces that composed a reproduction of a oil painting of a nineteenth-century whaling vessel. Joth carefully returned the piece to its respective pile.

"*Joth!*"

The angel lifted its head and stared up at the white-haired man standing over it. Joth recognized the old man as a friend of Lucy's named Ezrael. He was also Joth's friend, too. Ezrael seemed very frightened, judging by the color of his halo.

"Hello, Ezrael," Joth said pleasantly. "Why are you scared?"

Ezrael turned and pointed to where Lucy lay on the floor, flopping about like a fish on a gig. Joth's smile disappeared.

"What is Nisroc doing to Lucy?" it asked darkly.

"Nisroc is making Lucy cry," answered the muse.

The jigsaw pieces spilled from Joth's hands, instantly forgotten. And, without saying a single word, the angel got to its feet and stepped between the seraphim and Lucy.

* * *

To be of the elohim was to know no cold, no heat, no hunger, no thirst. There was no pleasure, but neither was there discomfort. But when the Fire closed on Joth, all that changed. One moment Joth dwelt in the sensory limbo of the angelic, the next it knew all pain.

It was as if the angel had been doused with boiling oil that covered every inch of its being, both inside and out. The elohim cried out, its wind-chime voice cracking, becoming hoarser and deeper in register. Great strips of its skin begin to peel away from its hands, like paint burning off a house, as fingerprints swam to the surface of all ten digits.

The feathers on the angel's wings began to smolder, then burst into flame. Joth shrieked like a wounded hawk and clawed at its back, but it was no use. Within seconds its proud wings resembled little more than burnt matchsticks. When Joth attempted to flap what remained, they crumbled to ash, leaving fresh scars on its shoulders.

Suddenly Joth was no longer a cipher—a void in the midst of creation. Nature, abhorring a vacuum, rushed in to fill the gap. The exact moment the angel's wings dropped away, a tendril of flesh, as fragile as a finger of new ivy, sprouted between Joth's legs, and its facial muscles jumped and twitched as its jaw line grew more square and an Adam's apple ballooned within its throat.

Hunger, thirst, cold, physical pain—all those things that were unknown to Joth a moment before were suddenly *all* it knew. The angel gave one final cry, like that of a baby entering the world, as marrow filled its hollow bones, tying it once and for all to the mortal sphere, and collapsed onto the floor, shivering uncontrollably as his bladder and bowels emptied themselves for the first time.

As the Fire retreated, reabsorbed into Nisroc's brass talons, the seraphim gave voice to a final ear-splitting roar.

"So be it: the elohim named Joth has Chosen," boomed Nisroc. "Your expulsion of the prodigal is now complete. The Host claims you no more. Go in peace."

The seraphim solemnly crossed its brassy claws over its chest as the portal opened behind it. The greater angel's fierce gaze sought out Ezrael, who was kneeling on the floor, cradling an unconscious Lucy in his arms.

The muse met and held Nisroc's stare. And, to his surprise, the seraphim's remorseless countenance softened somewhat, as it dipped its head in ritual acknowledgment.

* * *

Lucy opened her eyes. She was curled into a semi-fetal position, her arms wrapped around her head. She lowered her arms and saw Ezrael beside her.

"What—what happened?" was all she could gasp.

"Joth took the fire for you," Ezrael explained with pride in his voice. "See for yourself." He pointed to where Joth lay on the floor in a pool of his own filth, shivering like an unweaned pup.

Joth feebly raised his head and looked around. "Lucy?" he whispered hoarsely.

"Congratulations, Ms. Bender," Ezrael said with a weary laugh. "It's a boy!"

Lucy went to the shivering figure, careful to avoid the pool of urine. She gingerly stroked Joth's golden head as she took his hand in hers, squeezing it reassuringly.

"I'm here, Joth. There's no need to be afraid."

"It's so *cold!*" he said between wildly chattering teeth. "And my *bones*— they're so *heavy!*"

Lucy looked at Ezrael, who was leaning against the doorjamb, watching them with a faraway look in his eye.

"We have to get him to a hospital, Ez! He's sick!"

Ezrael laughed gently and shook his head. "No, my dear—he'll be fine. Besides, how would you explain to the interns at the emergency room your boyfriend's lack of a bellybutton, eh?" Ezrael pointed at Joth's stomach, which was as smooth as a lizard's. "Just clean him up, feed him and put him to bed—and be sure to climb in with him! He'll be right as rain in no time."

"But he's in *pain!*"

"No, my dear, he's just *alive*, that's all!" Ezrael chuckled as he reached for his gym bag. "He'll get used to it in day or two. It's up to you to show him the joy that also comes with living."

Lucy frowned. "You're not leaving, are you?"

"You don't need me anymore, Lucy. Nisroc and Preil are gone from your life forever—and I doubt Meresin will be bothering you much, either." Ezrael took a deep breath, smiling ruefully to himself. "Meresin's right, you know— these aren't the Dark Ages anymore. Nowadays his kind are only dangerous if you mistake them for benefactors, and you're far too clever to be seduced by the likes of him. And I think its time you and Joth got some quality time to yourselves, don't you agree?"

"You're not going to disappear on us, are you, Ez? I mean—we *will* see you again?"

"Oh, don't worry—I'll be around," the muse said with a smile.

* * *

Lucy spent every minute of every day in Joth's company, doing her best to live up to her responsibility as his tutor and guide in this brave new world. Since Joth no longer possessed an encyclopedic knowledge of Creation and all who dwelt within it, it was up to Lucy to school him on such things as what country he was in and the name of the street he lived on.

It was a great deal of work, but there was never a moment where she regretted her decision to open her heart and her life to the former angel. Even though she needed to be out looking for a job to replace the one she had lost, she chose instead to see the world anew through Joth's eyes. Their days were spent taking Joth out to Central Park and pointing to things like birds and trees and fish and asking him to name them for her. Joth was a quick study and soon mastered not only the names of animals and flowers, but reading, writing and mathematics as well. Lucy was as proud of his progress as she would be of her own child.

Their nights were spent in more physical pursuits, as Joth proved an eager, if unskilled, lover—but with great potential. After all, he *was* a quick study. But all idylls must have their end—and Lucy and Joth's came two weeks after the angel lost his wings.

As expected, the landlord had taken a dim view of her bedroom window being demolished. So when Lucy's rent check for the month bounced, the realty company that owned the apartment building wasted no time in slipping an eviction notice under the door.

As much as it upset her, there wasn't really much she could do. What little money she had saved was almost gone, since her budget wasn't prepared for feeding, clothing, and housing a second adult. She tried calling Ezrael's number, to see what help the old muse might be able to suggest, but all she got was a message telling her the number was no longer in service.

That left her with only one option, as much as she wished otherwise: calling her cousin in Arkansas and begging her for a place to stay. However, while she was certain Beth would be willing to find room for her, she doubted Joth would be as welcome. And there was no way she was going anywhere without him.

As she sat at the kitchen table, staring forlornly at the eviction notice, there came a timid knock on the apartment door. Looking out the spy-hole, she saw a blonde woman and a small child, both of whom looked vaguely familiar, standing on her doorstep.

Lucy opened the door. "Yes? Can I help you?" she asked, lifting her eyebrow quizzically.

"Are you, um, Lucille Bender?" asked the vaguely familiar blonde woman.

"Yes, I am," Lucy said, still slightly baffled. "What is this about?"

"My name is Carla Mearig, and this is my daughter, Penny," she said, gesturing to the little girl dressed in a sunflower print jumper with wavy, taffy-apple colored hair. "The gallery manager over at the Ars Novina gave me your address…"

"Lucy—who is it?" asked Joth.

The little girl smiled broadly and broke free of her mother's grasp, zipping past Lucy and into the apartment.

"*Penny!*" Carla shouted. "Come back here, young lady!"

"*There* he is!" Penny exclaimed, throwing her arms around Joth's legs. "I *told* you he was real! *Here's* my angel, mommy!"

"I'm *so* sorry, Miss Bender!" Carla said, blushing bright pink. "I've been having problems with her ever since her father became ill—"

"That's all right, Mrs. Mearig," Lucy said with a wry smile. "Why don't you come sit down and talk—seeing how your daughter's already in. You said the Ars Novina gave you my address—?"

"Actually it's Mrs. Uxbridge. Or, rather, it *was*. I've gone back to using my maiden name."

"Uxbridge—?" Lucy frowned, despite herself. *Now* she remembered where she'd seen the woman and child before. "The Matador Gallery?"

"Yes. I-I don't know if you've heard about my husband—?"

Lucy glanced over at the little girl, trying hard not to wince. "No. I've been somewhat, um, out of the loop lately. Please, sit down." She caught Joth's eye and motioned for him to take the child into the other room. "Joth, honey? Why don't you fix Penny some lemonade and cookies?"

Joth nodded and gave Penny a wide smile as he led her into the kitchen. "I like lemonade and cookies! Do *you* like lemonade and cookies, Penny?"

Lucy seated herself on the sofa beside Carla. "Now—what's all this about?"

Carla Mearig took a deep breath and looked down at her hands knotted in her lap. "Well, about two weeks ago my husband suffered some kind of—brain seizure. It cost him his sight and his sanity. The doctors aren't exactly sure what caused it, and I'm afraid I—I was drunk at the time it happened, so I have no idea what might have brought it on, either.

"All I *do* know is that whatever happened to my husband, Penny saw it. She keeps insisting that an angel flew into her bedroom and struck her father with a bolt of lightning! I know it sounds silly—but the child psychologists tell me it's a fantasy she's developed as a means of dealing with whatever *really* happened—"

Carla paused as a trill of little-girl laughter emerged from the kitchen. Lucy could hear Joth say something in his deep, gentle voice, which was followed by another child-like giggle.

"Is that your husband?" Carla asked suddenly.

Lucy blinked, somewhat taken aback by the question. Then she smiled and said, "Yes. Yes, he is."

"He must be an extraordinary man to draw Penny out so quickly," the other woman smiled wistfully. "I can't tell you how *good* it is to hear her laugh like that! I've barely been able to get her to talk to anyone since, well, since her father got sick."

"How horrible!" Lucy said sympathetically. "I'm sorry to hear about your husband, Mrs. Uxbridge, I mean Ms. Mearig."

"Call me Carla."

"Okay—Carla. As I said, I *am* sorry to hear about all this, but what has any of it to do with *me*—?"

Nancy Collins

"Well, since Page has been declared incompetent, I'm the one running the Matador now. While I was going through his office the other day, I found your name written down on some papers. I admit I don't remember much about the night of the opening at the Ars Novina—but I *do* recall my husband being interested in your work. So I took it upon myself to go back to the gallery today on my own—clean and sober. And, Ms. Bender, I must say I was genuinely touched by what I saw. And I would consider it a *great* honor if you would permit the Matador to host a one-woman show of your work. What do you say?"

Before Lucy could respond, there was another, much louder, knock on the door. "Uh, could you excuse me for second, Carla?"

The super was standing in the hall, chewing on his cigar while holding a large manila envelope in one hand.

"What do *you* want?" she scowled. "I've at least another week before you can kick me out."

"The new landlord told me to give you this," he grunted, shoving the envelope at her.

"New landlord?" Lucy frowned. "*What* new landlord?"

The super shrugged. "All I knows is yesterday some jerk bought this dump and he told me t'give you this."

Puzzled, Lucy closed the door and looked at the manila envelope. According to the return address, the new landlord was something called Azrael Realty. It seemed kind of heavy for a final eviction notice. Well, no point putting off bad news...

Inside the envelope was a letterhead, some legal-looking documents and what looked to be a birth certificate and a passport. Lucy fished out the letter and unfolded it. She recognized the handwriting immediately, even though the words were English, not arcane runes or mystic symbols.

Dear Lucy & Joth:

Consider this an unofficial wedding present: free rent for life. Yours or mine, whichever ends first. I've also enclosed identity papers for Joth. He'll need them if he wants to earn his keep.

All my best, Ez

Lucy looked up at the sound of Penny's laughter. From where she stood, she could see the little girl sitting at the table in the kitchen next to Joth. Penny was drawing something on the tablet Lucy kept by the window. Joth was leaning forward, watching the child with rapt attention.

For a half a heartbeat, Lucy glimpsed a blazing corona about her lover's head. As Joth leaned forward, the fingers of light radiating from his halo reached out and touched the pinkish-blue aura that surrounded the child's head. As she watched, Penny's halo strengthened, until it glowed from within like a cloud at sunset. Sensing Lucy's gaze, Joth lifted his head and smiled at her, his eyes golden as a tiger's.

"Ms. Bender?" Carla had left her place on the sofa to see what was delaying her hostess. "Ms. Bender—are you all right?" she asked, startled by the tears rolling down the other woman's face.

Lucy laughed and shook her head. "Carla—I'm *more* than all right. I'm *Blessed.*"

epilogue

O! for a Muse of fire, that would ascend
The brightest heaven of invention…
—Shakespeare, *Henry V*

The man worthy of praise the Muse forbids to die.
—Horace

The sky was blue and clear that morning, the air crisp and brisk off Puget Sound. All in all, it was an exquisite day for a double funeral.

Handel's *Water Music* was playing over the sound system as the mourners made their way down the center aisle and took their places in the pews. The immediate family sat in the front, along with the closest friends. Members of the press—easily identifiable by their Line-Of-Sight camera-headgear—jockeyed as politely as possible amongst themselves for prime coverage.

There were no caskets on display—but then, there were no bodies to place inside them. As was the custom with those whose physical remains could not be recovered, be it due to deaths via orbital re-entry or at sea, two life-sized holographic icons of the dearly departed revolved before the assembled mourners.

On the right was a projection of Lucille Bender, possibly the most influential and renowned artist of the early twenty-first century. As her image rotated, her features shifted from that of a silver-haired eighty-year-old grandmother to that of a fifty-year-old woman with laugh-lines and steel-gray temples, to a thirty-five-year-old mother holding her children in her arms, to a twenty-year-old wearing ragged, paint-spattered jeans and T-shirt and a mischievous grin.

To the left revolved the holographic image of Joth Angelin, Lucille's husband of fifty years. As Joth's image aged and rejuvenated alongside that of his wife's, it was obvious that he had remained a vigorous man, even well into old age. Looking at the octogenarian's broad shoulders and strong back, it was easy to understand why the couple had thought they could undertake such a hazardous voyage without any outside help.

Once everyone was seated, the music trailed off and a middle-aged man wearing the collar of a Unitarian pastor and a wireless broadcast mike stepped into the pulpit.

"Dearly beloved, we are gathered here today to honor the memories of two people who not only meant a great deal to us as friends and family members, but also influenced the world itself, as artists and teachers.

"Lucille Bender was one of the most famous and well-respected artists of the new millenium. Whether it be her early photographic work, her ground-breaking computer-generated light sculpture 'City of Angels,' or her brilliant lecture series on the nature of creativity, Lucy's name has become as familiar to our generation as that of O'Keefe, Avedon, or Wyeth. She lived a full life, right up to the end—one filled with romance and creativity, but most importantly, love. A love she shared for fifty years with her adoring husband, Joth, whom she proudly called her muse.

"Theirs was a unique and loving bond; one strong enough to weather both good times and bad, such as the loss of their son, Ezra. In the twenty years I knew them as friends and neighbors here in Seattle, I can't think of a single day when they were ever apart. When I saw the coverage of the Coast Guards finding what was left of their yacht on the NewsFeed last month, I was saddened by the loss of two wonderful, caring human beings. Yet, I was given some solace in knowing that, whatever may have happened, they at least died as they had lived—together."

* * *

Towards the very back of the chapel, seated in the pew closest to the door, were three mourners. The first was an older man with long white hair pulled back into a ponytail and eyes as golden as a cat's. Despite the somberness of the occasion, the bright colors of a Hawaiian shirt could be glimpsed beneath his jacket.

The second mourner was somewhat younger than the first, with hair the color of flame and eyes as black as a beetle's back. He was dressed in an impeccably tailored business suit and expensive shoes.

The third member of the group was a young man with broad shoulders and a smooth chin. His blond hair spilled down the middle of his back and his eyes were identical to those of his older companion.

"Heard enough?" Ezrael whispered.

Joth nodded that he had.

As the pastor began to introduce the first of the eulogists, the trio rose and left the chapel as discreetly as possible. As soon as they got outside, Meresin immediately prestidigitated a smoldering cigarette from thin air and took a drag.

"You're still chain-smoking those things?" snorted Ezrael. "They're fifty dollars a pack now!"

"Yes—I know," sighed the daemon. "It's a filthy habit. I really do mean to quit." The sephiroth turned his black gaze on Joth. "So—do you come to your funerals often?"

Joth shook his head with a melancholy smile. "This is my first one." He looked a good fifty years younger than the holographic image on display inside. "But I didn't come here for me."

Meresin dropped his cigarette and stamped it out with a cloven hoof. "Do not take this wrongly, for these things are difficult for one such as myself to fully grasp—but do you still miss her—?"

Joth gave a small laugh that bordered on a sob, then sniffed and coughed into his fist before answering. "I understand what you're trying to say,

Meresin. I take no offense. But to answer your question—yes, I *still* miss her. I shall miss her for the rest of my life—for however long that might be."

"Whoever composed that holo-icon of Lucy did a tremendous job," Ezrael said. "It really captured something of what made her special."

"Yes, it *was* particularly good work," agreed Meresin. "Perhaps I should track the editor down and offer him a job working for Terry Spanner, Jr.— his next series is "The Space Wheel After Hours." Zero-Gee Transvestite Sex and that sort of thing."

"Meresin—*please!*" Ezrael chided.

"Sorry," the daemon replied. "I didn't mean to drag work into this."

"The shipwreck was her idea, you know," Joth said softly. "The doctors had given her another three or four months—six at the most—before the cancer finally claimed her. I'd been artificially aging myself for decades, but we both knew that once she was gone, it would be impossible for me to continue without her. So she decided that we'd die together—or at least appear to.

"The girls didn't want us going out on the water by ourselves, but Lucy told them we were old enough to do as we liked one last time. We hated deceiving them like that, but there was no other way around it—not even my children know about me. We decided it was better that way.

"Lucy died in my arms the second day out. We were sitting on the deck, watching the sun set when it happened. She went easy—with no pain and no regrets. I wrapped her in one of the sails and weighted the shroud with the anchor from the dinghy." Joth fell silent for a moment, replaying in his mind's eye the last glimpse of his wife's body as it disappeared forever beneath the blue waters of the Pacific.

"Once her body sank beneath the waves, I radioed to Ezrael, who was waiting on the shore, and he came and picked me up in his own boat. We then used our combined magicks to summon up a storm strong enough to swamp the yacht. The rest you know."

The sephiroth nodded in the direction of the chapel. "What about your family—your children and grandchildren? Haven't you felt the desire to go to them? To see them?"

"*Meresin!*" Ezrael said loudly.

"Forgive me—tempting is the only thing I know."

"Yes, I *was* tempted, at first," Joth admitted. "When you lose someone as close as Lucy was to me, the natural instinct is to find solace amongst one's family. But I knew I could not do that without endangering everything Lucy and I had worked so hard for.

"In the month since our deaths were reported, I've come to realize my presence amongst my children and their families would be far more troubling to them than joyous. Their parents are dead—it is better they stay that way."

Ezrael glanced in the direction of the chapel. "Sounds like the service is letting out—we better make ourselves scarce, just in case some of your old friends have better eyesight than you realize."

They moved to the park across the way from the chapel, where they could watch the mourners file out of the building without being seen.

Ezrael glanced uneasily at his friend. "Are you sure you want to put yourself through this, Joth?"

The younger muse nodded, his jaw set. "I just want to see them one last time, Ez. To make sure they're going to be okay. For Lucy's sake."

In the fifty years they had had together, he and Lucy had made between them three children. The first, Ezra, had died as a child during the pox outbreak that forced them to flee New York City once and for all, over forty years ago. Now Joth stood and watched as his surviving children exited the chapel and stood in a small cluster, shaking hands and exchanging farewells with the other mourners and well-wishers who had attended the service.

Their oldest, Clio, was forty-one and had hair the color of a daffodil. Her eyes burned blue and clear, like sapphires held before a fire. Clio was standing beside her husband of ten years, Daniel. In between them was their son, Dorian. Joth felt a sharp pang as he spotted his first-born grandchild. Dorian's hair was the same vibrant blonde as his mother's—and his grandfather's.

At thirty-eight, Thalia was the baby of the family—and the very image of her mother. The resemblance was so strong Joth had to blink back the mist from his eyes. Thalia was with her wife, Candace. And, judging from the swell of Candy's belly, their *in vitro* clone was coming along nicely. Joth regretted that he would not be there to share in the birth of his newest grandchild, but he had no fear for the baby's future. Lucy had seen to it that their children, and their children's children, would be well provided for.

As he continued to watch, Joth spotted familiar faces among the crowd, as well as those he'd barely known. Friends, acquaintances, students and faculty from the local university where Lucy gave her lectures, all paused to pass along their condolences to the family. Joth noticed that Lucy's cousin Beth, hunched over her robo-walker, had taken the bullet-train up from Arkansas for the service.

Joth spotted Penny Uxbridge in the crowd. While her taffy-apple colored hair was now liberally laced with gray, there was no mistaking the halo that sparkled over her head. Joth was almost as proud of Penny as he was of Lucy. She had blossomed into an immensely talented artist in her own right—as evidenced by the clutch of reporters vying among themselves for a curbside interview with her.

After a few more minutes, the assembled mourners climbed inside their electric cars and buzzed off to their various destinations, leaving the street in front of the chapel deserted. Joth took a deep breath and turned his back on the empty street as well.

He would miss them—and never stop loving them—but the time had come for him to leave them to their own worlds and lives—and for him to begin anew.

"Lucy was a formidable woman—I envied you her, friend Joth," Meresin said with sad smile.

"What *you* need, Meresin, is someone to lure you away from the Machine," Joth said with a crooked smile.

Meresin shook his head ruefully. "I've had more sex partners than I've got hairs on my ass, but I've never had a lover. It's one of the Undivided Twin's little jokes that the Infernals, who are sworn to destruction, were given generative organs, while the Celestials, who toil in the belly of Creation, are without. Big laugh, right? Besides, those who are attracted to daemons are more interested in what we *are*, not what we *might* become. Only angels seem capable of inspiring such wishful thinking in humans."

"Some might call it hope," Joth replied.

"Indeed they might," conceded the daemon. "Now I fear I must bid you fond *adieu*, my friends. I have much business to attend to in Hollywood." Meresin cast off its human form and spread wide his bat-like wings, taking to the air with a single beat of powerful pinions.

As Ezrael tilted back his head, shading his eyes to watch the daemon's flight, he nudged his companion and gestured skyward. Joth looked to where the older muse was pointing and saw the gleam of what looked like hummingbird feathers pushing their way past the scales of the daemon's wings.

Joth laughed until his eyes brimmed with tears; eyes that burned as brightly as angels on fire.